The In Situ Murders

Dr. Zen Mystery, Volume 2

Lynn Emery

Published by Lazy River Publishing, 2021.

This is a work of fiction. Similarities to real people, places, or events are entirely coincidental.

THE IN SITU MURDERS

First edition. October 1, 2021.

Copyright © 2021 Lynn Emery.

ISBN: 978-1737379218

Written by Lynn Emery.

Chapter 1

Zen looked up at the same time as her new partner, Peter Navarro. They'd been assigned the task of opening a hatch in microgravity. All twelve had been split into two person teams. Navarro gave a soft grunt and went back to the task.

The woman clawed at the helmet of her space suit. Her brown eyes stretched wide as she panted and wheezed. "Shit. Shit. I can't do this. I can't breathe!"

"I'm sure her teammate will deal with it. He's closer anyway." Navarro clicked a final latch. "I got the hang of it."

Dr. Jeff Franklin, a NASA engineer, stopped only to throw a look of contempt at her. "For God's sake, get a grip on yourself, woman. We're not here to hold your hand."

"That's no act," Zen said.

Zen pushed off the curved wall behind her. In a few large jumps she ended up next to the woman. Her teammate's growing desperation to escape triggered her own sense of claustrophobia. Zen understood with sudden clarity the old concept of mass hysteria. In fact, another young trainee had paused to stare. He looked ready to toss aside the tool in his hands and rush for the nearest exit hatch.

"Shani, listen to me. Slow your breathing. You're going to be fine. You've got plenty of oxygen. Four team members are here to make sure you're okay," Zen said. She placed both of her gloved hands on either side of the woman's helmet. That forced Shani to look into Zen's eyes.

Ten minutes later, after walking her through a short emotion-regulation exercise and taking to her, Shani finished her set of tasks and the final two hours of their training session. They spent another thirty minutes in the chamber to readjust to normal gravity and shed the space suits. To their credit, most of the other team members gave her words of encouragement once they were in the locker-room. All except Franklin. Zen tried to reason away her growing abhorrence of the man. His lack of empathy didn't help.

"Now I know why a psychologist is a good addition to a space crew," Franklin said. He leaned against the wall of lockers.

"Clinical social worker."

"Hmm, same difference. Tinkering with the mind." Franklin smiled at her through his stylish eyeglasses. He tapped his temple with one forefinger.

She went back to gathering her personal items. The pompous physicist had two minor space missions under his belt. He'd made it clear he was annoyed at having to train with those beneath his professional stature. Never mind he hadn't been on a shuttle in four years.

"It certainly comes in useful, understanding human nature. Like people who believe in social hierarchies. Or people with perfect vision who wear designer eyeglasses. To be fashionable? Look more important? Some way to compensate, but for what?" Zen gave him a tight sideways smile that dissolved fast.

She banged the locker door shut without looking at him. At five feet six inches, he was the shortest of the new trainees. Two weeks of being around the man had brought out the beast in her. Between putting up with Navarro and him, Zen was more than ready to go home. Franklin didn't take the hint.

"Ouch. I'm assuming you'll use our interactions for the past days to add to your research, Dr. Batiste." Franklin nodded at her. "Did you attempt to provoke me as part of some experiment?"

"Nah, I just enjoy insulting snots who lack compassion. Good-bye, Dr. Franklin." Zen slung her crossbody bag over her head and walked off without looking back.

"Hey, Dr. Batiste. Wait up." Shani Jenkins hurried to catch up with Zen in the lobby of the NASA building. "Thanks for helping me decompress back there. Damn it, I'd been getting through just fine until then."

"Not a problem." Zen turned to face her. "And you can call me Zen. We've been underwater, under pressure, and floating in the void together. I think we're on a first-name basis."

At twenty-two Shani Jenkins was the youngest of the space trainees. With double degrees in geophysical and mechanical engineering, she had a bright future. But maybe that future meant her feet would stay firmly planted on Earth. The soft glow of her dark brown skin was back now that she was out of the harsh environment of simulated space. Zen had easily warmed to her. Shani reminded Zen of who her younger sister Lexi might have become had she lived.

"I don't know what the hell got into me. I want this so bad. Going to one of the lunar colonies, I mean. But now..." Shani's eyes went glassy with unshed tears she seemed determined not to let fall. She pushed out a breath as if practicing the breathing routine Zen had taken her through.

"Shani, with claustrophobia—"

"Mild, it's very mild. I can manage it," Shani broke in.

"And social anxiety, being confined with people on a space colony or one of the space stations will not be good for you," Zen went on.

"I work fine on teams, Dr., I mean Zen. You've seen me do it," Shani said, a note of pleading in her voice.

"Yes, you did. I'll be sure to put that on my debriefing summary and the feedback survey."

Shani hugged her hard and then pulled back. She wore a look of chagrin at her outburst. "Sorry. But thank you so much, Dr. Batiste."

"It's okay. You can offer a lot to the space program." Zen patted her shoulder.

"I want to see the moon, the stars, asteroids for myself. Not just in pictures or live streams," Shani said with zeal. She looked outside at the bright blue Florida sky.

Zen felt a burst of maternal warmth. She pulled out her tablet computer. "I can recommend you to an effective desensitization therapy."

Shani looked around. "I'm not, you know, mental."

"Seeking help is a sign of strength. You want the fastest and most effective way to get that anxiety under control, right?"

"Yes, I guess. But—"

"Treatment is strictly confidential if you're worried about NASA and private space agencies finding out. You've got time since this was your first training session. Most people have some kind of blip the first one or two times."

"Really?" Shani's tense expression eased as she gazed at Zen, still considering her options.

Zen pulled up her teenage daughter's favorite message app. Not only were messages private, but they weren't cached on a server somewhere. Nothing written could come back to haunt users. She didn't even ask if Shani used it. At her age, Shani probably had been using the app for ten years at least.

"I'll send you the info via Hit Me."

Shani grinned, her eyes bright. "Hey, cool. Old folks don't know about Hit Me."

Zen laughed out loud. "Bless you, child. You've just become my new best friend. My daughter for sure wouldn't put me in the 'young and with it' crew. What's your handle?"

"Uhura5.o. I can't thank you enough. I'm sure Dr. Franklin will try to kill my chances. Damn, I don't even want to think about what he's going to write. He might have even sent in something already. But you're famous. A good word from you will maybe cancel out his negative comments."

Shani chattered on in a mixture of hope and angst. Though worry seemed to be taking a firmer hold. Zen lingered longer to reassure her. She sent over the names of two colleagues, top therapists in the field of anxiety treatment. Two other space trainees joined them to exchange good-byes and wishes of good luck. Zen enjoyed seeing their enthusiasm help brighten Shani's mood. She turned to see Dr. Franklin studying the group. He gave a curt salute without approaching the others and strode through the glass doors. Navarro appeared at Zen's shoulder.

"Good riddance, eh?" Navarro gave a snort as he watched Franklin pause outside to talk a man and woman.

"Yeah, getting rid of irritating people is always nice. Like having a bad rash finally clear up," Zen muttered. She turned her back to him.

The others didn't notice any tension between them, or didn't give a sign if they did. They seemed to genuinely like Navarro, easily calling him Peter. He could be charming. Not at all like the stereotype of an introverted genius. A brilliant astrophysicist, Navarro had lately turned his interest to space environmental engineering. It made sense that he'd be assigned to the Office of Specialized Investigations, or OSI. The first investigative unit was created by the DOJ and NASA to handle outer space-related crimes. Navarro's research had led to advancements in space colony development. A lot of achievements and "firsts" under his belt; a list of letters after his name. Impressive. Except. He was also a suspected serial killer. No matter what Zen's boss said, she always added "SK" to the list.

Zen's own assignment at the OSI had been pretty nondescript at first. As a behavioral health specialist and expert in forensic sociology, her job was to assess potential lunar and space station crew candidates. When crime crept into the space program, Zen became an outer space crime fighter. At least that's the colorful description Astra, her daughter, preferred. Zen's investigative training at the Department of Justice had come in handy. Now she felt compelled to keep an eye on the latest addition to their nascent unit.

Zen succeeded in avoiding her new partner for the rest of the day. She didn't see Navarro until the next morning. They boarded a bus leaving their hotel at five thirty. Their boss, Clive Anderson, had arranged their flight from the private Airforce/ NASA gate at the Space Coast Regional Airport. Two other passengers, silent military types from the looks of them, were also headed out. Navarro nodded a greeting to Zen and found a seat without waiting for her to respond. The train slid silently along on the monorail. "The latest in 2086 technology," a digital sign flashed just over their heads as they rode, along with other commercial messages. Zen enjoyed the early morning scenery that flashed by as they traveled. Ten minutes later they were boarding the flight, a sleek electric plane that would take them to Virginia in just under an hour. Short-range airflight had been one of many benefits of technology invented in space. Zen settled into faux leather next to a window on an empty row. Navarro took the aisle seat. The plane could hold up to thirty people. Only about twenty were onboard. She made it a point to glance around at the empty rows around them.

"I thought we could have a talk," Navarro said.

"I'm not a morning person and I haven't had a coffee yet."

Before he could reply, a pre-recorded voice welcomed them aboard. They received safety instructions and details on how to access the Wi-Fi and other amenities. A smiling flight attendant reinforced they should secure their seat belts. Fifteen minutes later they'd been offered coffee, tea, and a continental breakfast.

Navarro patted his lips with a napkin. "Better?"

"Humph." Zen pulled up headlines on her tablet and pretended to be engrossed in reading.

"What will it take, Dr. Batiste?" Navarro said. The trace of his Spanish accent gave his voice a reassuring quality.

"Hmm." Zen continued to scroll through mostly uninteresting news stories.

Zen had managed to tolerate him by ignoring his attempts at non-work-related conversation. After the first month of his arrival, Navarro seemed to have accepted they wouldn't be buddies. That, combined with Zen replying "Hmm" and "Okay" to just about anything he said, had been pretty effective.

Navarro leaned across the empty seat between them. "You've seen the evidence that I was framed by a colleague."

"Uh-huh." Zen looked up at the flight attendant passing by. "May I have another cup of apple juice, please. Thank you so much."

She flashed a bright smile at the man, accepted the cup he held out, and went back to reading. Navarro hissed out a sigh next to her. He went silent for a few minutes longer. Then he took out his own smart device and tapped in commands. He read in silence.

"You should go to the RT or RNA news websites," Navarro rumbled.

"Humm."

"I'm not making small talk, Batiste," Navarro snapped. Then he lowered his voice as he glanced around. "I have a feeling we'll be briefed soon. Just look, damn it."

Zen's head snapped up at his tone. She finally looked at him full on. His olive skin and dark, wavy hair made him look like a handsome soccer dad. Yet his good looks didn't make him stand out. He could just as easily blend into a crowd. Peter Navarro seemed made for looking attractive and safe. The perfect camouflage for a lethal predator. His dark eyes blinked before he looked away from her. The man was isolated. Invitations from prestige universities to lecture had dried up. Articles about the investigation into his alleged crimes and personal life meant he had few allies. Most of his former friends and colleagues in the scientific community shunned him. Zen could almost see it all reflected in the haunted, lonely way he gazed at her. She felt a prick of... what? Guilt mixed with pity? Her father would call it her "bleeding social worker heart." Still, Zen fixed her face not to let it show.

She stole a glance at his tablet. Most of the major news outlets were bookmarked on her browser, so she quickly navigated to the RNA site. The Russian News Agency had a splashy heading in bright blue above a video: "Death In Space: Cover Up?" She connected her Bluetooth headset to listen. After a few minutes Zen looked at Navarro again. He nodded. They forgot their personal issues and started to talk in low tones to each other. Both their cell phones trilled at the same time. Messages from the boss.

They'd reserved a self-driven taxi while still on the plane and went straight to the office. Monday morning traffic was light due to the upcoming spring and Easter holidays. April sunshine made the day look bright. The boss was waiting for them in the conference room. Zen messaged Astra that she wouldn't have any days off after all. Her daughter, studying college courses from home, would no doubt easily pivot to plans with friends. Zen hated that they didn't see each other as much. Between Astra's classes, her social life, and Zen's work they seemed to only blow air kisses to each other in passing. But it couldn't be helped. Based on the reports she'd read they wouldn't get much mother-daughter time in the near future, either.

Zen and Navarro went through security in a few minutes. They stashed the carry-on bags in their respective offices and headed for the briefing. Hadley Truman, Clive's right-hand assistant, sat with her own tablet on the large oval table. Her long fingers flew over the keypad, but she managed to smile at them when they entered.

"Morning team. Coffee, yogurt, pastries," was her terse greeting. Her attention went back to the search again.

"Thanks. I can't stomach food midflight, even with the almost frictionless trips of modern travel," Navarro said. He poured coffee into a mug. He handed it to Zen and fixed one for himself.

Zen accepted it and moved to a seat. Clive cocked an eyebrow at her as he shot a glance at Navarro. Hadley cleared her throat loudly but didn't move her gaze from the tablet.

"Thanks, Navarro." Zen chafed at being treated like a rude youngster being reminded of her manners.

"It's been a month. I think you can call me Peter by now," Navarro replied in a mild tone.

"Yeah, thanks," Zen said.

Their boss pressed his lips together and turned to the screen that took up most of a wall. He stood with his back to them, studying the high-definition display in silence. No one interrupted his train of thought. Clive Anderson, at fifty-seven years old, was an intelligence veteran. He'd been assigned to the CIA, NSA, and the Department of Justice for thirty years. He'd worked for three US presidents in his career. When he talked, officials in government listened. Navarro spooned blueberry yogurt, patiently waiting. Zen studied the screen. The image, though familiar, was breathtaking. Blinking lights and the bright metallic surface contrasted with the ink-black vastness of outer space. Not quite emptiness though. Dots flickered as a backdrop, distant stars and planets.

"Star Flight Space Station. The third private space station to open; the first with commercial properties. Two hotels, six retail stores, three bars. It's like something out of an old twentieth century sci-fi movie. Minus the colorful aliens pulling up to buy drinks at a bar," Hadley said.

"None of them are totally private," Clive clipped. "They all have to be reminded of that fact every once in a while. NASA has research labs and offices on Star Flight. Their focus is on developing on-site resources."

"The official name is the In Situ Research Facility," Peter said in an even tone. Star Flight Space Station is the invention of some marketing person."

"Astra has been nagging me about taking our next vacation up there. Especially since I'm training for space travel," Zen said. She looked away from screen and at Clive. "But now I have an out?"

Clive face them again, both meaty fists jammed into his pants pockets. "Travel hasn't been restricted yet. The reporter hasn't gotten full details, and we're sure in hell not about to have a press conference. Not until we can get more information."

"Reporter? One?" Peter dabbed at his lips and sipped coffee.

"Only one cleared for outer space transport to Star Flight," Hadley said.

She tapped a remote. The screen split into three squares. One had the picture of a white man. He had a shock of red hair and an intense look in his greenish eyes. Clive shot a side glance at the photo with a grimace. Hadley clicked her tongue. Peter put down the coffee mug on the table with a thump.

"He looks harmless enough," Zen said as she glanced around at their solemn faces.

"Part of what makes him so good at digging up facts," Hadley replied. "Jacques Clairmont. Age, twenty-seven. He has a degree in biochemistry but pivoted to journalism in his second year at university. His mother is Belgian. He grew up in Amsterdam, London, and spent two years finishing up his degree at Rutgers. His father is Australian. He worked as a CEO for three top firms, which is why Clairmont got to travel so young. Estranged from said father because of the elder Clairmont's companies' less-than-ethical, if legal, actions. It's complicated."

"Oh great. He has daddy issues," Peter murmured.

"Ready to charge into any kind of authority figure. Sees deep state and corporate conspiracies everywhere. Let me guess. His parents divorced when he was young." Zen cocked her head to one side to gaze at the mild-mannered face.

"Correct, but the split was amicable, by all accounts. My friend Yaseera worked with Clairmont's mother on two UN economic projects. She's a powerhouse in her own right. Though she did focus on raising Clairmont and his two siblings when they were young," Hadley put in.

"Hadley, is there anybody you don't know?" Zen said.

Hadley chuckled. "In this instance it's purely a happy coincidence. Since he's a concern for us now, I did my research. I saw the names of those projects and remembered Yaseera worked as a liaison with the Indian and Pakistani governments."

"Okay, so what's happened that interests our interstellar crime-fighting team and we don't want a reporter to know?" Peter asked.

"Seriously—interstellar crime-fighting team?" Zen rolled her eyes.

"Thank our friend there," Peter said and pointed to Clairmont's photo. "He did a series of reports on your first cases at the lunar colony and Goddard's training camp."

"Which kicked off his interest in space. He's now a reporter for the Global Associated Press. Clairmont will find out eventually. I want us to get a head start on our investigation before he does. That way we'll mitigate damage, have some measure of control."

"What are we investigating?" Zen looked back the screen. She studied the space station again.

"Murder. What else?" Peter flipped open the case that held his tablet computer.

Clive tapped his knuckles on the conference table a few seconds. "The body of a forty-seven-year-old man was found at the Hilton Sky High Hotel two days ago. At first the officials at the hotel and Star Flight said he'd died of a heart attack."

"But he'd been entertaining three sex workers and drinking heavily; party drugs were found," Hadley added. "I've sent over a copy of the initial reports from Star Flight Security Agency officers."

Peter read the screen of his tablet. "A private police force, eh?"

Clive nodded. "Saves our government and the European Space Agency a lot of money. Two Space Command cops are assigned to work with them. They report to us, which is why we found out the death wasn't natural causes."

"Another guess; the big corporations that run Star Flight would rather not have the world know somebody died of a drug overdose in their luxe hotel in the stars," Zen said.

"Pretty much. They want to market Star Flight as a family destination. Our officers asked enough awkward questions that they finally fessed up."

"Good for them." Zen squinted at the shiny object in the sky, seeing it in a less-glittering light.

"Yeah, except now Star Flight cops are treating them like traitorous outsiders. All that cooperation and goodwill has dried up." Clive sat down and propped both elbows on the polished table surface. "Which is where you two come in. We knew this day would come, right? Two of our detectives going into space to investigate a crime."

"Oh goody," Zen drawled. Still, her pulse picked up at the thought of finally seeing Earth from space.

"When do we leave?" Peter frowned at no one in particular as he rubbed his jaw hard.

"We have a space shuttle leaving at six o'clock tomorrow evening. Weather will be just right after early-morning rain," Hadley replied. "I've made all of the arrangements."

Zen could guess why Navarro was worried about leaving. His wife had divorced him less than a year ago. He'd had a hard fight to even have weekend visits with their two small girls. His ex-wife had plenty of ammunition with a murder allegation and his uncovered secret addiction. To humanoid sex workers—bang bots, no less. Having the strong evidence that he'd been framed for the series of killings had helped. Along with months of in-patient psychiatric treatment.

"My daughters are scheduled to spend a school holiday with me in another three weeks," Peter said. "It's the first time in months. The judge ordered their mother to comply."

"Sorry, Navarro, but I can't say how long the case will last," Clive said with blunt force.

"I can't imagine they'll be on Star Flight that long though, Clive. I mean, LMPD and Space Command officers have made a solid start." Hadley gave Peter a look of sympathy.

"Who knows how long this thing will drag on," Zen murmured without looking up from the report on her own tablet. She could almost feel Hadley's admonishing gaze.

"NASA, the DOJ, and three foreign space agencies want us to wrap up this case. We've got more than one reason to move with all deliberate speed. Correct?" Clive's baritone voice rolled out like quiet thunder.

Navarro pushed his chair back to stand. "I'll start with the autopsy and other forensic reports. I see a full set of lab screens have been done. Bodily fluids from the victim, and a sweep of the crime scene."

"Good," Clive replied with a sharp nod at him. "Batiste, do a full psychological sweep of the victim first. Then move on to the staff who found him and work your way out. You have the personnel files of everyone."

"Yes, sir," Zen said. "Why was the victim on Star Flight, by the way?"

"Hassan Ahmad, US citizen of Saudi descent. He was an astrochemist who worked for a transnational company. They had a convention, one of two, at the hotel. His family is being notified as we speak."

Peter paused at the door. "Why the delay?"

"Yeah, if they thought it was natural causes, they should have been told," Zen added.

"Good question. I expect you"—Clive pointed at Zen and then Peter—"to deliver the answer to that, along with a list of others."

"Number one being if it was murder." Zen tucked her tablet under one arm. She grabbed her mug with her free hand.

"For a start. I've got a meeting at the White House. NASA is sweating about the effect on their In Situ facility, and Clairmont's boss is bitching about being stonewalled." Clive stood and brushed the front of his suit jacket. He wore a determined expression.

"You'll be able to handle them all, boss," Zen said with a grin.

"Pain in the ass part of this job," Clive retorted. Still, his expression was relaxed. Close to thirty years of dealing with powerful people meant titles didn't rattle him.

"Our prelim report will land in your inbox by five this evening," Zen said. She started to follow Peter out when Clive's voice stopped her.

"A moment, Zen," Clive rumbled.

Zen's internal antenna vibrated at the undercurrent in those few words. Clive didn't sound mad. He hadn't addressed her as "Batiste," or the more ominous "Doctor Batiste." And yet. She mentally ran through anything she might have done lately to incur his legendary wrath.

Zen faced him again. "Sir."

Peter glanced from Clive to Zen and then at Hadley, who remained seated. "We can compare notes before lunch, Dr. Batiste."

"We should dispense with formality by this time, Peter," Hadley said with a warm smile at him.

"Of course. I still feel like the odd man out so to speak. Because of... circumstances. I don't want to overstep." Peter blushed, gave a shy nod, and left the conference room before anyone could reply.

"To his point." Clive crossed his arms as he gazed at Zen.

"I haven't been mean to the new guy," Zen said. "I've shared information, told him where to find the restrooms, and I say 'Good morning' every day."

"In other words, the bare minimum of civility," Hadley murmured. She raised one dark blond eyebrow at Zen.

"Okay, look. The guy was a murder suspect. And let's not overlook that he could still be culpable for the disappearance of at least one person." Zen crossed her arms and looked from Hadley to Clive.

Clive's impassive expression didn't change. "Evidence supports—"

"Yeah, yeah. He was framed for six murders by another guy. I read the reports. But the facts are still the facts. They hung out together in the seedy underworld of sex workers, human and robot. How do we know they didn't commit murders together?" Zen stopped when Clive raised a palm for silence. She sighed and waited for the lecture.

"We've been over this, Zen. Navarro went through intensive treatment, medical and psychological. That, combined with solid forensic evidence, means he was given a second chance." Clive paced as he spoke. Then he stopped to stare at Zen.

"Transcranial magnetic stimulation to control violent outbursts. I know all about it, remember? I uncovered the project certain top officials kept buried. The procedure and post-treatment protocols aren't perfect," Zen said, referring to what was named the Lodestone investigation in their files.

"No, but from what researchers learned based on your fine work on the case, TMS treatment of those with antisocial behavior has improved by thirty percent," Clive replied, his deep voice even.

Zen blew out a long sigh. Then she rubbed her forehead. "I know, I know. We're approaching a new era, leaving behind the notion of locking people up for life. I can quote the study findings, too."

"Two police departments, the Maryland DA, and a court found the other man committed the murders. He's sitting in a maximum security prison. One of the two hundred criminals convicted of violent crimes deemed not suitable for or amenable to be included in the Lodestone treatment process." Clive nodded when Zen glanced at him in surprise.

"They were going to try on *him*? You've got to be kidding. Navarro is one thing, but that guy?" Zen shook her head slowly.

"Peter Navarro's work greatly contributed to the creation of 1-G gravity field generation, or GF as it's called. In fact, it can be argued it wouldn't exist without his groundbreaking research and development. Plans for expanding space colonies were accelerated. Space tourism is taking off." Hadley tapped a key on her tablet and a science news article replaced the image of Star Flight on the sixty-inch screen.

"Which is why he was approved for TMS and assigned to us. Too valuable to lose," Zen muttered.

"Yes," Clive said, his tone brusque. "Not to mention evidence he's *not a serial killer*. You think I'd accept Navarro or anyone on my team if I hadn't squeezed out every fact about him?"

"No, it's just..." Zen threw up both hands.

"He's being monitored by the treatment team. He has regular appointments. A special federal probation officer is assigned to him. Bases have been covered. Got it?" Clive gave Zen a pointed look.

"Yes, sir."

"Federally protected health information that stays between us three," Hadley put in.

"I appreciate you sharing that info, boss," Zen said in a chastened tone.

"I'm not ignoring your gut instinct as a criminologist or behavioral health expert. If you see any solid, and I do mean solid, signs the guy is unstable or at risk of any hinky behavior, take him down. But tell me *first*. Understood?"

"For sure."

Clive's smartwatch let out a soft notification tone. He glanced at it with a scowl. "I have to get moving. Hadley—"

"The report is in your encrypted inbox. The president's chief of staff has been briefed," Hadley replied with cool efficiency.

"You should rule the world, H." Clive gave her a grateful smile and marched out. He paused in the door. "Focus on Star Flight and the murder, Batiste."

"Definitely, sir." She watched him leave. "Don't say it," Zen blurted when the door shut, leaving them alone.

"I'm not going to fuss. I had the same misgivings," Hadley said.

"I have to work with the man, and now we're going into outer space. Being with him in the field requires a whole other level of trust, Hadley." Zen stared at the wide screen again.

"Believe me, Clive gets it. He wants you to concentrate on closing cases, not have to worry about your partner," Hadley said.

"But his patience won't last forever," Zen looked at her.

Hadley folded up her tablet and crossed to Zen. "We've got a suspicious death to solve. Not just for the victim's loved ones. There are wider implications."

"A billion-dollar investment in the first off-world destination for the public," Zen replied.

"NASA and the international corporations are antsy, to say the least. A lot is at stake. Do your thing, Zen. If anyone can get answers, it's you." Hadley flashed a smile of confidence at Zen and left.

"No problem. I'll just put it out of my mind," Zen grumbled to herself and went to her office.

Chapter 2

Later that evening, Zen sat at her long kitchen island while Astra prepared dinner. Nothing fancy. Astra was preparing her specialty, stir fried beef with Chinese veggies and homemade egg rolls. Zen had her mother to thank for Astra's culinary skills. They'd bonded over recipes since Astra was six years old.

"Lucky for you I cooked up a lot of frozen egg rolls last week. All we have to do is heat them up." Astra bustled between the six-burner stove, the convection oven, and the island.

"At this rate, you'll be good enough to open your own restaurant." Zen scrolled through personal emails and sipped wine as she waited.

"I'm committed to space research, like Dad. He sends love, by the way. Interesting that he's just coming back from the moon and you're about go." Astra grinned as she took plates from the warmer and filled them.

"I'm only stopping at the NASA lunar colony. Then I'll be at the space station. Not for long, so don't worry."

"Mama, please. I'm almost eighteen. For the hundred and fiftieth time, I can take care of myself," Astra replied.

"I don't care. Brianne is coming to stay with you," Zen replied in her best "don't bother arguing with me" tone. She felt much better knowing her brother's oldest child would be in the house. At twenty-two, Brianne was as serious about personal choices as she was about her studies in oceanography.

"I like my big cuz, but she's a little..." Astra shrugged as she stirred the vegetables. The fragrance of garlic, ginger, and soy sauce filled the kitchen.

"Level-headed, makes good decisions, grounded. I'm sure you meant one of those." Zen leaned back as Astra put a plate of food in front of her.

"Wound too tight. You even said that she tries too hard to please Uncle Brian and Auntie Gianna. They combined their names when she was born. That's a lot of pressure." Astra placed a small plate with egg rolls on the island.

"There is nothing wrong with being focused. Some might rub off on *you*." Zen paused to say a quick blessing over the food and then continued her lecture. She pointed a fork with noodles dangling from it at Astra. "School. Career. Parties should be a distant third."

"One time and I'm marked for life. Man!" Astra executed a perfect teenage eyeroll.

"Loni almost wrecked her car because y'all were playing too much and not paying attention. Which is how we found out you'd been drinking—"

"Loni was the designated driver. And I wasn't drunk. So, our favorite old school jam came on the system and we got carried away. I told Loni not to panic and call her dad."

"Right, because otherwise you four kids would have gotten away with it." Zen eyed Astra as she sliced a piece of the savory beef.

"We weren't trying to get away with anything. I just argued against getting you guys upset. Four sets of parents freaking out.

Well, at least Kalen's mom was cool." Astra grinned at her mother's snort.

"Kalen's got the 'cool mom,' which means he gets away with way too much in my opinion."

"Don't be judgy," Astra quipped.

"Humph."

"Didn't you have fun when you were young, or can't you remember back that far?" Astra smothered a giggle at the scowl Zen gave her.

"Ha-ha."

"Grandmother says you and Aunt Lexi got up to way worse," Astra said, seemingly determined to push more buttons by quoting Zen's mother.

"Which is why I want to head you off before you go too far, young lady," Zen replied mildly, sidestepping the trap.

"Grandaddy was cool about it," Astra said in an offhand way.

"They're not your parents," Zen pointed out.

"You're starting to sound like your mama more every day." Astra ducked when Zen aimed a playful swat at her.

"Maybe you don't need the car your father and I promised to buy. With public transportation, ride shares and—"

"Okay, okay," Astra blurted. "You're young, vibrant, the coolest mama ever. I'll make the Dean's List this semester. I promise. Anything else, just say the word."

"Yeah, I know your weak spots, too. And don't you forget it." Zen had no real worries about her only child but even a good kid needed guidance.

"Nobody knows the trouble I've seen," Astra mumbled.

Zen burst into loud laughter and Astra joined in after a few seconds. The family joke never failed to crack up Zen, her brothers, and their kids. Zen's paternal grandmother in Louisiana had taught all her grandchildren traditional African-American gospel songs. Grandmother Elise was a retired teacher. She couldn't stop drilling history lessons into her descendants even at the age of ninety-two.

"Ahem, speaking of Grandaddy," Astra murmured. She shot a side-eye at her mother and pretended intense interest in slicing her egg roll in half.

"We weren't talking about him," Zen said. "Your father says he might be in town next month."

"He told me. Nice try though. Back to *your* father, my grandfather. James Batiste. You should make up with him." Astra poked her mother's shoulder with one finger.

"Your dad might marry Minji. I'm surprised she's lasted almost two years. She has a possessive streak, if you ask me," Zen said. She and her ex-husband remained friends. His Korean-American girlfriend had been lobbying hard to be the next Mrs. Jordan Darensbourg. No doubt she was happy Zen had kept her maiden name.

"Mama." Astra put down her fork and stared at Zen.

"What? I'm not being catty. I like her. Well, not all that much, but—"

"Daddy can take care of himself, and you're not going to switch the subject. C'mon. What did Grandaddy do that you're still mad at him?"

Astra's voice held a note of pleading. For all her bravado, she became uneasy about family tensions. Her sensitivity sprang from the divorce. Zen felt a twinge of the old guilt. She and Jordan had worked extra hard to reassure Astra that her world wouldn't crash. Even so, Astra had a tendency to pick up any undercurrents of conflict. The effects of the seismic change in her childhood lingered.

"It's nothing you need to worry about, alright?"

Astra pushed vegetables and meat around on her plate. "He asked about you, which means you haven't talked to him in a while. I can tell he misses you."

Zen couldn't tell Astra the entire story. Not that Zen knew it all. Yet. James Batiste, expert in global space treaties and a visiting professor at three major universities. Retired CIA director. Except Zen learned during her last investigation that he wasn't retired. At least not when it came to global politics. Even her friend Chloé's digital investigation magic hadn't turned up much. On the surface, her father still loaned his expertise as an advisor to the White House when requested. As did a number of highly respected former government officials. Except Zen suspected there was much more to her father's "consulting" than met the eye.

Zen swallowed the lump of food stuck in her throat. The note of sadness in Astra's voice was real. She smiled and tugged on one of Astra's long micro-braids. "We'll work it out. You know how it goes. Every parent-child relationship hits a bump once in a while. Like you and that party..."

"Oh, no! Not again. Ethan didn't even trash his parents' beach house or anything," Astra protested.

"Thanks for reminding me you kids snuck off to the beach. In North Carolina, no less," Zen said.

"We're almost adults and his father said it was okay. Maybe he didn't mention how many of us would be there, but..." Astra heaved a sigh. "Fine. I'll become a nun and do nothing but study if you make up with Grandaddy."

"I said—"

"I heard what you told me, Mama. I also know you're leaving out a lot. It's something to do with work. I'm not asking for details, okay? Like Daddy says, you and Grandaddy can't talk about hush-hush government stuff. Just *call him*. He sounded a little sad when he asked about you." Astra rubbed her mother's shoulder. "I think you miss him, too."

"Okay, Little Miss Peace Maker. I hereby swear an oath to call my father and make nice with him." Zen said with her right hand raised.

"Tonight," Astra replied in a firm tone.

"Yes, before I go to bed. Now, let's enjoy this gourmet meal." Zen grinned at her and dug in.

Two hours later, Zen was sure Astra felt better about the state her of her family bonds. They'd laughed and talked about her college courses and latest crush as they cleaned up the dinner dishes. Now Astra was video chatting with her best pal Loni. Zen, dressed in her favorite leggings and sloppy sweatshirt, went to her home office. She logged into her computer to find three messages from Hadley and one from Peter Navarro. She couldn't resist looking in spite of her pledge not to let work creep into her home life. One quick scan wouldn't hurt.

Nothing earth-shaking. Hadley sent over the details of their flight off world. Shuttles to the moon and space stations had become routine in the past sixty years. They had flights on Luna Six, a shuttle operated by Space-Corp. Hadley's other messages had details about office duties assigned while they were gone. Peter supervised one male agent. Zen supervised three special agents who did security screens on space crews. Navarro's encrypted email was more interesting. Zen did more than skim his meticulous notes. She was soon pulled into the world of space tourism and a full description of Star Flight. The space station was known in official circles as In Situ because an entire third of the rotating wing held a NASA research facility. In Situ had developed advanced tech around developing resources on the moon and Mars. Space exploration was advancing rapidly as the means to extract water became cost effective. Scientists also worked on ways to generate oxygen. Another unit was working on materials to shield humans from the effects of radiation in space. The fourth section was making breakthroughs in Earth-like gravity fields.

Peter's email is what made Zen forget to call her father. He sent a full dossier on the murder victim and two persons of interest. Precise as any scientist, Peter stated it seemed too soon to label them as suspects. Zen looked over the three pages on them and agreed. Then she moved on to their victim. Hassan Ahmad, age fifty-three, had been in excellent physical health. No surprise since space travel required it. NASA and private space companies still had strict guidelines about tourists taking off from Earth. Two words explained their restrictions: legal liability.

Ahmad was an American citizen, fifth-generation Jordanian. He worked for a major mining equipment manufacturer. He and fifty of his colleagues from around the world had earned the trip to a trade convention, the first held in space. He was survived by his wife, two teenaged sons, parents, and six siblings. He had a taste for pole dancers, too much liquor, and one-night stands. The kids were staying with relatives while his wife accompanied him on the trip. She was still on the space station. What might turn out to be the crime scene, his hotel suite, indicated he had not been alone. Correction. Not the suite he'd shared with his wife. Ahmad had booked separate accommodations two levels away. His wife hadn't known about it.

"Tsk, tsk. But points for audacity," Zen murmured as she continued to read.

"Are you working or talking to Grandad?" Astra yelled from the hallway.

"Umm, I uh—" Zen tapped the keypad to close the documents just before Astra stuck her head in the door.

"Quit stalling." Astra, dressed in purple pajamas, crossed her arms.

When her desk phone trilled a soft ring tone, Zen picked up her wireless earbud. "Right after I take this important call about work. Now if you'll excuse me. And I promise to call him."

Astra jabbed a forefinger at her. "I'm going to call Grandad tomorrow and check." Then she disappeared.

"I'm still the parent around here, you know," Zen yelled after her.

"Whatever, Mom," Astra retorted, her voice fainter as she went down the hallway.

Zen connected to the call without looking at the digital phone display. She expected to hear either Hadley or Malone Ramirez. Malone had been her partner, the first two senior agents at the new space crime unit.

"Hello and thank you," Zen blurted. Only then did she realize the screen was blank.

"You're welcome, Dr. Batiste. But you might want to hear me out first," the male voice said. "My name is Jacques Clairmont. I'm with—"

"Global Associated Press. Pretty cool you're able to call me from space," Zen said. She began tapping her virtual keypad to activate a digital source trace.

"I'm on the terra side for now," Clairmont said, using the slang for being on Earth rather than in outer space. "I wanted to get a comment on why your unit is headed to the Star Flight Space Station."

"What do your sources say?" Zen activated the firmware in the phone system's router. Her computer whiz bestie Chloé had made it just for her.

"That the recent death of a businessman at the fancy hotel wasn't from natural causes. You're on the passenger list for the next shuttle leaving. I know because so am I."

"Interesting," Zen drawled. She divided her attention between listening to Clairmont and waiting for the results of her search. The app on her tablet opened. A map confirmed his call originated in New Jersey.

"I came here to get face-to-face interviews with his family. The authorities have kept me from his grieving widow. Did the feds order that she be isolated? That makes me think there's more to his death than we've been told."

"We who?" Zen replied.

"Stop the delay tactics, Dr. Batiste. I'm about to block all geolocation, so don't bother sending agents to detain me," Clairmont said.

"My goodness, Mr. Clairmont. Your imagination is on overload. As you no doubt know, any death in space is investigated. Even if the circumstances aren't suspicious. Section C, enacted in 2083, of article seventy-eight of the Outer Space Treaty of 2023—"

"Yes, the part added two years ago to cover crime in space. I get it. And until now international government space authorities have insisted crime isn't a problem out there. But the formation of your unit last year says otherwise. First there was the death at the first Mars colony twenty years ago. Then on the moon last year." Clairmont pressed on in a mild voice.

"Which we investigated and resolved. Human beings don't change because they're working in space, Mr. Clairmont," Zen said, fighting to keep her temper in check.

"Call me Jack, please, like my other American friends. We'll get to know each other during the trip and on the space station," Clairmont said in a jaunty tone.

"No, Jack. We won't," Zen clipped.

"We certainly aren't adversaries, Dr. Batiste. Or may I call you Zenobia? Such a lovely name, by the way. I won't presume to call you Zen, as your family and close associates do."

Zen pushed down the string of expletives she really wanted to spew. "Thank you, and no, you may not."

"Democracies are strengthened by a free and unfettered press. Journalists provide the public and governments with information we all need. Democratic governing has spread and persists. Despite the efforts of nationalists and other right-wing extremist groups."

"In other words, we're on the same side. I can trust you with inside information because you're working for the greater good. As opposed to earning more awards and money for getting a big story."

"Who says money and ethics are incompatible? Your investigation into the Goddard Space Corporation deaths in

Chile and on the NASA moon colony was impressive," Clairmont went on, brushing aside her sarcasm.

"Then you also know that several were confirmed as accidents. No lurid murder details to splash across headlines," Zen said.

"There was more to those deaths though, weren't there? Something the White House did a very thorough job of hiding. Training for space assignments was revamped, according to my sources. A shadowy research organization called Tetra was involved. Exceptional care taken to keep those details behind firewalls."

Zen smiled when the app zeroed in on his secure server. Clairmont had his IP address sent through six different routes to end up in Russia. It masked that he had a separate VPN that went through the darknet.

"By the way, it's illegal to access United States classified government files. That includes federal employee personal data, like phone codes," Zen said. She executed several keystrokes as she spoke. "Like you did when you reported on the Trachtenberg Project in 2080. You narrowly avoided being prosecuted in three countries."

Clairmont went silent for a few seconds. "A close call, for sure. So, you don't have a comment for me?"

"In accordance with US and international law, we want to make sure citizens are safe in outer space. Death investigations provide information on the possible effects of changes in the body caused by sustained visits off-world." Zen suppressed a chuckle when Clairmont hissed in frustration as she droned on. "Investigations by my department serve to assure the public that we cover all bases, even in the case of death by natural causes. Mr.

Hassan Ahmad had at least one undiagnosed health condition that we know of, which may have played a factor."

"I'm good at what I do. Something I'm sure your now-complete file on me reveals. I'll get the real story."

"Good-bye, Mr. Clairmont. My phone codes have been scrambled," Zen added. The system would automatically update cloud contact data on the devices of her family and close friends.

"Oh, I won't need to call you again. Now that you've opened a case, you have to give regular press updates. Also a provision of the Outer Space Treaty of 2023. I'll see you on our flight, Dr. Batiste."

Zen took small satisfaction is ending the call without replying. She slapped the "end" button harder than necessary. When the phone rang again, she muttered a curse word. Her father's name appeared on the screen. She took in a deep breath and let it out. Only then did she connect the called.

"Hi, Daddy. How are you and Mama?" Zen said, hoping her voice sounded sufficiently normal.

"We're both fine. Thanks for asking after I had to call *you*." James Batiste's basso voice rolled through her earbuds like thunder.

"I was just about to call and don't make a smart remark. It happens to be true. Your granddaughter has been petitioning on your behalf. She thinks we're feuding." Zen could always talk straight to her father. Her interactions with Enola Batiste, on the other hand, were a different matter.

"Nonsense. You did your job. I took care of certain complications that happened to have intersected with your investigation. I know my involvement was a shock. But you understand the nature of classified operations," James said. He could have been lecturing a class of special agents in training. He had, in fact, done so frequently during his career.

"Wow, that's a neat mental trick. You make decisions that keep facts from me, facts you should have trusted me with, and presto! You did nothing wrong."

"Listen, daughter, the longer you're in the company," James said, his reference to all US intelligence agencies, "the more you'll accept why certain decisions have to be made. I trust you, Zen. You should know that by now."

Zen tapped a finger on the oak surface of her desk. "Yes, Daddy."

"It's not a matter of right or wrong. but making the best choice in a tricky situation. Leave self-righteous moralizing to pompous preachers."

"Don't let Enola Lee hear you talking like that. Mama has you going to church more after almost forty years. She'll clean you up from those heathen ways yet," Zen teased.

"Humph. I enjoy making your mother happy. Plus, those church cooks make some mean potato salad," James replied with a laugh. "So, daughter, we good?"

"I thought we weren't feuding."

"You haven't called in three weeks. And the last conversation we had was brief. I know when you're irritated with me." James paused. "Well?"

Zen's heart softened at the deep undercurrent of worry in his voice. "We good, Daddy. Always."

"That's my baby girl. Ahem, so you're going on your first space flight, I hear. Your mother has become an expert on shuttles, the effects of space on the body, and more. I think she would work for NASA." James paused.

"Astra must be giving you daily briefings on me. Yes, I'm leaving tomorrow evening."

"I've reassured your mother that space shuttle flights are as routine as plane travel on Earth these days," James replied.

"I doubt that made her feel better." Zen shook her head. Her mother had traveled to more than thirty countries over the years. She still didn't enjoy flying.

"Call her tomorrow before you leave, Zenobia. I know you'll be busy preparing for that case, but…" James paused for a few seconds. "She doesn't fuss over you, and I know you've had differences over the years. But she worries."

"I know."

Zen heard the unspoken. He and her mother rarely talked about her younger sister's death. Not outright. Lexi's unsolved murder would always be the silent shadow that followed them. Even during joyful family gatherings, Zen would catch her mother looking at them all with unshed tears. Or her father would become quiet and go off on his own.

"Anyway, you know how she is. She's gathered all of her facts and keeps dropping hints about what you're doing," James said.

"You mean critiquing my every move. She's says I've gotten 'mixed up in crime.' Her church friends probably think I'm a major gang leader," Zen joked.

"Don't be silly. Besides, they've seen the news stories about you."

"Okay, now it's your turn. Go ahead. Lecture me on how the best intelligence and criminal investigators don't become the news." Zen sat back to wait.

"Give me more credit, Zenobia. You didn't have a choice. Anything connected to space is big news. It wasn't your fault.

Deaths at a space training camp and on the lunar colony? Couldn't keep that under wraps for long," James said in practical tone.

"Thank you."

"Madrid was another matter, though." Her father's voice dropped low. "Just be thankful I've kept the details from your mother."

"You told her quite enough," Zen retorted.

To be fair, the facts about her trip to Madrid had been sensational. Zen went to track a suspected serial killer. Who in turn became her new partner at the OSI by a breathtaking twist of fate. Her father seemed to read her thoughts across the miles from his home in Maryland.

"How's Navarro?" James asked.

"Clive and Hadley never cease to remind me that he was framed. That his treatment has been effective, and he's closely monitored." Zen sighed. "I don't know what the stress of launching into space will do to him, Daddy."

"You're the mental health expert. You see any signs he's unstable, on the edge?"

Zen thought for a few moments. "Honestly, no. Being a research scientist means he knows how to follow leads, test facts and theories. With additional investigator training and his knowledge of the space program... On the surface it's a brilliant decision."

James gave a short laugh. "I agree. Someone probably did one hell of a sales job to NASA, the White House. Not to mention your boss."

"Wait a minute." Zen sat straight. "You didn't—"

"No, Zenobia. I can't take credit for this one," James said. "The man is a genius. If any of those other space folks try to blow smoke up your ass, he'll know it instantly."

"Yeah. Perfect choice on an outer space crime fighting team. At least that's what this pain of a reporter calls us," Zen said with a grunt.

"You just be careful. I know you've come through your training with exceptional ratings. But if you need anything, let me know."

"Thanks, Daddy. Be sure to report back to Astra that we talked," Zen added in dry tone.

James laughed. "I don't know what you're talking about. Oh, and I'll tell your mother the trip is just routine inquiries for your unit. A dry run, even. No need to upset her."

"Oh, I'm prepared for the full Enola treatment when we talk tomorrow. Believe me," Zen replied.

"Don't judge your mother, baby girl. Think how you'll feel when Astra starts going farther from home."

"Gee thanks. I'll be mentally scrolling through all the ways Astra can get in trouble until two in the morning."

"Don't worry. You've got time yet before Astra starts crossing borders or going into the great beyond. Brianne is the perfect choice to stay with her. They'll be going to museums and art lectures instead of frat parties," James said. "Have a restful night. You've got some busy days ahead. Love you."

"Bye, Daddy. Love you, too."

Zen ended the call. She laughed at the thought of serious Brianne dragging Astra along to a science symposium. Then she went down the hall to Astra's room and knocked.

"You may enter the inner sanctum," Astra called out.

"Generous of you, considering I pay the mortgage," Zen quipped before she opened the door. She heaved a sigh at the state of Astra's bedroom. Clothes were thrown over the chairs. Even on her desk. Books were piled high in two corners, threatening to fall over. Astra sat crossed-legged on her bed, a plate of cookies to one side. "Seriously?"

"What? It's Tuesday and I have a busy week of classes and hanging with my friends."

Zen picked up two sweaters and sniffed them. "I guess you being smart *and* tidy is too much to ask."

"A messy room is a sign of genius," Astra replied.

"You just made that up." Zen made a neat stack of clothes to take to the laundry room. She picked up two textbooks and pointed to empty shelves. "You have a bookcase for a reason, you know."

"Thanks for the reminder. Did you come just to criticize me or is there another reason for this visit?" Astra bit into an almond butter cookie.

"I came to report that your call to Daddy was effective. We had a nice chat. Very warm, no shots fired." Zen sat down on the pale pink comforter across from Astra.

"Excellent!" Astra reached out and hugged Zen. A cookie slid onto the bed.

"Careful. Good grief." Zen giggled and hugged her back.

"You look more relaxed already. I didn't want you going off into outer space with unresolved issues between you. I always feel great after a talk with my dad." Astra sat back with a look of satisfaction.

"Tomorrow I'll call Mama. That way you won't have to check in with Daddy again. All is well." Zen patted her cheek.

"I haven't talked to Grandaddy since last Friday. He missed you. I'm glad he reached out." Astra popped the last piece of cookie in her mouth and chewed.

Zen started to hop from the bed and continue cleaning but froze in place. She blinked hard, mind whirling. Astra seemed not to notice. She chattered on about plans she'd made with her cousin Brianne. They'd been texting back and forth. Then Astra launched into a spirited account of school drama. Something about Loni having a beef with a girl who thought she'd messaged her boyfriend. Zen only heard disjointed snatches of Astra's story.

"You didn't call Daddy tonight?" Zen cut in when Astra finally took a breath.

"Uh-uh. All day has been crazy. I emailed two papers I barely finished on time. Then Loni called, and Brianne—"

"You couldn't have told him about my shuttle to Star Flight, then. I didn't even know until today," Zen murmured.

"No way. I always leave that kind of breaking news to *you*. I don't need another lecture on talking too much," Astra declared. Then she proceeded to do just that by continuing her story. "So, then Talisha said to Loni—"

"And you're sure you didn't talk to Daddy today," Zen broke in.

"Things were wild, but I think I'd remember talking to my own grandfather. Anyway, I don't know why Loni entertains schoolyard drama. We're college girls now and..." Astra gazed at her mother. "What's happened?"

"Nothing. Don't stay up too late." Zen headed for the door.

"Okay. Speaking of drama," Astra muttered with a sigh as she watched her leave.

Zen padded down the hallway to her office again. She shut the door and prepared for her own late night of searching. She intended to find out if intelligence and global diplomacy legend James Batiste was somehow connected to her new case.

Chapter 3

Tuesday dawned, a crisp and sunny April morning. To prepare for her first space flight, Zen got up early for a run. She left at six and returned by seven-fifteen. Brianne arrived at eight full of energy and with a full slate of activities planned. Zen watched with amusement as her niece and daughter sparred over the schedule.

"Good God, Bri. You're like my kindergarten teacher. I swear, if you mention nap time we're gonna have a problem," Astra grumbled. She stuffed buttered toast into her mouth and glared at her cousin.

Brianne offered Astra a slice of apple. She grinned when Astra snatched it with a grudging glare. "You're welcome. I looked at your college program. You'll be ahead of the game if you follow my advice. There's a lecture at the Smithsonian that you should find interesting."

"I Iumph." Astra shot Zen an accusatory side-eye.

"At least be open to her suggestions," Zen said. She smothered a giggle when Astra's glare fired up.

"Humanoid innovations as a means to explore dangerous environments," Brianne said, reading a flyer. "Like going deep into the ocean without a submersible or working on a planet with no atmosphere. Or one toxic to humans. Personally, it makes more sense to understand this planet better before we blast off. Not to mention find ways to clean up the pollutants poisoning it."

"But you have to admit, finding another Earth-like planet would be cool. And then there's the possibility, or I think probability, of finding alien life," Astra countered.

Zen listened as they debated their favorite topic, the wisdom of spending billions on space versus saving mother Earth. "You girls have such interesting conversations. Brianne, I'll get the dishes. You two get going."

"Are you sure, Aunt Zen? It's no bother. The first lecture doesn't start for another hour or so," Brianne said.

"I'm about to fix my own breakfast, so I'll have to clean up anyway," Zen replied.

"The *first* lecture? How many are you dragging me to, Bri?" Astra planted both hands on her hips.

"Besides which, we'll be doing dishes while you're gone anyway," Brianne said to Zen without looking at Astra.

"Wait a minute. There's no reason we can't do takeout and meal delivery. Pizza, Chinese food, Greek, anything we want can be here in minutes," Astra said, her voice rising. "Mama, talk some sense into her."

"And housework," Brianne pressed on. She raised an eyebrow at Astra.

"Okay, now you've gone too far." Astra playfully tackled Brianne.

Both giggled and howled in pretend rage. They ended up down the hallway, trading jokes about each other. Zen shook her head with a laugh. Minutes later they were dressed and ready to leave. The kitchen doorbell chimed. A tall figure was silhouetted behind the curtain that covered the window of the door.

"I'll get it. Well, well." Astra shot a grin at Brianne and stage-whispered, "Mama's new good, good thing."

"I get to meet him! I can already tell he's fine." Brianne's hazel eyes glittered with gleeful anticipation.

"I'm going to get you both for—" Zen broke off when Astra opened the door with a dramatic flourish.

"Good morning, Special Agent Ramirez," Astra declared. "You may enter."

Dressed in a navy-blue sweatshirt over jeans, Malone strolled in. At six feet three, he looked well-built without having bulging muscles. He'd been Zen's first partner at the nascent Office of Special Investigations, the nondescript name for what they did. Criminal investigations in the space program. Malone was still in the Air Force, a member of their military police force. He was also a trained astronaut. He'd gone on three flights, in fact. After their first case, he'd been recruited by the Department of Justice to train the first fully staffed space police force.

"Hello, you little scamp. Teasing your mother again, I see." Malone grinned and pinched Astra's cheek as he walked inside.

"Certainly not. This is my cousin Brianne. She will dutifully report back to my uncle everything about you. So, be on your best behavior," Astra replied.

"Yes, ma'am. Pleased to meet you, Brianne." Malone performed a mock bow.

"Aren't you supposed to be at work?" Astra wiggled her eyebrows at him.

"I took a day. Can't let my lady fly into the great unknown without seeing her off," Malone replied.

"Whoa!" Astra and Brianne said in unison with matching wicked grins.

"You two, out." Zen affected a scowl.

"Bye-eee." Astra grabbed her backpack from a stool at the kitchen island.

"Have a great morning, guys," Brianne added. She followed Astra through the door. The sound of their chatter and giggles drifted back after it closed.

"Now you see what I have to put up with." Zen shook her head.

"Hey, you gotta expect it. I'm your first serious boyfriend since your divorce." Malone pulled Zen against his muscular body. "Hmm, you smell like sunshine. And bacon."

"Is that your romantic way of saying you haven't had breakfast?" Zen accepted his kiss and pulled back.

"I went to the gym early and had a smoothie. But that was at five o'clock. I could eat, now that you mention it."

Malone didn't wait for Zen to move. He went to the refrigerator. In short order he'd heated up veggie breakfast sausage, made toast, and poured glasses of mixed berry juice. They sat at the island while he ate and Zen had her second mug of coffee.

"Nervous?" Malone wiped his mouth with the napkin Zen handed him.

"A little," Zen admitted.

"Good. I'd be more worried if you'd said no. Hydrate. No heavy meals."

"Yes, and thank you. I've gotten the lecture from Jordan already." Zen put down her mug when Malone gazed at her. "I won't have any more after this."

"Coffee is a diuretic. You don't want to spend fifteen hours of that trip peeing. Getting out of those suits for runs to the ladies' room will be a workout You'll be exhausted by the time—"

"Really, Malone?" Zen slapped his shoulder. She took one of four sausage links from his plate and bit into it.

Malone laughed. He got up and made two slices of toast for Zen. Then he put the plate in front of her. "How is your ex, by the way?"

"Working hard as usual, but fine. He says 'hello.' "

"Tell him 'Hey' for me. Good guy." Malone nodded and sat down to eat again.

Malone and Jordan had sized each other up. Then decided they were okay. Jordan wanted to get a look at the man who would be around his daughter. Malone wanted to get the measure of Zen's ex-husband; see if he'd be a problem. For his part, Jordan was reassured because Malone was a devoted father to his two little boys. Zen expected them to be friends after a time.

"Hmm." Zen stared into her coffee.

"And speaking of James..." Malone pushed aside his empty plate.

"Mind reader," Zen said with a smile that faded fast.

"Bet I wasn't the only one you called last night about him. So, what did Chloé root out in the virtual world?" Malone lifted one dark eyebrow.

"I'm not saying I did or didn't. But if I did call an *unnamed* friend, then she or he didn't find much. My father has decades of experience burying his tracks. Not to mention his own 'unnamed friends' to help." Zen heaved a sigh of frustration and gulped more coffee.

"And you've run out of time to get intel before you blast off," Malone said with sympathy in his dark eyes. He rubbed her shoulder.

"Exactly. Navarro is still digging. Maybe he'll have better luck. He sure knows about hiding secrets and shadowy activities," Zen replied with a frown.

"Your new partner is being watched closely. He's complied with all the conditions of his treatment and parole." Malone shrugged when Zen looked at him. "Hey, I want to make sure you're safe."

"My hero," Zen drawled and kissed his cheek. She got up and poured her own glass of juice.

"Now what? You go to the moon first. By tomorrow at nine, Earth Easter time you'll arrive at the space station. You'll need another few hours to adjust physically. Time spent in the gravity cube to get used to the difference in space." Malone sipped more juice as his brow wrinkled in thought.

"The In Situ research team is close to finding a way to create 1 g in space. But at least we have the cubes," Zen replied, referring to rooms where space travelers could spend time in Earth-like gravity.

"Yeah, and creating oxygen and ship fuel on site is making longer space exploration way less costly. Still, I don't get why anyone would want to hang out at a hotel out there. It's cold and empty, except for chunks of rock the size of buildings speeding at you." Malone shook his head.

"Excitement. Private companies see dollar signs. Voila, hotel suites that are basically outfitted 1 g suites. Guests can switch them off, with approval from hotel management. Then they can have a weightless experience for short periods," Zen said, repeating the background report from Hadley.

"Humph. I'll keep that bit of info from my boys. They'd drive me crazy begging to go. Besides, I don't have the cash for three shuttle tickets." Malone grinned.

"Not to mention how busy you are training a cadre of space jedi to fight for truth and justice." Zen laughed when Malone let out a groan.

"Don't even joke about it out loud. We're just cops who happen to have outer space as our beat." Malone paused in the act of drinking more juice. He lowered his glass. "Damn, when I say it like that..."

"Exactly. Jedi," Zen quipped.

Malone had been recruited to help train what had essentially become a police force in space. His officers covered five lunar colonies and all three space stations. Six countries sent men and women to be employed by the Global Police Agency. The GPA had been created after sometimes-contentious negotiations overseen by the United Nations Security Council. The five major governments agreed that the new space police force would be an organ of the United Nations. Malone technically worked for the UN, but the United States still had outsized influence. Russia, China, Africa, and Japan kept a close eye to maintain a balance of interests.

"Our public information office has done a great job of making us seem less..."

"Like characters from a sci-fi movie?" Zen put both arms around his narrow waist.

"Yeah. My people have secured the scene. Statements were sent to Clive. They continue to interview guests. About thirty or forty were cleared to return home. No connection to the victim, nowhere near the wing he was in, no reason to keep them on the space station. We have their information in case they need to be questioned again," Malone said, switching to police officer mode.

"Right." Zen let go of him and started to clean up, her mind already in space.

His officers were the equivalent of uniformed police officers. For now, Zen and Peter were like senior homicide detectives. Three junior special agents were training to do major crime investigations.

Malone watched Zen move around the kitchen for a time. She loaded the dishwasher. Wiped the quartz countertops. Put the carafe of juice away. Zen acted on auto mode, going through the motions of what she'd done so many times before. Malone finally cleared his throat.

"Okay, here's one thing you should know."

Zen face him, a dish towel still in hand. His tone and serious expression pulled her back to earth. "Yes?"

"And you didn't hear this from me." Malone drummed his fingers on the kitchen island's surface.

"Nothing could make me talk. Go on." Zen hung the towel on a rack and sat next to him.

Malone sighed. "I've gotten word, nothing confirmed, that humanoids are being used by private companies. They've advanced so most people don't notice they're synthetic."

"Isn't that still under discussion and negotiations between the major powers?"

"Yeah, well, the private space companies and robot manufacturers got tired of waiting. The tech is moving way faster than global political bickering. The use of humanoids is still uncharted territory. No laws explicitly stop companies from using human-like robots," Malone replied.

"Right. NASA and governments have been using robots for over a hundred years. Technically, they're just fancier versions," Zen murmured.

"Except they have way advanced artificial intelligence, cameras, and microphones built in to record data to a cloud and—"

"Super spy capabilities. Government and corporate espionage would escalate astronomically. Pun intended."

Malone nodded with a frown. "A threat to world peace times ten. So, you can see why a treaty on the use of humanoids is important. Big companies are operating in space like world governments. They have their own security units."

"Are we talking turf wars?" Zen looked at him.

"Fortunately, it hasn't gotten to that level. Yet. Now with this murder." Malone's expression turned grim.

"Your people are pretty sure Ahmad didn't die from natural causes," Zen said.

"Nothing confirmed, but the circumstances don't pass the smell test," Malone said.

"You think a business rival took the guy out? Damn, if that's the case..."

"Hey, at this point I don't rule it out. We've had to step in to head off some pretty heated conflicts between companies. None of this is public knowledge. The battles between big companies, the humanoids in space. None of it. Keep your eyes open and your back covered," Malone said.

"Damn." Zen blinked at him. "There's a reporter—"

"I know. GPA officers are expecting you. One of my best, Sergeant Wyvette Young, will be your liaison. She's been on Star Flight for about a year. Young has experience running circles around Clairmont. She's also the one who got the tip on humanoids."

"There's a lot of prejudice against bots, you know. Paranoia fueled by sci-fi fiction about killer robots. Then there's the religious bigotry about them being unholy or some such nonsense." Zen grimaced with distaste.

"Well, the other stuff Young suspects won't help. She thinks bang bots are being used as entertainment in the two hotels. At the bars as well," Malone said.

"Robots used for sex work. The range of ways human beings find to get freaky is amazing," Zen said with a snort.

"Sex dolls have been used for generations. I don't get it, but..." Malone seemed at a loss for words.

"They talk, have synthetic skin, systems to make them warm. I've been told they're very lifelike. Some even argue that they are become self-determining beings. That they have civil and human rights."

"Okay, you've gotten too philosophical for me. I'm a simple military cop. They're machines. Period. And the entire subject is kind of weird."

"I didn't say I agree. Honestly, I don't know what to think." Zen sorted through a maze of thoughts and emotions about the issue.

After a few moments of silence, Malone nudged her. "Hey, you could ask your partner about it. Navarro has loads of experience with bots."

Zen turned to Malone, who looked back at her with an impish half grin. "Very funny. Now what do I tell Clive?"

"Everything. He hates not being informed by his team members." Malone drew a finger across his throat to emphasize Clive's legendary wrath.

"Yeah, volcanic eruption of epic proportions," Zen replied with a melodramatic shudder.

"Which you faced down a time or two and lived to talk about."

"Hmm, I have loads of practice living with James and Enola Batiste." Zen's smile turned to a frown in seconds.

"He knows about your case. Doesn't mean he's got his fingers in it," Malone said, reading her expression.

"If I confide in him about the bots, the corporate trouble brewing..." Zen slapped the quartz counter surface. "Damn it. Why can't he be a normal retiree and play golf or go fishing?"

"Maybe if you lay your cards on the table, he'll share information with you. He wants your trust, right? Make him earn it." Malone took one of Zen's hands in his.

"Hmm. Maybe when I get back. Let him wonder about what I find out on the station for now." Zen leaned against Malone's strong shoulder.

"If he doesn't have a source on Star Flight or the moon already," Malone replied and kissed her forehead.

"Thanks for the reassurance. You really think his reach goes that far though?"

"I think you should concentrate on rest, clear your head before you leave tonight. You've got an intense fourteen to twenty days ahead. Got Astra's childcare all arranged?"

"Ooo-wee, don't let her hear you even joke about her needing a babysitter!" Zen chuckled. "Brianne will be here for a week. Then they'll spend spring break from studies with my brother. After that, a few days with my parents."

"No time with her dad?"

"Jordan's knee-deep in a new assignment. He'll be on the Isis Space Station in about eight or nine months," Zen replied, her mind still on her new case. Jordan was not only an astronaut, but a doctor. He'd become a specialist in medical research in space.

"Cool. Well, I prescribe relaxation after the workouts you've done." Malone stood behind Zen to rub her shoulders.

"Do you, Dr. Ramirez?"

"Stress release is the best medicine," Malone murmured. His lips brushed her ear.

"A massage sounds like just the thing." Zen sighed at his firm but gentle touch. Muscle tension from the puzzle buzzing in her mind melted away.

"Hmm, yeah. Whole body." Malone pulled her up and wrapped both arms around her.

Two hours later, Malone had showered and left. Zen did indeed feel centered. Tender moments with him had made a big difference in her attitude. He had her back. Her daughter would be in good hands. So, Zen turned laser-like focus on packing a few personal items for her trip. She chose five shirts, all lightweight fabrics that didn't take up much room. Her three pairs of knit slacks were the same. All rolled up in packing cubes that took up little room in her carry-on pack. Her natural hair was done in thick braids. Any extra toiletries she might need could be bought at a space bodega on the moon or one of two on the Star Flight. Zen put her bag near the kitchen door and went to her home office. She read through Peter's reports and Hadley's written briefings several times. When Astra and Brianne returned, she put work away to spend time with them. At three in the afternoon, she kissed her daughter and niece good-bye.

Zen took an AI self-driven taxi to the airport. A military electric plane took her to Florida in less than two hours. Her fellow travelers were a mix of young Air Force members and a few serious types dressed in civilian clothes. Zen couldn't help but steal side glances at them. She wondered if one of them worked for her father. Forty minutes later they arrived at the Air Force base just outside of Orlando. Only five of the men and women boarded the shuttle bus for Cape Canaveral. Zen kept an eye on all of them. Not one gave any sign they were watching her. One young woman, dressed in her uniform, struck up a casual conversation. Nothing unusual.

By the time Zen got to the space shuttle site, she had talked herself down from being so suspicious. Peter had already arrived and was being fitted with his suit for travel. They prepared in a section only for government employees. He looked totally calm.

"You ready?"

"As anyone can be facing g-force, almost two days on a rocket, and murder." Zen spoke low even though no one was near them.

"Nothing like the other trips I made. This is research of a very different sort."

Peter patted down the flexible mylar and Kevlar, a new version created in the last twenty years. A network of sensors in the fabric monitored the vital functions of wearers. What looked like a small backpack was sewn in with the oxygen generator. Two small containers of water were woven into other compartments. Those were back-up supplies in case the space shuttle's systems failed. Their helmets were now optional after the first fifteen minutes or so. Most travelers kept them on during the flights. Automatic snaps and locks allowed the helmets to be quickly clicked in place. Connections to tubes would deliver air and water.

"I read your briefing with added information about humanoids and fighting between the private space companies. Interesting."

Peter started to say more but stopped when an Air Force officer came in. The woman nodded a greeting to them, suited up with expert moves in minutes, and left. Zen watched her leave and then turned to Peter.

"All unconfirmed. Stick to what we know. So far, no indication that Ahmad's death is related to his work," Zen said.

A cheerful space shuttle attendant appeared in the doorway. He wore a light blue shirt tucked into navy slacks, the standard Air Force attire. "Dr. Batiste, Dr. Navarro, time to board. I'll lead you to your seats. Your row is separate from the seven civilians on board."

"Thanks," Peter said and led the way.

Zen started rhythmic breathing to settle her nerves. Anxiety mixed with excitement made her a bit dazed. She listened to the flight instructions of the attendants. Then they buckled themselves in for the ride. The force of lift-off pressed them back against the bucket seats they were in. Another twenty minutes went by before they were weightless in space. Zen marveled at how quiet the ride became once the boosters stopped firing.

"A significant improvement from twentieth-century ships. Fuel is lighter," Peter said.

He spoke in an even tone, like a college professor starting a lecture. His voice came through clear in the audio speaker in Zen's helmet. She blinked at the odd tingling in her skin. For a moment she considered looking out of the window to their left but decided against it.

"Quantum vacuum," Peter said.

Zen started at the clear voice coming through the compact speaker in her helmet. "What?"

"Pioneered in 2020 by a scientist called Pais. He was a genius. I and two of my colleagues built on his research. Friction is reduced using quantum vacuum. Less friction, faster space travel."

"Right." Zen's growing jitters at being shot into a dark void started to recede, replaced by annoyance.

"That, along with refinements in gravitational—"

"I get it," Zen broke in.

"We're cruising and oxygen levels are normal. Helmets are now optional. If conditions change, follow instructions," a pleasant AI voice announced. "Gravity optimum has commenced. You may now move about the cabin for short periods."

A cheer went up from several passengers. A smiling flight attendant appeared and handed out cups of juice. The refreshments were designed to increase hydration. Additional vitamins and minerals also helped combat space sickness.

"Interesting how the human touch makes such a difference. All of the technology we have, but people still prefer a human to AI attendants." Peter waved away the offer of refreshments from the attendant.

Zen accepting a cup of mango lemonade. One sip made her sigh with satisfaction. She stared into the cup. "This stuff is amazing."

"Formulas that not only taste delicious, but deliver nutrition the body needs to combat disorientation caused by space flight," Peter said.

The flight attendant appeared as if on cue from him. "Trail mix packed with protein and antioxidants."

"Thanks," Zen said with a side glance at Peter. She accepted the bag with dried fruits, nuts, and dark chocolate. "Don't tell me. You helped design menu options for dining in space."

Peter smiled and shook his head. "No, and I apologize for sounding like a know-it-all. My flawed attempt to distract you from distress."

"I'm fine." Zen plastered on a smile. The shuttle shifted and her yelp spoiled the courageous façade.

"It's okay, Dr. Batiste. Everyone goes through it the first three trips at least," Peter said. He patted the back of her hand that gripped the seat arm. Moments later he left his seat.

"Damn, get it together," Zen mumbled. She closed her eyes. When footsteps approached, she opened them to appear cool.

"Enjoying the ride?"

Zen turned to find the reporter in Peter's seat beside her. Jacques Clairmont wore a suit with the news agency logo on it. "I will once you're gone."

"We both go after the truth no matter where it leads. In this case, into the great expanse." Clairmont waved a hand toward the window.

"You should be on the stage, the way you love drama." Zen settled into her seat and looked straight ahead.

"So, we're not going to talk candidly about why the famous Dr. Zenobia Batiste going to Star Flight?"

"And it only took you a few seconds to figure it out. Impressive." Zen tapped on the entertainment unit in front of her. She scrolled through the options, pointedly ignoring Clairmont.

A bulky man's deep voice bounced in the shuttle cabin. He blocked Peter's path back to their seat row. "Hey, you. Navarro is your name. I saw stories about you on the Global Newsfeed."

"Excuse me, sir. You're in my way." Peter's voice stayed level.

"Some kind of freaky stuff with bang bots. Sick if you ask me. I was at the Harris Air Force base when they caught you. My sister was stationed there, too. I think they covered up the real story. You were as guilty as that other psycho. Framed, my ass." The man swayed.

"Sit down, Will," another man said through tight lips. "You guzzled too many bourbons last night." He looked at Peter. "Sorry."

"The effect of alcohol can be heightened in space. Just get him some juice and let him sleep it off," Peter said calmly.

"Hey, don't talk over me like I'm not here." Will swayed as he jabbed a finger at Peter. "Now everyone on board knows who you are, sicko."

Clairmont managed to wedge himself past the man to stand between them. "Look, you don't want this kind of trouble."

"How about you mind your business." The man poked Clairmont's chest with the same finger.

"William Mulligan, AI engineer contracted with the Air Force. Navy vet with two tours in the conflict between China and Russia," Clairmont replied fast, rattling off the man's details.

"Who the hell are you anyway?" The man frowned at Clairmont. He blinked hard as if trying to focus.

"A reporter for the Global Associated Press. Which means I could plaster your picture all over the internet. Drunken Temple Corporation employee brawls on space shuttle. Dr. Navarro is too valuable to NASA and the White House. So, guess who'll get kicked back to Earth? Spoiler alert—it won't be *him*." Clairmont glanced at Peter and back to the man.

"You don't know anything," the man muttered. Despite the buzz hanging on after hours of drinking, Clairmont's words seemed to sink in.

"That pretty lady on row six you're trying to impress looks anything but right now." Clairmont jerked his head toward the woman in question. She wore a frown that communicated distaste.

The flight attendant marched up seconds later. Her congenial expression gone, she looked capable of manhandling him. "Sit down, *sir*."

The man leaned back as if her words had pushed him. "I was just asking the guy—"

"Now." The flight attendant pointed to a seat four rows away. "I've arranged for a change. You'll be more comfortable on row twelve."

"Thanks," the man's companion said. He grabbed two compact bags and pushed Will ahead of him. "Shut the fuck up. I'm not losing this job because of you. Asshole."

"Listen to your colleague, Will," Clairmont called after the men. Then he beamed at Peter. "You're welcome."

"I didn't need your help." Peter brushed past him to stand next to his seat. He glanced down at Zen.

"Clairmont was just explaining how we're all on the same team." Zen looked from Peter to the reporter.

"I doubt that very much." Peter's stony gaze bore into Clairmont. "We're not giving you any statements. Classified government business is not for public consumption on gossip news sites."

"So, you're on a top-secret mission connected to the death of businessman Hassan Ahmad," Clairmont shot back, undeterred. He flinched when Peter took a step closer to him. "Easy."

"You'll very much regret any such news release, young man," Peter growled.

"A free press is the cornerstone of democracy," Clairmont replied.

"I got that lecture from him, too," Zen retorted.

Peter glared at Clairmont. "Reporters don't care about the lives they destroy. Why confirm facts? We'll get the story out, grab the public's attention, make money, and worry about the truth later."

"I reported what the authorities released. Nothing in my story was a lie or distorted," Clairmont said. He held up both palms as if they could shield him from Peter's wrath.

Zen switched her focus from Clairmont to Peter. His dark eyes glittered with animosity. His mild-mannered science nerd demeanor had disappeared. In its place appeared a man capable of violence. Zen stood, ready to get physical if necessary. She didn't doubt that Peter tipped on the edge of grabbing Clairmont around the throat.

"Navarro, take a breath." Zen nodded at Peter and faced Clairmont again. "I think it's time for you to find your row and stay there. Away from us. Yeah?"

Clairmont gazed past Zen at Peter for a few moments of tense silence. Then he walked backward a few steps. "Yeah. See you on Star Flight."

"You good?" Zen watched Peter's hands clench and unclench three times.

Peter motioned for her to sit again. He dropped into his seat. He stared straight ahead as through the seat before him. Zen dealt with the flight attendant, who was eager to make sure the trouble had passed. The woman kept glancing at Peter even as Zen answered her query if they needed anything. Peter never looked at her. Once the woman left, Zen risked placing a hand on Peter's arm. He blew out air, opened both fists, and flexed his fingers.

"It's not going to be a problem," Peter murmured. "You should have told me first."

"I don't—"

"About the humanoids on Star Flight, possibly on the moon as well. You talked to Clive and Hadley, not me. We can't be effective if you people don't trust me."

That word again. Trust. Zen wasn't sure either her father or Peter had earned it just yet. She sank back into her seat and gazed out into space. Empty darkness stretched before her. Too many unknowns, but she'd have to sort through them all. No choice.

"I'm not in Kansas anymore," Zen whispered.

Peter turned to her. "I'm sorry, but what has the state of Kansas to do with anything?"

"It's a line from a movie made over a hundred years ago. This girl, Dorothy... forget it." Zen performed a neat trick Malone had taught her, forcing her mind to go blank with a repeated phrase. Peter went quiet beside her.

Chapter 4

They arrived on the moon without any more hiccups. Clairmont stayed well away from them. Zen hoped he'd continue to avoid them but knew better. He was onto a juicy story. No way would he let it go.

"Welcome to Luna One, the original NASA colony on the moon. We pioneered traveling and living in space. A unique international, government, and private partnership that opened up new worlds of possibilities." The automated voice continued for thirty minutes. They had been led to a comfortable lounge, part of the transition process. A created atmosphere of mixed gases helped their bodies adapt to the change. Four sets of screens scattered around were visible from the sets of seating arrangements. A coffee and juice bar stretched along one wall. Pastries and fresh fruits were available. Two refrigerated vending units sat in a corner One held yogurt, milk, and soft drinks. Another had sandwiches and salads.

"The gravity level here seems so like home," a woman said.

The screens switched on and a chirpy redheaded model beamed at them. "Welcome, friends. Please enjoy the amenities provided. Improvements in environmental engineering make colony living so comfortable you won't know the difference."

"Yeah, except we're only one accident away from dying," a man retorted.

"Shut up, Han," another man said.

"Just stating facts," the man replied.

"Safety is top priority here on Luna One and all four colonies established. NASA and the European Space Agency work closely with private companies to develop and maintain several layers of systems. Our backups have backups," the woman on the screen said.

"AI programming. They respond to comments. A way to combat incorrect information spread among passengers," Peter said to Zen as he stirred cream into a paper cup of coffee.

"Wow," Zen murmured. She gazed around at their fellow passengers. Several them stood before the screens in rapt attention.

"Gives us time to physically and mentally adjust. First-timers focus on the vids. Experienced space travelers just keep checking their text and email messages," Peter said with a smile.

Zen blinked back from gawking at a video tour of a nearby lunar colony. "Very effective. I stopped thinking about instant death in an airless vacuum of moon dust."

"Notice how the video changed after comments from Mr. Doom over there?" Peter nodded toward the man called Han.

"Amazing." Zen had gone back to watching the show prepared for them.

The upbeat redhead had been joined by a movie-star-handsome young man with dreadlocks. He began a smooth pitch for upscale apartment living in a new residential development. Zen was pulled into his spiel. Then a short comedy sketch show came on. Peter's voice pulled her away from a joke about Martians. They were now alone in the lounge.

"The next trip will take less time. We should be at Star Flight in three hours or less." Peter glanced at his smartwatch.

"Right. The transition is very effective. A few more artificial potted plants and I'd swear I was in an airport on Earth." Zen brushed back her braided hair. She debated looking into a mirror and decided against it.

"You look fine," Peter said. "Being an astronaut suits you."

"My skin feels dry as that moonscape." Zen brushed fingers across her forehead and frowned. "Anyway, the main thing is to hit the ground running. Make the most of our time."

"Agreed. Mrs. Ahmad has been giving the security forces a hard time. She wants to leave the space station and take her husband's remains back to Earth. His family has raised protests as well. Muslim traditions are that burial take place within twenty-four hours of death," Peter replied.

"Kind of obvious that wouldn't happen. Not unless she wanted him buried here." Zen swept a hand out at the rocky landscape on the other side of thick glass.

"There are unmanned rockets that take supplies to and from Earth in a few hours. Clive and the local law enforcement had a challenge. They didn't want panic to spread about a murder. Yet they couldn't release the body so fast."

"Which is how Clairmont got wind that Ahmad's death might not be natural," Zen replied.

"And not just him. Colonies are replicas of small towns on Earth. But then you're the expert on social environments."

"You read my dissertation on the possible development of criminal patterns in space communities? Of course you have."

Peter faced Zen with his arms crossed. "And all seven of the journal articles you published. I'm sure you know about my life in microscopic detail, down to the name of my second-grade teacher."

"Mrs. Bailey. You showed an interest in science at an early age," Zen replied in a mild tone. His famous intense dark gaze no longer unnerved her.

"Ah, yes. The social worker. You don't just gather facts. You put them into an environmental context to get a complete psychosocial profile of your subject."

"I'm not constantly assessing you, Navarro," Zen said.

"Of course you are. I would be doing the same thing in your place."

Zen turned from him and went to the buffet of food selections. She grabbed a bag of dried apple and pineapple chunks. "I'll interview Mrs. Ahmad and the mistress. You can talk to the medical examiner. Then the hotel manager."

Peter followed her a few moments later. He placed a donut covered in powdered sugar on a small paper saucer. He sat on a nearby chair and munched on it in silence. "A division of labor. Sounds good."

She pointed to the donut. "I'm surprised. I would have thought you'd be strictly health food."

Zen studied his lean, fit frame. He wasn't built with muscles like Malone. Still, Peter wasn't the stereotypical scientist, either. His white skin wasn't pale, his body fragile from lack of physical exertion. He'd split his time between long hours of study and laboratories with working out. Not that a killer needed to have the strength of a grizzly bear to be lethal.

Peter held up the donut. "Glucose for energy. This isn't coffee but ground java with golden milk. Caffeine free."

Zen's reply was cut off by a beep from her smartwatch. She put down the bag and read a message. Hadley had sent an update. "Mrs. Ahmad is here. On the moon, I mean. Not literally here at the shuttle port."

"Good." Peter ate the last half of his donut and wiped his hands.

"Might as well get started. Officer Young is on the way over. Before she gets here tell me about the beef you have with Clairmont." Zen studied him. She almost could see the wheels turning in his head.

"Clairmont made his name on my back. Stories about humanoids and their rights had been his thing before. He had a former colleague working as the press secretary for a government official. She got wind of the investigation of my... about me. Luckily, a homicide detective with morals didn't settle for the easy win and a promotion. When he found evidence that cleared me of three murders, he followed the leads. Not that Clairmont cared. He did an entire syndicated series on trafficking in so-called 'bang bots.'" His mouth twisted as if the words were bitter root on his tongue.

"Oh. Shit." Zen wasn't thinking about Peter's life being upended.

"Yes. If Clairmont thinks there's an underground use of humanoids on Star Flight, he'll be all over it like a rabid dog," Peter said.

Zen walked over to the window and gazed out. A moon rover rolled off along a path. She imagined its destination was the array of city lights in the distance. Two more vehicles appeared. In another decade, traffic might resemble a small city on Earth. Minus the fossil fuel pollution, she hoped. A moon city with all the trappings, including crime. Her thoughts bounced around. Then it hit her. She faced Peter again.

"Maybe he'll be distracted and leave us alone," Zen said.

"I hardly think so. Once Clairmont gets onto something, and especially now he knows I'm involved?" Peter glowered as if the unpleasant subject of their conversation stood in front of him.

"Not if we drop bread crumbs for him to follow. Hear me out," Zen added when Peter waved at her in dismissal. "We have info about the illegal importation of humanoids. Well, unauthorized."

"Right. Legislation hasn't kept up with technology in that area," Peter replied.

"Yeah. Anyway, investigating that isn't our turf, so to speak. Definitely not our priority. But—" Zen paced in a circle. "We plant stories for Clairmont to follow about the bots. He's good at digging up details."

"Something I know all too well," Peter retorted, the trace of his Spanish accent deepening with dismay.

"A careful set of clues. Let him dig up the facts, and the security corps can clean up the problem. The FBI and Interpol will swoop in to finish the job. Prosecutions, exclusives for Clairmont." Zen spread her arms out.

"Send him down a carefully controlled and constructed set of rabbit holes." Peter rubbed his jaw as a slow smile started. "Quite an unconventional yet ingenious plan."

"Like you said, Clairmont has an interest in humanoids. And he's relentless when he's onto a story. Might as well use those traits to our advantage."

Peter's expression turned solemn again. "Mr. Anderson impresses me as a standard operating procedures kind of commander. Would he agree to such a strategy?"

"Clive knows the value of an unconventional plan." Zen took out her tablet. The email she needed to send would be too long to tap on her smartphone. "Now if I can just rely on the satellite signal for a connection to Earth."

"The connection is fine. I sent a note to my oldest daughter. She has a set of tests coming up and I wanted to wish her well." Peter's usually impassive face softened. "She still values my opinion."

Zen glanced up at him for a second before going back to her task. With each day she saw more of the humanity in him. His caring concern for his children seemed quite real. Zen filed away another piece of the Peter Navarro puzzle to think about later. She'd still keep an eye on him.

Her message got through to Hadley. Zen glanced at her watch. It glowed Earth time as seven o'clock in the evening in soft green numbers. It had taken them thirty hours to reach the moon. She wasn't surprised Hadley answered promptly. A young woman with smooth brown skin and a soldier's bearing entered the lounge. Zen concentrated on her direct message exchange with Hadley.

"Sir, Ma'am. I'm Sgt. Wyvette Young with the Lunar Metropolis Police Department." Sgt. Young shook hands with Peter. Then she turned to Zen with a look of expectation.

"Hi. Give me a sec," Zen said with a fast nod and looked down again.

Peter smoothly took over with full introductions. "We're sending communications back to our office, Sgt. Young. We can get going shortly."

"Of course, sir," Sgt. Young replied.

Their voices faded into background buzz as Zen continued her mission of explaining her rationale to Hadley. At first it seemed Hadley might balk at the maverick maneuvers required of her. Hadley, more than Clive, was the true "by the book" veteran of the US intelligence service. Yet Zen appealed to her desire to take a more active role in cases. Plus, Hadley didn't mind pushing boundaries so long as they did it as a team. Zen needn't have worried. Hadley, meticulous as ever, only probed specifics to look for holes. Satisfied there were no obvious downsides, Hadley jumped onboard.

"Done. Hadley is certain Clive will agree. He's not too happy about Clairmont. Sorry if I seemed a bit short a minute ago."

"No problem, Dr. Batiste. I'm here to provide any level of assistance you and Dr. Navarro might need." Sgt. Young looked from Zen to Peter. She opened the door for them and then led the way. "We won't need to suit up to leave the shuttle port. Environmentally controlled corridors connect us to five other villages in this sector. Oh, we call them villages but they're more like neighborhoods in this colony. They've gotten big enough to have their own village councils to take of minor governance. Of course, the colony commander is where the buck stops. On the moon at least. That goes for the four private colonies, too."

"Government's long arm crosses into outer space," Peter murmured.

"Indeed. We need order," Sgt. Young replied with a crisp tone in true military fashion. "Commander Okoro has been effective in pulling together lunar leadership."

"Amazing task given six countries, the European Union, and three private conglomerates are in the mix," Zen said.

Moving sidewalks hummed, ferrying people on either side of a wide avenue. Others chose to walk along a standard paved path beside it. Two feet of curb composed of some sturdy plastic-like material separated the pedestrian sections from the "street." Golf cart-type vehicles of various colors zipped by carrying multiple passengers. The curved, domed ceiling was at least forty or fifty feet overhead. Various shops were in additional pods along the way.

Sgt. Young took them to a parking area. A rover had the Lunar Metropolis Police Department medallion in silver and blue on both doors and the hood. "Here we go. This baby is equipped to go outside, too. Oxygen unit on back in case suit helmets run low. That's for longer surface trips, of course."

Peter seemed mesmerized by their surroundings. "I hadn't realized the colony had progressed to this degree."

"Yeah, well, since more companies have set up shop it's gotten a bit too touristy for me. I remember the days when it was mostly space professionals and soldiers," Sgt. Young replied as she drove past a coffee shop full of people.

Ten minutes later they pulled up to an impressive-looking entrance. The United States Space Command logo was above two wide doors. They slid open and closed automatically as people entered or left. A woman dressed in the LMPD duty uniform came out to greet them. She saluted Sgt. Young, waited for them to exit the vehicle, and drove off. Zen and Peter followed Sgt. Young inside a wide lobby. Workers in civilian dress moved around like in any other office. There were also women and men in both police and military uniforms. Sgt. Young took them down a hallway. She stopped at a desk to announce them. The twenty-something police officer who manned a desk picked up his headset. He swept Zen and Peter with a gaze as if assessing their threat level.

"Good evening. Commander Okoro will be with you in a minute," he said to them and then announced them.

"He's expecting us, but he got pulled into a meeting last minute. Happens a lot. Always something popping off lately." Sgt. Young's smooth brow furrowed.

"A major uptick?" Zen looked around. The officers seemed to be moving with a sense of urgency.

"More people, more trouble," Sgt. Young retorted.

Peter appeared to scan the area around them out of more than casual interest. He appeared relaxed, but Zen sensed an underlying tension. She'd worked with him long enough to know when he was on guard. When he noticed Zen studying him, he gave a slight nod. When Sgt. Young got pulled away by another officer Peter gestured for Zen to move closer.

"There was a disturbance in one of the villages, as they call them." Peter inclined his head toward a group of three men. Two were police; a third wore an Air Force uniform. "I only heard snatches, but—"

A different older officer marched to them. Sgt. Young broke off her discussion with the other officer and snapped to attention. The man's iron-gray hair contrasted with a youthful face. He could have been anywhere between forty and sixty. His crisp nod to Sgt. Young acknowledged her deference. Then he pivoted to face Zen and Peter.

"Welcome. I'm Lt. General Walker. Commander Okoro is waiting," he said and gestured for them to follow. He walked off without waiting for them to reply.

Zen and Peter exchanged a glance before following him down a short hallway. Another desk with a young soldier seated sat outside a door. Captain Walker tapped a keypad and the doors slid apart. They entered a spacious office. The wall behind the desk had a floor-to-ceiling window. A lush forest scene splashed with sunlight seemed within reach. Zen gasped.

"Dr. Navarro and Dr. Batiste, thank you for coming." The man behind the desk stood.

Zen did a quick mental review of the background Hadley had provided them. Commander Okoro was at least six feet six inches tall by Zen's estimation. He had the look of a leader. Okoro was a general in the United State Space Force on Earth. Here, he was commander in charge of all operations on the moon. A native of Senegal, his family had emigrated to America when he was ten years old.

"I'm sure they're eager to meet with the Lunar Police to wrap up their investigation," Captain Walker put in.

"We are," Zen replied, though both men looked to Peter. "We'll interview witnesses. Examine the scene. That sort of thing."

"Understood," Commander Okoro beamed back at her. He came around the desk and pointed to a seating area. "Please, sit."

Peter waited for Zen to go first. She sat in one of five dark blue leather chairs arranged at a round table. Peter sat next to her. A woman came in carrying a tray laden with cups and two carafes. The aroma of coffee gave the office a congenial atmosphere.

"You'll be leaving for Star Flight in a few hours." Captain Walker sat erect. He didn't touch the steaming mug set before him.

Zen glanced at Peter and then at Captain Walker. "We will. But the victim's wife is here, we were told. She's our first stop."

"Hmm." Lt. General Walker wore an impassive expression.

"I've been in touch with Police Chief Collier. He's tied up at the moment. Sgt. Young will be your contact," Commander Okoro replied with an easy smile. "I'm sure you'll have everything you need for an expeditious visit. LMPD works closely with the security guards employed by the private companies. Very thorough, in my experience."

"I'm sure. We have time to complete our enquiries. I believe the White House and the Pentagon have informed you about our unit."

"Yes," Lt. General Walker clipped. He pressed his lips closed into a stiff look of disapproval.

"There is some thought that the Space Command could have developed a criminal investigation unit. In the same way that your unit was invented," Commander Okoro said, his tone genial. "Cream?"

Zen blinked at him. "What?"

Commander Okoro's white teeth against his dark brown skin seemed to gleam. "For your coffee." He poured when Zen nodded in response. "Amazing age we live in. Here we are floating on a ball in space that for thousands of years humans gazed up at in wonder. And we have simple Earth pleasures like lattes and sushi."

"Spacecom has been tasked with military operations only since its inception in 1985, sir," Peter put in, his tone respectful yet firm. "Keeping criminal investigations in the civilian realm is logical for a host of reasons. Hopefully, there won't be a need for warfare skills in space. Though we know tensions with Russia, China, and Africa continue."

"And we've been briefed that private corporations with competing interests have clashed as well," Zen added.

"Disagreements are inevitable, but we always manage to mediate parties onto common ground," Commander Okoro replied, his good humor intact. "Makes for dramatic fodder to be reported in news stories back home. Much more mundane in reality."

"Good to know," Zen said and smiled at him before she sipped coffee.

They continued their meeting for another twenty minutes, the commander's version of chit-chat over coffee. He gave them a virtual tour of the lunar colonies and explained the technology that provided gravity and oxygen. Peter dived into the details with great interest. When they were finally shown out, Sgt. Young was waiting for them in the lobby. She stood erect, both hands clasp behind her back. Only when the Commander and Lt. General Walker left did she speak.

"The crime scene at Star Flight is secure. I'm keeping tabs on it, so no worries. I mean, it's different than Earth since you needed so many hours to get here. But our officers have control. The evidence custody chain has been maintained," Sgt. Young said.

They walked through the building and to the main lobby once more. People parted to let them pass. Gazes followed them as they progressed. Zen tried to grab onto the vibes. Not hostility, exactly. Peter's head swiveled as he walked. He seemed determined to examine every corner of the command center. The rover sat outside when they went back onto the walkway. Once they'd climbed in it, Peter turned to Sgt. Young.

"Please brief us on the disturbance." Peter's voice had a balance of politeness and authority. Not a question.

"Umm." Sgt. Young started the rover's engine and they pulled into light traffic. "There was a fight at one of the bars. It's a favorite hangout of Spacecom soldiers. It's been handled."

"I see." Peter gazed at her, waiting for more.

"I know you both must be tired. I'll take you over to the Marriott Residence Inn so you can get some sleep, shower, and a meal. Mrs. Ahmad is staying in a fancy short-term rental in one of the villages. I'll bring her over to our station for you in the morning. Or what passes for morning out here. We're at the tail end of our night cycle. Lasts about thirteen days. Then we'll have thirteen days of sunlight. Gets hella hot and cold here, which is why our geodomes are embedded halfway in the side of hills or mountains," Sgt. Young said.

Peter and Zen by silent agreement let her talk without interruption. Sgt. Young kept up a congenial stream of chatter until she dropped them off. After registering, Zen and Peter went to their separate second-floor rooms. Zen sent direct messages to Astra and Malone after settling in. She slept for twenty minutes and then was wide awake. Glowing red numbers on the digital clock displayed that it was three a.m. Earth time. Zen lay in the darkened room trying to drift off but finally gave up. Minutes later, dressed in comfortable sweats and sneakers, she went down to the first floor.

She went to the kitchenette off the lobby. Another room had a television taking up most of one wall. The twenty-four-hour news channel was on but the sound muted. Peter sat on a small sofa with his tablet, reading. Without interrupting him, Zen wandered around more. The front desk was fully automated. A console allowed guests to enter their reservation data. Only then would they be issued key codes for their rooms. The inn had two floors. Maintaining the air and gravity was still too expensive for multi-level buildings for most businesses. Seeing nothing of interest, Zen went back to sit in front of the television.

"You couldn't sleep either, I see," Peter said without looking up.

"Space lag, I guess." Zen yawned. She found the remote for the TV and turned on the English subtitles.

"The sound won't bother me," Peter said. He dropped the tablet on the arm of the sofa. Then he stood and stretched. "I was looking over updated notes from the office."

"Um." Zen watched the news anchor talk about stories from various countries.

"I haven't seen anything about Ahmad or the space station," Peter said. "Or maybe we shouldn't talk about work. Just try to wind down. We're going to have a busy two or three days at least."

Zen stretched her legs out and yawned a second time. Not that she felt anything close to drowsy. "You get the feeling folks are looking forward to seeing the back of us?"

Peter strolled around the room. He picked up and put down several paper magazines. Then he gazed at artwork on the walls. "Commander Okoro was a bit more subtle than Walker. Still, his implicit message was clear. Get in and get out of his domain."

"Yeah."

Zen looked down at the arm of her comfy chair. A six-inch console had a digital channel guide. She scrolled through it and found a local lunar station. She switched the channel using a remote. As she hoped, the last news broadcast of the previous night replayed on a loop. Two attractive anchors wore serious faces as they took turns giving reports.

Peter stopped his circuit of the room and faced the television. "I think there's a DVR function."

"You're right. Automatically records and stores programs for six hours. Let's check it." Zen tapped the console. She found the stored version and started the newscast from the beginning.

The female anchor, her brunette hair cut in a bob style, assumed a grave face. "A disturbance in the village of Halo shocked residences of that typically peaceful upscale community. Let's get an on-the-scene report," the female anchor said.

"Not him again," Peter said with a grunt of distaste when Clairmont appeared on the screen.

"Good evening, Layla. Residents are expressing concern about their quality of life being at risk. Here's what we know. At about four o'clock this afternoon two men got into a heated discussion at the local food shop. Apparently, friends of the men took sides. What started out as a simple dispute turned into what one witness described as a free-for-all. Now a source tells us one of the men who started the altercation is a Space Command soldier. Police showed up, and I haven't been able to confirm any more details. I'll stay on the beat to get the facts. This is Jacques Clairmont reporting from Halo Village."

"Thank you, Jacques. News Six attempted to get a comment from Commander Okoro's office. We're told he will issue a joint statement with the LMPD chief in another day or so. Quote, 'The investigation into the incident is ongoing."

The female anchor went on to another story. This one was about shoplifting at a lunar bodega. The owner gave a spirited interview with wild hand gestures to punctuate his outrage.

"So, they think crime is getting out of hand. What did they expect with the rise in population?" Zen said with a shrug.

"Most people who emigrate here can afford the shuttle transport prices. They can also pay the rents or even build their own homes. A few executives with the four major space companies have brought their families here. Most have set up house with mistresses," Peter replied.

Zen gazed at him and then back at the television. She hit the mute button on the console. "I shouldn't be surprised. Living a double life is a breeze when you live off the planet. So, local cops and Okoro don't want their Earth commanders to know there's an uptick in crime."

"And possibly the first drug-related death on a space station is especially unwelcome. Hence their wish to see us leave quickly," Peter added.

"They better cooperate is all I know." Zen frowned at the prospect of hostile locals.

"I doubt Commander Okoro or the lunar police will outwardly block us. Besides, we have the medical examiner's report. Ahmad's heart stopped, which looks like natural causes. But a toxicology screen revealed he'd been administered the designer drug Jump."

Zen shook her head. "I don't understand why humans need to create new ways to self-destruct. Weed is legal."

"It's become too tame on the party scene, especially underground. Danger and defying the rules is part of the high. Developing new drugs in space is legal for medical treatments only."

"Okoro had plenty of great press for breaking up a drug-trafficking scheme in one of the private colonies," Zen said.

He nodded. "And now we might uncover unpleasant facts about serious crime."

"Not to mention humanoids being secretly shipped into space." Zen studied Peter for his reaction to her observation.

Peter maintained an impassive face. "Exactly. Two forms of trafficking right under his nose? No surprise Commander Okoro would like us back on Earth quickly."

"You think they'd go as far as hiding stuff from us? That would be worse for Okoro's career than a few drug dealers and bang bots," Zen retorted.

Peter grimaced with disgust. "Humanoids deserve the same respect as human sex workers, Dr. Batiste."

Zen felt a flash of guilt at his admonishment. "You're right. I should know better. I suppose it's because I've never met any face to face yet. Are they really so lifelike?"

He shifted from one foot to the other as he looked away from her. "Their construction has become quite... sophisticated."

"Maybe we should talk about this, Peter. And stop calling me Dr. Batiste. Makes me feel like my grandmother." Zen tried a joking tone but Peter's stiff frown didn't ease.

"Facts surrounding my... situation have been distorted. Very much misunderstood." Peter fidgeted with his hands and turned away from Zen.

"Look, we're facing challenges here. We need to be a united front. That means no secrets; lay out any issues that might make our job more complicated. So, please know I'm not asking out of prurient curiosity. Your behavior toward female humanoids was described as addictive, sometimes violent." Zen let her words sit in the heavy silence between them for a several seconds. "I need to know if—"

"I won't be triggered if we encounter humanoid sex workers. I assume that's what you're asking. My treatment included systematic desensitization." Peter faced Zen again, chin up. "I'll release the treatment summaries for your review, if that will relieve any concerns."

"I've read them already, Peter," Zen said.

"So much for treatment confidentiality." Peter's face twisted with anger. "Then you know all about my so-called obsession."

"Look, Clive has our unit cleared for the highest level of security access. We damn sure don't gossip. Our investigations are—"

"Yes, yes, I know. Top secret, among the most sensitive because of global space politics." Peter waved a hand of dismissal. He paced in a circle and stopped before Zen. "No matter what I've done or been accused of, I'm still a person."

"We're not in a controlled therapeutic environment."

Zen watched him pace in silence. Minutes stretched on. She wondered if arranging immediate transport for him back to Earth was an option. Then he stopped and faced her. His impassive façade had snapped back into place.

"I need to tell you the whole story then. Things even my neuro-psychiatrist doesn't know."

Chapter 5

Two hours later Sgt. Young picked them up from the hotel. They sped along a domed boulevard. Mrs. Ahmad had insisted on leaving the Star Flight Space Station after her husband's death. She was staying in an upscale lunar short-term rental. Sgt. Young launched into a spirited account of how difficult it had been to get the woman to cooperate.

"I guess she thought leaving the space station would give her more leverage. She's still demanding her husband's body be released," Sgt. Young concluded. The rover passed a residential block.

"Looks like any nice urban neighborhood in New York, DC, or Baltimore," Zen remarked. Trees were planted in spots carved out of the space-age sidewalks. Small front yards had flowering plants.

"Some of those are fake. But the local horticulture folks have come up with hybrid flowers. The rich folks can pay for those pricey lamps that grow plants," Sgt. Young replied with a grimace. "I mean, if you want the same thing, just stay on Earth. Me personally, I like the moonscape."

"There's only so much that can be done to make outer space like Earth. Science has its limits," Peter said. "Your alien experience won't be spoiled any time soon, if ever."

Sgt. Young's grimace turned into a smile. "Hope to see Mars one day. I hear a Mars Metro PD is in the works. Even heard about plans to colonize Titan."

"The only moon or planet known to have rivers, lakes, even a sea or two," Peter said. "Manned flights can reach it in under three years now."

"Yeah. I could have a new life out there before I'm thirty-five."

Sgt. Young turned down a narrower street. Official-looking buildings lined up on either side of it. She'd taken them to the civilian administrative sector. She parked outside of the police station in a reserved spot. Officers came and went, some serious. Other appeared more relaxed.

"What about your family on Earth? Marriage, kids?" Zen said.

Sgt. Young cut the engine and turned to Zen. "I choose adventure."

"Sometimes there's little to leave behind," Peter said in a heavy tone.

Zen shot a glance at him. Meanwhile, Sgt. Young hopped out of the vehicle. Minutes later they were in an interview room, waiting. An officer had been dispatched to pick up Mrs. Ahmad and hadn't returned yet. Zen made sure they weren't being recorded or observed. She blocked any wireless or wired transmissions with a tap of her smartwatch. The tech wizards had come up with that handy app.

She looked at Peter. "About your story—"

"My *story*. You'll reserve judgement on whether to believe me," Peter said. His blank face gave no hint of anger.

Zen blew out air. "Okay, you're brilliant. You have Asperger's Syndrome. Relating to other people is... challenging. You can relate to humanoids in a special way. But the aggression toward them? That seems like displaced rage against human females."

"Not just females. I, uh, I had some encounters with males as well," Peter said quietly.

Zen leaned forward across the table. "Something else that got missed?"

"I refuse to go into my childhood and family history. Suffice to say there are incidents that shaped me. The point is, I had some measure of control. Though admittedly once I found escort services that specialized in more intense needs—"

"People who like inflicting pain during sex," Zen broke in.

"I sought treatment years ago. Is that in the reports? I never hurt my wife. Her tastes were much different than mine. Mild bondage only," Peter replied.

"Please, I don't need the details."

Peter wore a pained smile as he gazed back at her. "You're not willing to lift the veil on my marital state but will peer into every other nook and cranny of my life."

"Your wife didn't do anything. We don't want to subject her to more scrutiny," Zen said.

"You're right, of course. She's been through enough. All because she fell in love with me, had children. I never hurt her. Or my girls." Peter swallowed hard.

"I know."

"Of course you do," Peter said, his voice barely audible. He stared at the bland gray wall instead of at Zen.

"Look, as a clinician I understand that symptoms can be very specific, but—"

Peter looked at Zen, his dark gaze intense. "I realized humanoids were more than bits of input, output, and storage circuitry. I'm not saying they feel emotions," he added when Zen's eyebrows arched.

"But to say you fell in love with a robot?" Zen kept her voice low. She couldn't resist glancing at the camera set in a corner of one wall.

Peter started to reply when the door opened. He whispered, "We'll talk later."

Sgt. Young gave them both a pointed look, her face a mask of repressed anger. She shot a side eye at the woman who pushed past her into the room. "Sir, ma'am, Mrs. Ahmad—"

"I am quite sure they know who I am. I have been held hostage here, my husband deprived of the dignity of proper last rites."

Mrs. Ahmad held her chin up to look down her aquiline nose at them. Her long, dark hair was pulled back into a bun. She wore a scarf, high-neck blouse, and long skirt. Still, she managed to look like a fashion model. Her makeup was flawless. Her olive skin smooth. At forty, she looked at least ten years younger at first glance. She could afford the best cosmeceuticals.

Peter stood. "We apologize for any distress delays have caused. Our main goal is to find out what happened to your husband. I can assure you we've taken all measures possible to be respectful in this most unusual tragedy. You've faced a terrible loss in extraordinary circumstances. Condolences on behalf of the American government and the European Space Agency."

"Well..." Mrs. Ahmad exhaled after a few moments. "Finally, someone with a sense of decency, some feeling for what I've gone through."

"We only want to get all of the facts, Mrs. Ahmad," Zen added. Judging by the way the woman's expression tightened again, Zen decided to let Peter take the lead.

"I know the facts," Mrs. Ahmad snapped, slipping back into attack mode. "I've been shouting the facts from the rooftops. I have three sons. What will their professional and personal prospects be if gossip gets out? My husband was not perfect, but at least he provided a good future for his children. I accepted his habits for what they were."

"I'm so sorry to belabor painful details," Peter said and pulled out a chair for her. Mrs. Ahmad sat without hesitation.

"I know about you," Mrs. Ahmad said.

Peter flinched at the implication of her words. "I can assure you—"

"You know what it's like to have your life laid bare, judgements placed on your head far beyond the truth of your flaws," Mrs. Ahmad pressed on. She leaned toward him as if pleading for understanding.

"Mr. Ahmad had a mistress, more than one over the years. I also know he tended to be discreet, careful of your feelings. Though nothing can mitigate the disappointment of a faithless spouse." Peter's expression and tone were full of empathy.

"My Hassan took it as a matter of course that he would have mistresses. Nothing his parents or mine said made a difference. After my third son was born, I accepted his periodic... lapses."

Mrs. Ahmad looked down at her tightly clasped hands. She kneaded the straps of her Valentino handbag. Zen resisted the urge to blurt out a dose of hard reality. Her Hassan had kept mistresses throughout their twenty-year marriage. At one point he juggled two at the same time. And cheated on them and his wife. The man had way more energy than the average cheating husband. But instead of breaking the flow, Zen kept her mouth shut.

"A Mrs. Stephania McDougal accompanied him," Peter said with care. "You weren't aware that she had taken an earlier shuttle to the station."

"Of course not. You think I would have agreed to come and be humiliated in this fashion?" Mrs. Ahmad shot back with heat. Then her outrage softened when she looked at Peter. She sniffed and searched in her purse. "I'm sorry. The stress, having to tell my sons."

Peter turned to Sgt. Young. "May we have—"

"Yes, sir." The young officer snapped to and disappeared. She returned moments later with a container of tissues and a glass of water.

Mrs. Ahmad dabbed her nose with delicate motions and took a few moments to sip water. Then she looked at Peter. "The truth is..."

Peter followed her gaze as it darted to Sgt. Young and then to Zen. He nodded and Mrs. Ahmad's shoulders dropped. He cleared his throat and nodded encouragement. "Unless it pertains to the adjudication of crimes, we'll keep all sensitive personal details from the press."

"That damned reporter," Mrs. Ahmad spat. Then her frown softened around the edges. "At least *you* appreciate the value of propriety."

"Sgt. Young, we can finish up and meet you later," Zen said as a quiet aside to the police officer.

Sgt. Young blinked at her and then at the widow. Understanding seemed to dawn on her. She gave a crisp nod and slipped out the door. Zen did her best to fade into the background. Peter appeared to work a kind of magic on the prickly woman.

"I tolerated Hassan's behavior for years. Why?" Mrs. Ahmad cast a quick glance at Zen as if anticipating her question. "I know it sounds archaic in these times of robots and rockets, but for my sons. Both our families believe in marriage as a stabilizing element for children and society. The first time it happened, I thought it was because of my preoccupation with the boys. Small children require all of a mother's time. And I loved every minute. Sometimes more than I enjoyed being a wife. So, I made an effort. But he strayed again. And again."

"It wasn't about something lacking or being wrong with you," Peter said.

Zen studied him, fascinated with the way he connected to the woman. He established a rapport any therapist would admire. The proud woman told Peter details of more affairs, arguments and family blow-ups.

"I even forced him into marriage counseling. Looking back, I have to be honest. I suspected he saw outer space as the perfect location for sexual freedom." Mrs. Ahmad clutched a wad of tissues in one hand.

"Which is why you were determined to come with him," Peter put in.

Mrs. Ahmad nodded slowly. She sighed with a short laugh devoid of amusement. "He didn't object. Put on a perfect act about being excited to travel with me. And I was fool enough to believe him."

"When did you realize something was off?" Peter said in a soft tone.

"He'd vanish for hours. I didn't say anything, but I accessed his business account and saw his itinerary. He wasn't attending meetings or seminars. Liar," Mrs. Ahmad frowned. A tear slid down one cheek and she swiped it away.

"Did you confront him?" Peter prompted.

Zen went still, holding her breath. They might be on their way home sooner than she thought. Peter Navarro, former suspected killer, had turned out to be a gifted homicide detective. Mrs. Ahmad hesitated for a few seconds before answering.

"Not immediately. I wanted to see how far he'd go. As it happened, he met my low expectations. I followed him to another part of the hotel. I heard him and that woman moaning through the door. But that's not all. I followed him to a different wing and room the next night. And a different party scene. Two women."

"Please write down the section and number for us. We'll interview them as well." Peter produced a small e-notepad from a pocket of his jumpsuit. He handed her a stylus and watched as Mrs. Ahmad wrote on it. Then he took it back.

"You don't need to waste time on those *ahrat*," Mrs. Ahmad snapped, using the Arabic word for whores. Then she wore a bitter smile. "Talk to the other one—Mrs. McDougal. She found out Hassan was playing her as well. They had a terrific fight. Can you believe it? She's not his wife, but she expressed outrage. Not to mention she's married. Her husband didn't seem to care what she did. He was oddly nonchalant when I told him about his wife's sluttish behavior."

"How long have you known about Mrs. McDougal and when did you tell her husband?" Zen stared back at her when Mrs. Ahmad shot her a heated look.

"It's very important that we know," Peter interjected before Mrs. Ahmad could boil into anger again.

"I didn't *know*, but I saw the way they looked at each other on the shuttle flight. So, I kept an eye out. Hassan tried to keep me busy with shopping and excursions. As if he cared about me having an enjoyable time. It was about his pleasure, not mine."

Zen glanced at Peter and spoke after he gave a subtle tilt of his head. "Where were you—"

"At the time Hassan died? Having a drink with a very handsome and younger man at the Moonlight Lounge on level eight. We went to his room. I almost lost my nerve. Then I thought about Hassan grunting like a pig with all those other women. I'm glad I did it," Mrs. Ahmad said with defiance. "I felt wanted, desired as a woman."

"We'll need to confirm your whereabouts," Zen said, keeping her voice calm to avoid another explosion from the woman.

"I paid for my drinks with Hassan's credit card, so I have receipts. I was there for almost an hour before he arrived. Fillip Bergman. Level eleven. He's young, more... energetic than Hassan." Mrs. Ahmad smiled as if savoring the memory of her revenge.

Peter took over being the kind, sympathetic cop once more. They questioned Mrs. Ahmad for another thirty minutes before they let her go. Sgt. Young returned to lead her out of the station.

"So, Ahmad partied hard. Our witness list just grew," Zen said once she was alone with Peter.

"Hmm. His mistress. Her husband. Mrs. Ahmad. They all had reasons to be very unhappy with him." Peter gazed down at his e-notepad with a slight frown.

"LMPD and the security detail on the space station need to clean up drugs on their turf. And unregulated sex work." Zen leaned back in her chair with her arms folded. "We won't be away from our kids as long as we thought."

"Humph." Peter continued to frown.

"I'll update Clive and have Hadley give us info on Mr. and Mrs. McDougal and this Fillip—" Zen snapped her fingers as she searched for the name.

"Bergman," Peter murmured as he took out his tablet and tapped the screen.

"Yeah. You get with Sgt. Young to track them down and arrange for us to interview them. What?" Zen said as she studied his puzzled expression.

"Space travel is still expensive. Your average sex worker couldn't afford to set up business out here." Peter continued to focus on his tablet as he spoke. "Which means someone with means must have sponsored them."

"A rich, space-age pimp. How colorful," Zen retorted. "But you make an excellent point. The lure of big money tempted someone to import special entertainment against the rules?"

"You said yourself, criminal laws haven't kept up with the times. Someone, more likely a consortium, decided the benefits balanced favorably against the risks. At worse, they would be fined. Multiple global governments and corporations have enough to deal with. Their employees get to have a good time."

"Yeah. But like my father says, it's all fun and games until somebody ends up dead." Zen sat straight again. "The authorities don't sweat the party girls and drugs. Keeping oxygen and water flowing, managing operations, growing food keeps them busy."

"Along with a hundred and one other things they have to consider. Government research, private companies working on projects—there is a lot going on. The value of new products and processes being developed alone is huge. I keep a hand in the field despite a considerable loss of prestige. Two former colleagues haven't cut me off completely." Peter looked at his tablet when a tinkling bell notification sounded.

"That's... nice."

"They've attended symposiums and conventions in space. One is even excited that he might get to Mars," Peter explained with a smile. "They're young and don't fit the stereotype of socially inept scientists. Like me."

"In other words, they like to party in between coming up with inventions that change the world," Zen quipped.

"I feel quite paternal toward them," Peter replied and went back to reading.

"We've stepped into a hell of a mess, Navarro." Zen drummed her fingers for a few seconds on the titanium table. "But there's good news."

Peter looked at her. "I fail to see it."

"No murder. Everything points to Hassan overindulging in his two hobbies, sex and getting high. Commander Okoro and the police chief can handle the other stuff. Let's wrap this up."

"We still have to visit the space station. There is no way around it," Peter pressed on when Zen started to speak. "Bergman is there. So are Mrs. McDougal and her husband. And we should examine the crime scene at least once."

"We could have the police bring the witnesses here, but you're right. Looking at remote video of the scene is no substitute for being there." Zen frowned at the blank wall before her.

"You don't like being in space?" Peter said.

"Hmm, no, it's not that. I'm used to it now. Every now and then I feel... wobbly, though." Zen shrugged.

"Walking in low gravity is hard. And the air generators create molecular oxygen. The gases used in the process can cause a slight lightheaded sensation."

"Fascinating. No, I'm just thinking about the prospect that Okoro and the LMPD might hide things from us. All the more reason to visit the crime scene ourselves," Zen said.

"And interview witnesses away from here," Peter said in a tone barely audible. He darted a quick glance around the room.

"Pretty sure we're okay." Zen tapped her watch to indicate her blocking app.

Sgt. Young tapped on the door and then entered the interview room. "Mrs. Ahmad blasted my ears for fifteen minutes before an officer drove her off. Thank the stars she's gone. She seems to like you though, sir."

Peter blushed. "I simply tried to balance empathy with questions."

"You handled her with skill. Not bad for a socially inept nerd," Zen said. Even beneath the compliment, Zen thought of the psychological profile of psychopathic killers. Most could be charming and persuasive when on the hunt for victims. Sgt. Young's voice shook Zen out of her musing about her partner.

"Ma'am, we have video feed. Latest in high def and speed cameras to give you a close look at the hotel rooms. I set up for a live chat with Berman and the McDougals, still at the Sky High Hotel. In secure rooms, of course." Sgt. Young smiled at them in turned. "Figured those were your next moves. Which do we do first?"

"Neither. We're going to Star Flight as planned," Zen replied.

Sgt. Young blinked as if Zen's words had struck her in the face. "But you can save time by using the feeds. Our officers have a full forensic inventory of items found. Reports are done. Chain of custody has been maintained. You can check with my captain if you—"

"It's not a judgement of your thoroughness, Sgt. Young. I can assure you. However, OSI has procedures," Peter said before Zen could respond. He looked at Zen as though sending a warning.

Zen bit back a tart explanation that might have included an expletive. "Right. OSI procedures. We examine the crime scene, make our notes. Consult with local authorities."

"Then I'll let my chief know. Authorization for the next shuttle to the station shouldn't take long. An hour or—"

"I arranged flight on a NASA vehicle taking supplies to the In Situ research site," Peter put in smoothly. "We leave in an hour. So, we should go."

"Yes." Zen nodded to him with a smile and looked at Sgt. Young.

Sgt. Young gaped at him for a second before she recovered. "I'll, uh, let the local cops still at the hotel know you're coming. I'll drive you to the departure site."

"Thank you for all the help, Sgt. Young. You've really aided us in our work here on the moon." Peter beamed at her and gestured to the door.

Sgt. Young shifted from one booted foot to the other as she spoke. "Of course. We want to figure this stuff out. First death on Star Flight. Anything I can do to speed things along. Not that we want to do a rush job or anything."

"Is there something you want to tell us?" Zen said, cutting in before she could continue.

"Ma'am?" Sgt. Young went still.

"Our interview with Mrs. Ahmad was quite interesting." Zen watched her words sink in.

"Jealous wife, cheating husband. Old story, huh?" Sgt. Young forced a stiff smile.

"Are there recreational drugs and sex workers on the space station?" Zen asked.

"We hear rumors. The private companies hire their own employees. What those people do on their days off to earn extra is... sex work isn't illegal in space. Most stuff isn't for now. My dad calls it the Old Wild West up here. Part of the reason he wasn't happy I signed up. Dad loves those hundred-year-old westerns. He—"

"Sgt. Young, seriously." Zen broke in. "We can chat about your father's taste in movies later. Sex and drugs, on the space station. Maybe here on the moon?"

"No," Sgt. Young blurted out with force. "We keep things clean on Luna. None of the nonsense they let go on at the space stations."

"They?" Peter said.

"Not here. Please." Sgt. Young didn't glance around, but her stiff posture made clear they were watched.

"We're not being recorded," Zen said quietly.

"I'll go with you to Star Flight. I think my boss will give the okay."

Sgt. Young spoke in a conversational tone as she led them out. They went down two halls to a side door with a line of police vehicles. Peter went along with a glance at Zen. She pushed down the itch to pull more information out of the young officer. Sgt. Young chose a different vehicle to drive them. The interior was newer than the last one. Five minutes later they had pulled away from the police station.

"The chief and my captain know the signals were blocked. Didn't take much for them to figure out it wasn't a glitch in our system," Sgt. Young said as she drove. "They really want to know what you know."

"Then we'll tell them once we get back from Star Flight," Zen replied. She settled into the leather seat.

Their first stop was the hotel to pick up their bags. With just enough time to freshen up, Zen hurried to her room. She scanned the interior of neutral colors and nondescript furniture. Nothing seemed out of place. Then again, an expert could search without leaving a trace. Then she hastily secured her carry-on. Ten minutes later she rejoined Peter in the lobby. A hotel employee stood at the front desk. The woman beamed at them.

"I hope you're enjoying your stay," she said. "You can call our concierge number any time. Our AI is top of the line, but we also provide the human touch here."

"We're fine, thank you." Peter flash a brief smile back at her and then turned to Zen and whispered, "I doubt anyone wasted time here."

"You had the same thought, huh?" Zen looked around.

He nodded and led the way out. "Sgt. Young is in a difficult position. She suspects there is some level of corruption in her department. She thinks it nothing more than a concerted effort to look the other way."

"So, that means she doesn't know who to trust," Zen whispered back. She pulled on Peter's arm until he stopped. "They're not very good at covering."

"I'm sure they assumed distance from Earth gave them a certain insulation from scrutiny." Peter pointed to the rover. "We should go."

Zen glanced at her watch. "Right. Don't wanna miss our ride."

On the way to the launch section, Sgt. Young expressed frustration with her job and colleagues. Her desire for an assignment on Mars or another planet was motivated by more than a desire for thrills. Yet she didn't think her fellow officers or bosses were crooks.

"Look, this is a tough gig. Adjusting to space is a stress, ya know? Forget going outside for a walk. That's a whole thing getting all geared up. Once the novelty of walking around on the moon wears off, you're pretty bored. So what if people party a bit too hard? Besides, jump isn't illegal. Most of the sex is consensual and nobody gets hurt," Sgt. Young explained.

"Until now," Zen said.

"Yeah. Damn it." Sgt. Young hissed through her teeth.

"Sounds like a speech you've heard often," Peter said.

"Look, I'm no snitch. And I've tried looking at it as no big deal. But now... I had a feeling bad shit was gonna go down one day." Sgt. Young exhaled as if relieved to speak freely. "Excuse the language, sir and ma'am."

"No worries," Zen said. "Sgt. Young, have you ever considered your colleagues might be doing more than just looking the other way?"

"You mean bribes?" Sgt. Young glanced at Zen and back at the smooth, paved avenue. "A couple of the officers have upgraded their living spaces. Two have private rovers. The fancy models made in Sector 51 of Colony G—"

"The third Goddard Corporation colony. Luxury homes for mining executives," Zen said with a grimace. Her first investigation hadn't won her any friends at the private space conglomerate.[1]

"Right. But I'm not naming names because like I said, no proof. They could have second jobs. And we've gotten pay increases thanks to Congress." Sgt. Young nodded to herself.

Zen glanced at Peter, who sat in the back seat of the rover. "True. We're not trying to blow things up. But if we find evidence of wrongdoing, Sgt. Young..."

"Understood, ma'am. I'm just saying, ninety percent of the officers, police and in Space Command, are good people. Not perfect, but—" Sgt. Young huffed out another sigh. "I don't want to see their lives wrecked because of extra pocket change."

"One death, possible murder, is a sign that the situation will only get worse," Peter said in a somber tone.

Sgt. Young's hands tightened on the steering wheel, but she didn't say any more. Zen glanced back at Peter again. His expression said he knew about life going downhill fast. Zen wondered if he was thinking about his own spiral into obsession. His life, professional and personal, had unraveled. Not to mention becoming a suspect in a series of brutal murders.

"Here we go. No space on this one for me. I'll have to take the next flight out. I'll catch up with you in a few hours." Sgt. Young frowned in distraction. She didn't get out of the driver's seat but instead pointed. "Entrance C is for NASA transport departures."

"Thank you, sergeant. We'll be circumspect and weigh all of the facts before taking action," Peter said as he hefted his bag from the floorboard.

"Appreciate the consideration, sir," Sgt. Young replied with a crisp nod. She drove off the second Zen's feet hit the ground.

"Did you—" Zen started but a booming voice cut her off.

"You must be the Earth dwellers hitching with us. Welcome! Dr. Irene McCoy here." A tall woman with blond—almost white—hair strode over to them with a hand out. "We're a small town out here. Not a lot of turnover or new faces," she declared in a crisp Irish accent.

"Dr. McCoy, thanks for accommodating us on short notice," Peter said and accepted her handshake. "This is my colleague, Dr. Zenobia Batiste. Dr. McCoy is a medical researcher and biochemist with the European Space Agency. She's also a top neurosurgeon. We met at the Bio International Convention in Amsterdam back in 2084, I believe."

"Hi," Zen said and winced at the strength of Dr. McCoy's grip.

"We're taking the Andromeda shuttle. I'll be at the controls, but don't worry. I'm a licensed shuttle pilot."

Dr. McCoy continued a stream of animated chatter with Peter. Zen let him keep up their side of the exchange as she looked around. The local lunar shuttle port was a duplicate of the one they'd arrived at from Earth, only smaller. Most of the flights leaving transported NASA and other government personnel, including UN observers. Security protocols were tight since classified tech passed through at times.

Twenty minutes later they sat side by side, strapped into their seats. The Andromeda shuttle was all function. No flight attendants or snacks here. Fewer seats allowed for equipment to be loaded. Storage bins overhead carried more supplies. Only one other passenger boarded. After another ten minutes the shuttle undocked and took off. Once they were in flight, a light signaled they could take off their helmets.

Zen glanced around the cabin. The other passenger sat at the far end as if he wanted privacy. He seemed intent on reading from his tablet. Still, she kept her voice low. "You shouldn't have made promises to Sgt. Young."

"My purpose was to reassure her so she wouldn't feel guilty and do something rash. Something that might put her in danger," Peter replied quietly.

"You think we're about to uncover something bad." Zen let out a groan at the serious look he gave her in return.

"Commander Okoro and Captain Walker don't impress me as men who like being opposed. And if Ahmad's death wasn't an accidental overdose..." Peter tilted his head to one side.

"Then someone is willing to kill to maintain the status quo," Zen said after a few moments. "Welcome to the outer limits."

Chapter 6

The trip turned out to be more enjoyable than Zen or Peter had expected. They passed by the Isis Space Station. The scale of the giant double wheel-like structure made Zen gasp. One section of it spun in seeming slow motion. Peter explained the physics of how it maintained Earth gravity in most units. Orion sat farther away in the direction of Mars, a way station for longer space exploration trips. Photovoltaic panels captured solar and electromagnetic energy from other stars. Zen didn't understand most of what Peter said. Instead, she marveled at the beauty of it. Andromeda floated against a blackness of space. Points of light, stars and planets, scattered in the distance beyond it. For a time, Zen forgot the dismal circumstances of their journey. Two hours later they arrived at Star Flight. The docking port was surprisingly busy.

"You'd think we were in one of those sci-fi movies," Zen said as they walked along a ramp. "I wouldn't be surprised if aliens strolled by and waved."

Peter laughed. "Given the vastness of space, the odds against stumbling onto sentient life are quite small. And, they may not be friendly."

"Geez, let me dream at least. I've got to get some pictures for Astra." Zen used her smartwatch to capture images. "Astra might be ready to hop on a ship to take off once she sees these."

"It is extraordinary," Peter agreed.

People dressed in space suits hurried around as if on serious business. Most were dressed in comfortable attire, jumpsuits or pantsuits. Smart fabrics made for space served multiple purposes. From monitoring vital functions to radiation protection, clothes were tools. Still, fashion hadn't been completely abandoned. Colors contrasted with the sterile metallic gray and white of most surfaces. A rainbow of blue, purple, and green seemed to be shades most favored this season.

Dr. McCoy beamed at them as she strode forward. She'd spent thirty minutes making sure her cargo had been registered. Then it had been loaded on a flatbed pulled by a Jeep rover.

"Ready for a tour of In Situ?" she said.

"After our interviews. And we need to visit the crime scene," Zen replied fast. She suppressed a grin at the crestfallen expression her partner wore. She knew the astrophysicist in him would happily spend days wandering the labs.

"Ahmad's death was accidental. I thought you two came to tie up minor loose ends. You know, paperwork. Governments love paperwork." Dr. McCoy lost her good-humored attitude for the first time. She looked from Zen to Peter as if seeking reassurance.

"The use of a designer drug and possible sex trafficking in space are for the moment not approved. Both are against regulations, if not outright crimes," Peter put in smoothly.

"Right," Zen said. She silently thanked him for fixing her blunder.

"Hardly," Dr. McCoy replied with a grunt. "This way. Just a quick ride to the research sector. We could walk but it's crowded with pedestrians around lunchtime. Anyway, back to the unfortunate businessman; I assisted in the postmortem. Evidence of sexual activity, traces of the drug jump in his system. We don't much stress about a bit of sex, drugs, and space boogie as we call it."

"Maybe you should," Zen muttered.

Dr. McCoy stopped and faced them. "Until now the worst security had to deal with were loud parties and trashed hotel suites. Most of the people responsible paid more than enough to cover the damages. We're not a hotbed of bad behavior, no matter what you've been told."

"But you must agree that a death changes the game," Peter put in.

"Hmmm," was Dr. McCoy's only reply. She looked less pleased to see them.

They followed her to a mini-monorail. Compact train compartments held a few passengers. As Dr. McCoy had said, most people were on foot. The train track sat only about ten feet above "street level." It glided along, making little sound. Their short ride was so effortless, Zen might have wondered if they'd moved at all.

"Here we go. You've been cleared but you still need to scan your ID," Dr. McCoy said. They went through a set of pocket doors. Security personnel checked their bags, took their prints, and scanned the barcodes of their digital identification. Then they went to the administrative offices. Trim men and women, none had to be older than twenty-five, bustled around desks.

Down a long hallway they went to an office. Its interior was distinctly utilitarian, unlike Commander Okoro's elegant one.

"Dr. Gregson and I are co-directors of the In Situ Research Center," Dr. McCoy said with a gesture of her head to the man.

"Good to meet you," Dr. Gregson said and shook hands with Zen and Peter in turn. He was tanned with thinning blond hair. He exchanged a quick glance with Dr. McCoy. "I understand you wish to get started right away."

"Indeed. Thank you for arranging a room for us." Peter smiled at them both.

"Not at all. Awful business. We assisted by storing the remains. Dr. McCoy and Dr. Elliot, she has a medical practice locally, performed the postmortem. Lucky for us, Dr. Elliot was a coroner back home. Escaped the gritty reality of urban crime for the adventure of space."

"She followed accepted forensic documentation and preservation of evidence. Nothing more than overzealous partying," Dr. McCoy added.

"Naturally, we treated the widow with sensitivity. Even so, she wasn't surprised at the circumstances," Dr. Gregson said.

"She knew her husband had affairs, you mean," Zen said.

"Hmm." Dr. Gregson nodded and exchanged another look with Dr. McCoy. "She was the one who suggested we check for drugs or designer alcohol, and to see if he'd entertained... female company."

Zen laughed at the delicate description. "Dr. Elliot, we've heard there may be sex workers at the hotel."

"Sex work isn't illegal on Earth. Criminalizing carnal pursuits is distinctly antiquated. Yes, I know our home office at

NASA and various governments frown on it out here. But..." Dr. Gregson shrugged.

"And yet Hassan Ahmad is dead," Zen replied in a dry voice. She decided to embrace the bad cop role.

"Yes, very sad. He did have an undiagnosed heart abnormality. Though usually not fatal, certain unregulated street drugs can trigger typically benign premorbid medical conditions," Dr. McCoy said.

"I agree with Dr. Elliot's findings, although my field is engineering and chemistry," Dr. Gregson put in. "Her summary fits with all the other circumstances and evidence."

"He pushed his body too hard after space travel. He died from an overdose of fun," Zen said.

"Exactly. One of the reasons we lobbied against changing the name and character of the station. But we didn't have the final say-so in the direction things took." Dr. McCoy squinted in disapproval.

Zen caught the implication that NASA and ESA shouldered the blame for allowing private interests to take over. The name Star Flight came from private companies who saw the commercial potential for space tourism. Though the In Situ research facility came first.

"The price tag for the space station was high. Plans for Star Flight, or whatever you want to call it, always included private corporations," Zen said.

"Yes, but the base technology that made it a reality came from *us*, global governments and scientists," Dr. Gregson asserted. "We've allowed control to slip from our hands. When profit motives take center stage, we see what happens."

"We have military security staff in government sectors of the station. The rest? The responsibility of Black Rock," Dr. McCoy said, referring to the private contractor who'd won the bid to provide guard services.

Peter looked past the co-directors to a digital image on one wall. The space station map had sector labels. "They cover a lot of territory then."

"Yes. I'm sure you have a lot of questions for them," Dr. Gregson replied. "We have excellent relations, but they're paid by big business."

"Are you saying they've let things slide and don't share all information with your security team?" Zen asked.

"I'm just saying they may have a different view on what needs to be reported. As far as we know, the party culture on In Situ has been fairly... laid back. Wouldn't you say, Irene?" Dr. Gregson looked at his associate.

"I don't know firsthand, Greg," Dr. McCoy said with a small laugh. "From what I've heard from younger staff, it's mostly harmless frat house kind of stuff."

Dr. Gregson smiled back at her and faced Zen. "As you may have noticed, most of our team here at In Situ is below the age of forty. Median age thirty-three, I believe. Irene and I are ancient, both closer to fifty than forty."

"He's being diplomatic," Dr. McCoy retorted. "I'm fifty-two and Greg is a mere child of forty-five."

"I wouldn't dare speak on a woman's age. You don't look a day over thirty-five," Dr. Gregson replied with a short bow.

"Which explains why our working relationship thrives," Dr. McCoy joked.

Zen studied them both as they talked. Their fair skin was unlined. Neither looked older than their late thirties. Anti-aging medicine had benefited from space research along with other fields.

"Isolation is a real challenge even with the expansion of space populations. Then there is boredom, the sameness of seeing familiar faces twenty-four seven. We're also a species that loves to roam. Only so many places to go here. The social dynamics could lead to clashes, aberrant conduct." Zen watched the research scientists for reactions.

"Dr. Batiste is a forensic sociologist and social worker. She's studied individual and group behavior. Her dissertation on social environments in space colonies is considered groundbreaking." Peter turned to Zen with a look of genuine respect.

Zen blushed at the indirect compliment. "My point being we shouldn't assume space populations are immune to criminality. Space residents are wealthier and more educated than the general public on Earth. But people are still people."

"Very interesting. I'm sure your reputation for solving crimes is well deserved. I've read the news stories, Dr. Batiste. Though it seems not all of your conclusions proved valid," Dr. McCoy replied with a side glance at Peter. "What looks obvious can trip up even the best brains."

"True, but as my father loves to say, if it looks like a duck..." Zen smiled at the two research scientists.

Peter cleared his throat. "Maybe we should proceed with our interviews first and then tour In Situ."

"Right. Thanks for the insights," Zen said.

"I'll show you to the living units," Dr. McCoy said with a quick glance at Dr. Gregson.

Zen followed her out and Peter trailed behind. Dr. McCoy gave them an abbreviated tour as they passed through sections, explaining the purpose of each. A full tour, which would include the research labs, and a presentation would come later. Dr. McCoy left them to get settled. Their rooms were surprisingly spacious, each with an en suite bathroom. Sgt. Young rang Zen's room an hour later. They met the police officer in a common area. The lobby was decorated with large potted plants, and simulated sunlight came from lamps above.

"Wow, nice." Sgt. Young gazed up at the domed ceiling. Blues skies with a smattering of fluffy clouds were displayed overhead. "High-def digital Earth environment décor."

"The luxe villages in your lunar colony are pretty nice," Zen replied.

"Yeah, but not like this. Even the pricey modular homes don't have courtyards with sky," Sgt. Young said as she pointed up.

"Don't be surprised if some developer decides to build one on the moon," Zen joked.

"I doubt it. Interest seems to have shifted from living on the moon to Mars and Titan," Peter said.

"Dr. Navarro is right, ma'am. The moon is mostly for miners and company execs. Not a lot of ways to make it homey like Earth," Sgt. Young agreed.

"Even Mars and Titan will attract only the most adventurous and scientists. Migration in any numbers will be limited until we find a habitable planet or exoplanet," Peter added.

"In other words, there is only so much tech can do to make space livable for us puny humans. Fine by me. Anyway, let's get to the witnesses." Zen pulled up the names with locations on her tablet.

"Two are still at the hotel. I've arranged a meeting room for you there. I managed to track down two party girls seen with Ahmad in the days before he died." Sgt. Young gestured for them to follow her.

"Good work, sarge," Zen said as they walked.

"Wasn't easy, but I've got friends who work at the hotel. And I know the chef who does their meals. He owns the restaurant franchises at the hotel. Had to arrest one of his employees who was stealing. So, he feels like he owes me." Sgt. Young kept up chatter giving them more info. They rode a train to the hotel.

"You must spend quite a bit of time here," Peter said, looking around with interest as they moved through sections.

"Security can detain folks, but LMPD does official investigations that lead to prosecution. And they can't charge people, of course. I also come here when I have days off. Good places to eat, shops, and they've got three nightclubs. Even have free concerts in the park on level five. This way."

"So, you're here for business and pleasure," Zen replied.

"Basically, you could say this is my beat."

Sgt. Young waved to three people working the expansive registration desk. She took them to the manager's office. The short man seemed anxious to help them on their way. No doubt eager to have less negative attention that might affect bookings. After assuring him they would be discreet, Zen and Peter proceeded to the crime scene.

The suite had been roped off, but not with crime scene tape. Sgt. Young explained that the company had negotiated the less-conspicuous method. Zen and Peter looked around for no more than thirty minutes and then left. They interviewed Mr. and Mrs. McDougal separately. Zen took the wife while Peter dealt with the husband. The only notable result was how matter-of-fact the husband was about his wife's affair. Zen and Peter reconvened two hours later to compare notes. Both had recorded their meetings. They listened to each in turn.

"So, Mrs. McDougal had full permission to have an affair?"

"She requires more... physical attention than he. He made a show of assuring me it didn't bother him, or at least he accepted their differences," Peter said after his audio ended.

"But you didn't buy it." Zen looked up at Peter.

"He's human. The man loves his wife and is more afraid of losing her. Tolerating her affairs is the lesser evil."

"Affairs?"

"Ahmad was her latest love interest. Well, not exactly love. Didn't she say?" Peter asked.

"She made it seem like Ahmad was a true soul mate in every way. The usual, 'His wife doesn't appreciate him' line. I got the impression she had real feelings for the guy," Zen said.

"Her husband emphasized the opposite. He's sure it was just sex, that his wife would never leave him."

"So, either he's lying to cover up a motive for murder or..." Zen arched both eyebrows.

"Mrs. McDougal was in love. Ahmad had multiple sex partners at the hotel. She finds out, confronts him, and things get violent," Peter replied.

"Giving him a drug doesn't sound like a crime of passion. I'd expect an enraged jealous lover to bash his head in. Shoot him or stab him," Zen said. "She finds out, bides her time, and gives him the drug. Nah, doesn't fit."

"Why not?"

"Mrs. McDougal is emotional. Drama is the woman's middle name. She went from tears to rage when I told her about the other women. I'd say she was the bash-in-his-head type. But it could have been an act."

"People lying to the authorities during an investigation. Say it isn't so," Peter retorted.

"What's next?"

"Let's hope the party-girl witnesses shed some light on this."

Sgt. Young brought two women to the hotel, a woman with dark brown skin with blond hair and a pale brunette. Neither looked happy to be there. They interviewed the African woman first.

"Imirah Suri," was her short reply when asked her name. "I'm African and Turkish," she corrected when Peter tapped notes. "Get it right."

"Thank you," he said.

"I didn't know the guy. He looked cool, had one of those shiny black credit cards. The waiters all seemed to know him. We ate and drank the best. So, when he invited me to party, I was down," Imirah said. "I don't know that other girl. We kinda hit it off after we both met him."

"How much did he pay you? We're not investigating sex work, so don't worry," Zen added when the woman's expression turned sour.

Imirah studied Zen first, then Peter. She shrugged. "I accept gifts. Living here can be expensive. I work at the Chez Café, a little eatery on level two. Not a lot of money. I came just to experience life in space. Nothing better for me on Earth. If you know what I mean."

"Hmm. Who sponsored you?" Zen asked.

Imirah scowled at her. "I don't have a pimp, if that's what you mean. Now unless you are charging me with somethin', I'm done." She pushed the chair back and stood.

"Thank you for speaking to us. We'll be in touch." Peter came around the table, pulled the chair away, and opened the door for her.

"No need. That's all I know," Imirah retorted and flounced out.

The other woman was subdued. Zen studied her round face. She had the delicate features of a schoolgirl. Where Imirah wore the bright plumage of an exotic bird, Emme Gaida was understated in appearance. Her dark hair was cut short to complement her features. She wore a row of three silver stud earrings in each ear. Yet her charcoal-gray blouse and matching slacks clung to her curves. She gave off just the right hint of promised sensuality. When she entered the room, her movements flowed like water. Every gesture seemed to be an invitation. She appeared at ease until she saw Peter. Zen caught the hesitation even though she recovered quickly. Peter, tapping in notes, didn't look up at first. When he did, he caught his breath.

"Emme," he breathed.

Zen gazed from the woman to Peter as they sat in stupefied silence, staring at each other. She let the seconds drag on before she spoke. "Stay here, Ms. Gaida. Navarro, outside."

When Peter didn't move Zen lightly punched his shoulder. He seemed to snap out of his daze. Zen watched him stumbled as he stood. Then Peter seemed to collect himself with effort. His movements were stiff as he walked out. Emme Gaida avoided returning Zen's pointed look. When Zen was out in the hall, Sgt. Young approached.

"We got a suspect? Dr. Navarro came out looking sick." Sgt. Young stopped when Zen raised a palm.

"Make sure Emme Gaida doesn't leave that room. I still need to question her. Right now, I need a few minutes with my partner," Zen clipped.

"Yes ma'am," Sgt. Young murmured. She gestured down the hallway in the direction Peter had gone.

Zen nodded acknowledgment and marched off. She found Peter leaning against a wall with his forehead pressed to it. "You're going to tell me about you and Emme Gaida right *now*." She stopped when a research employee gave them a curious look as she walked past.

"When I..." Peter inhaled deeply and then blew out a harsh breath. Another employee walked by and he averted his face. "Not here."

"Fine," Zen snapped.

She strode down two doors and to the second room they'd been assigned. The door panel went green when Zen tapped in the code to unlock it. Once the door whisked shut, Zen faced him with a scowl. Neither sat at the table in the room.

Peter took a deep breath. "Emme was one of the women I used to see when... I mean, she and I were..."

"She's a sex worker," Zen said after a few moments of watching him squirm and search for words.

"No, I mean, in a manner of speaking. She provided what is sometimes called the girlfriend experience. I paid her rent and other expenses. We'd spend hours talking. Sometimes we didn't even have sex. We became close. I thought we... were in love. She was very good at her job." Peter scrubbed his forehead as if trying to rub out bad memories.

"And?" Zen pushed.

"I was naturally quite disappointed to learn my feelings weren't reciprocated. I tried to talk to her. I was persistent. Very." Peter looked at the ceiling.

"You're telling me you stalked her?"

Peter flinched at the question. "I may have been desperate not to lose her."

"How long ago did this happen?"

"It's been about seven years since our last encounter. The police were called. I didn't tell them about our arrangement. My wife didn't find out." Peter exhaled again. "I thought she understood me. Anyway, after that blow I turned to impersonal sex workers and then humanoids."

"I didn't see that in the file on you." Zen frowned. How did Hadley miss such a choice detail?

Peter shook his head. "It happened long before the problems I had with humanoid sex workers. Emme was a graduate student at the time. I thought she'd finished school and gone on to a normal career."

"She financed her education and paid the bills with sex work."

"No, she didn't have multiple men. Only me. Emme wasn't... isn't a prostitute," Peter insisted.

"Navarro, she partied with Ahmad. You really think she and the other woman came to this space station to be low-wage waitresses? I'll bet good money they have a sponsor." Zen paced around the metal table.

"She was a smart student, very talented," Peter replied.

"Yeah, she's got talents alright. They got her on a very expensive floating piece of hardware in space. Surrounded by men and women who make lots of money. You're going nowhere near this interrogation."

"Emme isn't a suspect. We don't know—"

"The only reason I won't get you shipped back to Earth is because of how much trouble it would be. Anyway, you're going to help me crack her."

"Zen, listen to me. I know Emme, knew her. Once we got over the tension of our failed... relationship—"

"Please," Zen said with a snort.

"We became cordial, on good terms. Though I admit we lost contact a few years ago. But I followed her progress. She graduated, moved to Miami and, well, I lost track of her after a time. Plus, my wife and I had our first child and then another. My work, family life, and a rocky marriage—in short, life got in the way. I didn't make an effort to seek Emme out but assumed she was doing well," Peter said and went back to rubbing his forehead.

"You found time for a colorful secret life though."

Peter's expression stiffened. "I made mistakes, terrible mistakes. Losing my family, the damage to my career, time in prison, and forced treatment aren't enough punishment? Another man was arrested for those murders."

"Did all of the facts come out about you though?" Zen said, her tone relentless. "Oh, yes. I read your treatment summaries. You had a taste for roughing up sex workers, Navarro."

His shoulders slumped. "I don't remember everything."

"Say what now?" Zen peered at him through squinted eyes.

"The treatment caused problems with my memory in certain areas. The doctors speculate the brain stimulation may be the cause. It could be I'm blocking out certain details to protect my psyche." Peter pulled out a chair and slumped onto it.

"So, in other words, you may have killed and can't remember. Or so you say." Zen stood and studied him in silence. The look of misery that twisted his normally blank expression looked real.

"I wish I could dredge up every memory. I deserve to suffer for what I've done. To my family, my colleagues whose work was questioned because I was their collaborator. But I'm sure I didn't kill anyone," Peter said with a shudder. "I know what you're thinking."

"Hmm," was all Zen could manage. Her mind raced with this new big problem on her hands. She could have easily had Navarro placed on leave if they were on Earth. But they were far from home.

"Maybe I was brilliant at covering up my crimes," Peter said when Zen didn't respond.

"Damn it. I need a second pair of eyes not tied to the lunar colony or Star Flight. If the LMPD is looking the other way—" Zen heaved a sigh.

"Sgt. Young will resist turning against her fellow officers. Commander Okoro has his career to think about." Peter sat straight after a few moments. "I certainly didn't expect to find someone from my unsavory past here. I'm sorry for the complications it has caused."

Zen paced for a few moments. She raked fingers through her African braids, done specifically for this trip. "You swear you didn't lay a hand on the woman? I mean in anger."

"No, that I do know for sure."

"Okay, so you can still be on the case. Just nothing related to her. If she's hooked up in this even more... well, I'll deal with it later. You trace how both women came to be out here. Contact Hadley to get on it."

"I will. Do you think Sgt. Young should help you interview Emme, I mean Ms. Gaida?" Peter looked a bit less dismal, having been assigned a task.

Zen sat across from Peter. "Yes. I'll tell Clive about this hiccup in the investigation."

"I know. I was bound to cross paths with someone from my previous activities, I suppose," Peter murmured.

"Well damn, how many women we talking about?" Zen shot back.

Peter blushed pink and wore a self-conscious smile. "Not nearly as many as the media would have you believe."

"Enough that you bumped into one in outer space." Zen stood, hands on both hips. "Might as well get back to it. You start digging."

"And Sgt. Young?" Peter stood to face Zen. His composed, impassive demeanor had dropped back into place.

"I'll tell her you aren't feeling well and—" Zen stopped at his skeptical frown. 'Yeah, sounds like an obvious lie to cover up something."

"Tell her we discovered new information and I'm going to check in with the office," Peter offered.

"Then she'll want to know what new information. Not telling her will look like another cover-up," Zen countered.

"You think she's reporting back to her chief and Okoro then." Peter rubbed his jaw.

"She doesn't have much choice. If she's not part of wrongdoing then we'll put her in a tight spot. And if she is..." Zen shrugged.

"She'll intensify efforts to prevent us from uncovering the truth," Peter added.

"Yeah, and call in reinforcements to track our moves and keep us in the dark," Zen added with a grimace.

"You think we're in physical danger?"

Zen didn't answer right away. After a few seconds she shook her head. "I don't think so. These folks would have to be really stupid to try something. NASA, DOJ, OSI, and God would come down on 'em. Well, the God part is a teeny exaggeration," Zen joked.

"I get the logic," Peter said with a grin. Then he grew serious again at the gravity of their discussion. "So, we must be cautious in what we reveal."

"Screw it. Tell her something that's basically the truth. The interviews haven't resulted in any big shockers, routine stuff. Two space hookers partying for profit. You'll be doing more background checks to verify their accounts. We're dividing our efforts to be efficient." Zen gave a short nod. "Ready. Set. Go."

Peter followed her out. They went back to the larger meeting room and made their explanations to Sgt. Young. If she was skeptical, Sgt. Young did a good job of hiding it. She seemed to accept the change in plans with enthusiasm, in fact.

"I don't get to interrogate suspects much out here. Not on something serious like a possible murder. Mostly I do paperwork and deal with petty stuff," Sgt. Young said. She rubbed her hands together.

"I'll do the talking," Zen said.

"Of course, ma'am." Sgt. Young lost none of the sparkle in her eyes.

"I can find my way back with the digital directions app. We'll meet up later to compare notes," Peter said and left them.

Sgt. Young watched him walk away and turned to Zen. "He looked shook up before."

"He's fine. Come on," Zen replied in her most matter-of-fact tone. She led the way back into the room.

Chapter 7

Emme sat straight when Zen and Sgt. Young entered the room. She seemed to adopt defensive posture complete with a hostile glare. "Unless you're charging me with a crime, I have a right to leave."

"Thanks for your cooperation so far, Ms. Gaida. And no, you're not under arrest."

The word made Emme flinch but she recovered fast. "Right, because I haven't done anything illegal."

"Special Agent Navarro and I will need to check your story. I'm sure your employer at the café will confirm that you work there."

"He's—" Emme pursed her lips for a few seconds. "I mean, you're with the Lunar Police Department?"

"No. We're federal law enforcement. We conduct special investigations of incidents that happen on space colonies and satellite facilities like Star Flight." Zen sat and watched as the information sank in with the young woman. She could almost hear the wheels.

Sgt. Young sat down a few seconds after Zen took her seat. Emme's suspicious gaze bounced between the two of them. She squinted as if that would help her read them better. After a few seconds, she appeared to relax a bit.

"Okay, well, I don't know what happened to Hassan. We didn't see him the night he got killed," Emme said.

"I never said someone killed him," Zen replied with a frown as she leaned forward.

"I mean, why else would there be such a big deal about him dying? Police asking questions, federal cops showing up in space. Pretty obvious you think he didn't just keel over from a heart attack or stroke." Emme looked from Zen to Sgt. Young and back. "I'm no CEO or rocket scientist, but I'm not stupid."

Zen studied her in silence. Emme gazed back at her, unfazed. "How long have you known Ms. Suri?"

Emme blinked hard a few times. She paused before answering. "We've known each other since school in London. I was an exchange student for a year, undergrad. She's from there—England, I mean. She moved to D.C. after finishing."

"Interesting. She told us you met here. Why would she lie?" Zen raised one eyebrow.

"She's scared is one answer. I don't know. Ask her," Emme shot back and pressed her lips together.

"When and where did you meet Hassan Ahmad?" Zen pushed on.

"Not that many places to go for a drink, right? We were bound to meet him." Emme shrugged and glanced away.

"Which doesn't answer the question," Sgt. Young put in.

"We were at Club Venus one night. He said he'd just arrived that morning. He didn't waste time finding a party," Emme replied in a tight voice. She scowled at Sgt. Young and then looked at Zen.

"Three days before he died, then," Zen said.

"If you say so." Emme examined her lacquered acrylic nails. The bright turquoise color had silver strips down the middle.

"That night club is very exclusive. Waitressing pays that much out here?" Zen glanced at Sgt. Young.

"Uh, no. Ms. Gaida and Ms. Suri must be supplementing their income in some way," Sgt. Young replied in a flat tone.

"Look, guys like to treat us, okay? We don't have problems getting dates out here. Andre knows us, so we get in," Emme snapped.

"I'll bet he's happy to let 'entertainment' come in for the rich guys," Zen replied.

"I'm not a common prostitute. And if you're going to accuse me, I want a lawyer!" Emme shouted and slapped the tabletop.

"You won't be arrested. NASA and the big corporations have the authority to deport you. I'm assuming you read the terms and conditions." Zen's calm response and words had the desired effect. The heat evaporated from the young woman so fast Zen could almost hear the hiss of steam.

Sex work on Earth had been decriminalized since 2045 but was regulated. Anyone traveling to the colonies or space stations had to accept a list of rules governing behavior. That included refraining from criminal acts and a prohibition against sex for pay. Prostitution tended to attract crime, something Zen had studied while pursuing her doctorate in forensic sociology. Activists had campaigned for decades to make sex work legal in America. They'd argued that it would reduce crime. That turned out to be wrong for a variety of reasons. Men and women drawn to that career continued to be preyed on. Zen had concurred with previous research. People who hired others for sex saw them as objects. Violence continued to be a serious occupational hazard.

"We're not druggies," Emme finally blurted out. "I mean, we're not addicted like a lot of—"

"Good money is hard to resist. Especially when you get used to it," Zen observed.

Emme stared at Zen for a few seconds. "I want to talk to you *alone*."

Sgt. Young stood without hesitation. She glanced from Emme to Zen with a look of speculation. "I'll be outside if you need me."

"Thanks." Zen turned her attention back to her witness.

"I assume you didn't tell that space cop about Peter and me." Emme wore a smug half smile. When Zen didn't reply she went on. "That means you don't entirely trust the local authorities. You're right not to."

"If you've got something to give me just spit it out. I'm not going to play the game," Zen retorted.

"I would win a bet that the lady cop isn't telling you everything. Even if she doesn't know it all, her boss does. And you'll win a prize if you play the game. It's called mutual benefit. Information for giving me a pass so I can stay on the space station and keep my job. It's pocket change but I like it." Emme's smile wavered in the long silence that followed.

"Only if that information is useful," Zen replied after a few more beats of letting her worry.

"Promise you won't report me as a sex worker. We're being recorded, so you can't go back on your word. I only got gifts. It's not like we set up shop for-real for-real." Emme pursed her lips into a pout. The expression made her look even younger.

Zen gave her a cool smile. "As it happens, we're not being recorded right now. I wouldn't have to keep any promises even if we were. And it wouldn't be up to me. Commander Okoro and Star Flight CEO have the final say."

Emme's eyes narrowed. "Then maybe I should be negotiating with one of them."

"You could try. Hassan Ahmad is dead. They're in full control of this floating hardware. You want to put your life in their hands? Go right ahead." Zen sat back with her arms crossed.

"You're saying they... that somebody murdered Hassan?" Emme's skin went pale until it almost seemed translucent.

Zen had surprised herself with the shot-in-the-dark comment. Yet she made sure to keep her calm pose. "If you or your girlfriend didn't do it, someone did. Or at the very least is covering up the dirty circumstances of his death. What kind of party drugs were you taking with him?"

"We didn't sell him jump or swag. He had that powder when we got to the suite," Emme burst out and then realized her mistake.

"So, you did illegal drugs with him along with your gal pal. What's swag?" Zen shot back.

"It's a designer drug made here and on the moon. The rush doesn't last longer than three hours and it doesn't show up in your system. A test hasn't been developed yet," Emme said.

"What are the effects?"

Emme heaved a sigh as if resigning to the fact that she had to talk. "Most get a giddy kind of high. Makes you want to party. Guys get erections that last hours. But there are bad effects. Some people get aggressive or take dangerous risks. One guy ended up in an airlock without a space suit. At least that's what I heard. The official report said he got drunk on liquor and wandered in there."

"Okay," Zen replied, making a mental note to follow up on the death. "Tell me about your visits with Hassan Ahmad. Everything. People who partied with you, where, and when."

"Hassan was a beast. By that I mean he was fun. Always up for a good time, ya know? And generous with drinks, tips, the works. He could go for hours when the music was pumping and bottles of expensive liquor kept flowing. He wasn't a druggie, more into recreational use. Anyway, that night—"

"The night he died," Zen cut her off. "When you claimed you hadn't seen him."

"He was alive when I left at around two that morning. I had a shift. Two other guys and girls were in the room snorting and guzzling like crazy. Imirah wasn't ready to go, said she didn't care about losing a shit job. I think she was into Hassan. Thought he was her platinum ticket."

"How so?"

"He really got into her 'exotic looks,' he said. Imirah indulged one of his kinky fantasies of being tied up and choked out. While she... you know, sat in his lap."

"Details," Zen prompted.

Emme shook her head and smiled. "We had a wild two days with that guy. He paid me to watch once. They were both naked. Imirah riding him until he was whimpering. Me sipping champagne while another guy or girl felt me up. Except the part I didn't like was him handcuffed with a scarf around his neck. She'd tighten it until he said the safe word. Sometimes he'd almost pass out but still be begging her not to let loose."

"That night the good times went bad and he didn't wake up," Zen put in.

Zen's statement wiped the grin from Emme's face. "What—no. *No.* That's not what happened! I swear he was alive. He snapped out of it after they finished. I saw him. He was high and exhausted, sure. Imirah knows how to bring you to the moon and back. But when I left them, he was breathing."

"Maybe he didn't recover. You panicked. Partying and drugs in exchange for rough sex is one thing. But when somebody ends up dead..."

"No, no, no. Imirah met up with me later. She laughed about how much money he threw at her. Said it was the best orgasm of his life. Claimed he'd pay our way back to Earth if we promised to keep seeing him. He was gonna set us up in our own house and everything," Emme said. More words spilled out in a rush. "Why would we kill our big opportunity? He was about to be made the R&D head of the company he worked for. He was a chemist, had come up with three new miracle drugs. He managed to negotiate to keep part ownership of the patents."

"Research and development," Zen murmured.

"Right. Hassan talked big, but he wasn't lying. Imirah did a background check. We found the Earth articles about him. I don't know. Maybe he helped invent that new party drug, somebody found out, and wanted to shut him up. Or cut him out of the profits." Emme breathed fast as though she was running a marathon. Then she sank into her chair with a bleak look on her face. "That's all I know. I swear."

"Hmm." Zen scrutinized her in silence for a time. "Tell me about you and Dr. Navarro."

Emme blinked in confusion at the abrupt change of subject. "Peter didn't do drugs if that's what you're asking."

"Did he ask to be treated like Ahmad or hurt you?"

"Look, I..." Emme looked away. Then she faced Zen again with a fierce expression. "He's a nice guy, okay? And he didn't kill those women like you said he did."

"You kept up with what was happening with him. I thought you wanted to stay away from Dr. Navarro, filed reports because he stalked you," Zen replied.

"I wasn't in love with him but I didn't hate the man. He just got a bit too intense. Took things too far."

"Got violent?"

"No, not exactly. He liked rough sex, but he never drew blood. Just left a few bruises. But he seems different now. I don't know..." Emme gazed ahead at the wall with a slight frown. Then the pensive façade faded into one of suspicion as she glanced at Zen. She shifted in the chair like she was sitting on spikes. "Why are you making me talk about him? This is about Hassan dying."

"Wow. You'd rather be questioned about a dead guy than talk about Peter. Strange loyalty to an ex-stalker." Zen wore a baffled frown for a few seconds.

"His wife found us; she followed him a few times. I didn't sign up for drama or to be a stepmother. She stalked me, not him. Vandalized my townhouse. Showed up at all hours screaming obscenities. I called the police one night. Peter begged me not to say it was her," Emme confessed.

"So, his wife was violent and not him?" Zen wore a skeptical expression.

"He went on so about how it was all his fault until I felt sorry for the woman. But she's not exactly a pitiful victim. When he got in trouble, she took real pleasure in it."

Zen considered additional details about her partner. His story had more layers than expected but it didn't mean he was innocent. Still, Emme was on target. They were there to talk about Ahmad.

"You have a history of getting rough with customers. You hook up with your friend Imirah and she's even more into it. Except Hassan Ahmad doesn't survive the festivities. Nothing kills a party like a corpse."

"Imirah can tell you. She was with him longer than me," Emme exclaimed with wide eyes.

"Wow, you threw her under the speed train real quick," Zen clipped.

"I didn't mean she killed him. You got me all messed up." Emme's eyes went shiny with tears that then rolled down her cheeks. She combed trembling fingers through her brunette hair.

"Let's go back over your story. Or I should say your *stories*. First you acted like you only partied with Ahmad once and you didn't see him the night he died. Then you admitted being with him more than once, including in the hours before his body was discovered." Zen sat back with her arms folded. "I didn't mess you up, Ms. Gaida. You can't keep your lie straight. The truth is in there somewhere. Maybe the answer to how Ahmad died."

Emme shook her head during Zen's speech. She looked around as if searching for an escape route. After twisting her hands for a few moments, she huffed out a sigh. "Okay. Okay. Imirah and I have been friends off and on for a while. Neither one of us are made for sitting in an office on somebody else's schedule. So, we like to party. Men and women like to treat us."

"Treat? Interesting spin on prostitution," Zen said.

"It's legal," Emme shot back.

"Go on."

"He liked to party hard—Ahmad, I mean. The man lived dangerously. And he was obnoxious but thought he was Mr. Charm," Emme said with a snort of derision.

"Dangerous how?" Zen sat forward.

"He liked to brag and toss in a few insults to other people while he was at it. In his mind, he was the smartest guy in every room. Always seemed easygoing and fun until you got past the surface. I wouldn't be surprised if somebody did kill him. Including his wife."

"You're saying she knew about his behavior," Zen said.

Emme shrugged. "I told Imirah he was bad news. Always upping the stakes. He liked that his wife knew. He'd even drop hints to drive her to the edge. Hassan said she was very uptight, into appearances and her pride. Plus, she liked the lifestyle. Houses, travel, meeting the rich and powerful. He implied her family looked down on him, but they liked his money. His wife was the same."

"Did she confront him or show up?"

"We never met her. Then we did some snooping and found out he had a mistress. And she's here at the same convention with her husband." Emme let out a short laugh. "Hassan was something else."

"Take me through the days after you first met Mr. Ahmad," Zen said and tapped the screen of her tablet. Her agency recording app blinked on.

"Again? I do have a job. At least I hope I still have it. News travels fast around this place. You're going to pay for my ticket back to Earth," Emme said with heat in her tone.

"Dr. Zenobia Batiste with US Office of Special Investigations. April 25th, 2086, on the In Situ Space Station, also referred to as the Star Flight Space Station in commercial space tourism circles. Please state your name and age. Also, your passport number." Zen returned Emme's scowl with a look of calm resolution. "If I arrange your departure, Ms. Gaida, you'll walk off that shuttle ramp right into the arms of special agents. Unless you give me a story that I can confirm which clears you of suspicion."

Color drained from Emme's face. She pressed her lips together for a few seconds before she started talking. Two more hours of sharp questions left Emme looking drained. She'd lost any attempt at bravado by the time Sgt. Young showed up to usher her out. Zen sent brief secure messages to Peter. She read two messages from Clive and Hadley. She was so intent Zen didn't hear Sgt. Young return to the meeting room.

"Ma'am," Sgt. Young clipped.

Zen looked up to find the young policewoman standing with a tense expression, legs apart. "Sorry, I wasn't ignoring you."

"You want to tell me what is really going on? I can't help with this investigation if I don't know all the facts." Sgt. Young stood between Zen and the door. They gazed at each other in silence for several seconds.

"Have a seat," Zen said finally.

Sgt. Young sat down with her back straight. "I have experience interviewing witnesses. I can talk to Imirah Suri again now that you've squeezed her friend."

"How did you—"

"I saw the look on the woman's face when she walked out of here. She couldn't get away fast enough. But she did leave, which means you didn't get evidence she contributed to Ahmad's death. Playing off two witnesses against each other is a common strategy."

"Okay," Zen replied mildly.

"I was in ROTC from middle school until I finished college, ma'am. I took criminal justice courses early on. Learned US and international law. Decided I wanted to be a civilian cop more. I'm not trying to impress you, just telling you who I am. I'm younger than you, but I wasn't born last night." Sgt. Young gazed at Zen as if waiting.

"Thanks for the reminder not to underestimate you, Sgt. Young," Zen said.

"Ma'am." Sgt. Young put traces of respect into her voice, like a good soldier facing a superior.

Zen gave Sgt. Young a rundown on her interview with Emme Gaida. Although she skipped around implications about LMPD officers, Zen could tell Sgt. Young wasn't fooled. "Peter talked to Mr. and Mrs. McDougal. No big reveal from either of them."

"You going to hit Mrs. McDougal with Ahmad's extracurricular activities? Smells like motive to me."

"Ahmad inspired motive all over the damn place, but we don't know that he was killed by someone," Zen said.

"Looks like to me it's shaping up that way, but I'll reserve judgement," Sgt. Young added when Zen started to speak. "Follow the evidence."

"Exactly." Zen cocked her head to one side when Sgt. Young didn't leave the chair. "What else?"

"You think LMPD has dirty cops. Maybe including me."

"Like you said, space is still a small town. Officers check incoming cargo and equipment. They know what goes on and where it happens better than anybody here. The underbelly so to speak. Drugs and prostitution wouldn't thrive without help." Zen expected a hot denial. Instead, Sgt. Young wore a blank look for a few seconds. "Well?"

"Star Flight has gotten a rep as a place to really get loose. In the last year or so we get more visitors. More trouble. Rich folks have the same vices as poor folks. They just have a sheen of polish on 'em. At least until you look close." Sgt. Young sounded like a cynical cop over twice her age.

"The night clubs probably contribute to the good times, huh?"

"I have a friend who works at the Ogun Space Station. That's the main reason they tightly regulate who opens shop there. The African Union thinks Star Flight has been allowed to get out of control," Sgt. Young said.

"They could be right," Zen replied with a sigh.

"Nigeria throws its weight around as the richest African country. Back home they're slipping into totalitarianism. It's spread to Ogun SS. There's middle ground between 'everything goes' and an iron fist," Sgt. Young said.

Zen looked at her sharply. "You've given this some thought."

"I keep my eyes open, yeah. Maybe I've been too willing to give some of my fellow officers the benefit of the doubt. As for command... permission to speak freely. Off the record for now."

"Go on."

"Commander Okoro feels overlooked by his superiors. Captain Walker plays on his resentment, feeds it. He's angling for Okoro to screw up bad." Sgt. Young watched Zen.

"He's ambitious, wants to move into that seat," Zen put in to complete her thought.

"My chief just wants to avoid getting crushed between them. His focus is on getting back to Earth. His job hasn't turned out to be the ticket to fame and fortune he'd hoped. Add to that his wife hates it here. We've had to smooth over trouble his two kids have gotten into. One of which involves public intoxication. They're teenagers," Sgt. Young said with a slight grimace as if that explained it all.

Zen gave a short laugh at the look on the young officer's face. "I feel his pain."

"My point is they're all distracted. Which could give an opening to bad actors. On both sides of the law."

Zen started to reply when her smartwatch hummed. The vibration on her wrist pulled her gaze to the display. "Let's go. Peter has the final postmortem report."

Sgt. Young led Zen to the El-train only used by officials. They rode in silence in the elevator. The glass front gave them a view of levels as they traveled up. Then the car moved perpendicular, transforming into a train. Ten minutes later they arrived at the In Situ research center. Peter met them in the lobby and led the way to a meeting room. He tapped in a code that opened the door and put the "In Use" sign on.

"I think you've got more news for me," Peter said seconds after the door whisked shut. He glanced at Sgt. Young and back to Zen.

"Emme Gaida has been moonlighting. No surprise there. I didn't think being wait staff at a café financed her lifestyle," Zen replied mildly. "She also told me how she knew you."

Sgt. Young hissed in a breath as her only reaction. Her neutral expression stayed in place. "Sir, did you know she was here?"

"Did you know unregulated dangerous drugs and prostitution was on Star Flight?" Peter clipped back.

Sgt. Young took a step closer to him. "You accusing me—"

"While you were collecting gossip, I was doing real police work, *your* job." Peter pointed a forefinger at her chest.

Zen wedged herself between them. She pushed Sgt. Young against the far wall as the young officer seemed likely to throw a punch. "Stand down. Both of you."

"For the record, no. I had no reason to think I'd meet up with anyone from my past out here. Why would I?" Peter shouted.

"Because you've had a colorful life featuring a cast of thousands, based on reports," Sgt. Young yelled. "You've got nerve, passing judgment on my department."

"So, reading sleazy tabloids is considered solid investigative technique out here? No wonder so much is going on under your nose," Peter said.

"Enough!" Zen glared at him.

The door lock chimed before it swung open. Dr. McCoy stood with a security officer. She glanced at the three of them in turn. "Is there a problem in here we need to know about?"

"We're comparing notes is all. A spirited exchange of ideas," Zen replied. "Nothing we can share."

Dr. McCoy continued to stare at them with a slight frown. The security officer craned his neck to look around her. "I see."

"Everything is fine. We'll let you get back to your schedule. Thanks."

Zen walked forward until Dr. McCoy took the hint. Dr. McCoy backed out of the room but looked in through the narrow window set in one wall. The security officer also gazed at them in curiosity for a few seconds. Then they both left.

"These rooms are soundproof," Peter said. When Zen and Sgt. Young looked at him, he shrugged. "I read up on the entire station, all sections."

"Okay. Deep breath, everybody." Zen pointed to the chairs around a table. They sat as though obeying the teacher in a class of unruly students. "Let's put our cards on the table. Peter does have what you call a 'colorful' past, Sgt. Young. But all evidence points to him not being a serial killer."

"Thanks for the ringing vote of confidence," Peter muttered with a grimace.

"Did you really fly to Madrid and break into his apartment? Like, wow." Sgt. Young shook her head.

"You really shouldn't believe everything you read on newsfeeds, sergeant," Peter muttered.

"I didn't break into his apartment. Technically, I did but... Let's focus on here and now," Zen said with a sigh.

"My point exactly. As opposed to dissecting my life." Peter sat straight.

"Unfortunately, your past is part of our investigation, Peter. Which means you stay away from Emme Gaida." Zen watched him.

Peter stared at the wall as though to avoid their gazes. "No problem. Ancient history."

"The last thing we need is to have Commander Okoro demand you two be called back to Earth," Sgt. Young put in.

"I haven't seen the woman in years. *I said it's no problem*," Peter said, his voice rising with each word. He glared at Sgt. Young.

"And you, Sgt. Young, will need to follow leads no matter where they take you. Including to the doorstep of fellow police officers. Emme Gaida danced around questions of police or security involvement in drugs or sex work. She's scared." Zen frowned as she thought about the interview.

"She should be. Here's the report on the forensic examination of Ahmad's body. The jump was substantial in his system, but it didn't kill him. The presence of petechiae in two internal organs indicate strangulation. But not the ordinary type. The doctor thinks the drug rendered him easy to subdue." Peter pulled his small tablet computer from a pocket of his jumpsuit. "His throat wasn't damaged, though."

"Maybe a norphene bag was put over his head," Sgt. Young said.

"A what?" Zen asked.

"Norphene is an advanced kind of plastic used here. Developed for use in space. One of many products developed that became widely used in other industries, like food packaging," Peter said.

Sgt. Young nodded. "Right. We have them at the lunar colonies. Snack bags, freeze food in 'em. They provide a tight seal to keep out water, contaminants, and   "

"Air," Zen said.

"Jump has unique properties which make it dangerous. Users also feel numb to danger. And it lowers oxygen in the bloodstream," Peter put in.

"Not my idea of a good time. Give me a good wine any day." Zen took Peter's tablet to scan the report.

"Breaking the rules has always been part of the thrill of illegal drug use. Part of the reason most of them were decriminalized," Peter explained. "So, drug traffickers came up with new ways to thrill their customers."

"Taking stuff that can kill you just to party. People are crazy," Sgt. Young retorted.

"You have no idea." Zen gave a short laugh. "I made a career of dealing with people doing 'crazy' things. That was before I got into law enforcement."

"Okay, so maybe they were playing those near-death sex games. One partner chokes the other one until they're light-headed. They claim it gives you an out-of-body orgasm. We had one case here, married couple. The guy almost died. An executive with one of the space mining companies. That was some hot scandal when the details got out. Thanks to a reporter." Sgt. Young wore a sour look.

"Let me guess. Jacques Clairmont with Global Associated Press," Peter said.

"Nothing gets past that guy. He digs up more dirt than a moon excavator," Sgt. Young replied.

"Fits Ms. Gaida's profile. She and her friend let the good times get out of hand. She now says they were with Ahmad that evening. But she claims he was alive when she left him with Imirah Suri," Zen said.

"Humph, friendship doesn't trump getting charged with murder," Sgt. Young joked. "I say we drag their asses in for harder questioning. Turn 'em against each other."

"But they don't have a real motive to kill the man. He worked on sensitive projects. There are rumors of industrial espionage. I talked to two of his co-workers. Neither of them liked him very much," Peter said.

"No surprise based on what Emme Gaida said about him." Zen studied Peter.

"One of them said Ahmad might have been in secret negotiations to defect to a competitor. He could use the threat as leverage to get a promotion and a better compensation package," Peter rushed on.

"Murder to keep an employee from going to another company? Sounds like a stretch to me." Sgt. Young wore a skeptical frown. "Look, the simple answer is usually the right one. Two bangers for cash milk the target a bit too hard. Find the source of drugs or a fellow party pal, maybe both, and case closed."

Peter turned to Zen. "Don't you see? The information about his employment tensions corroborates Emme's, Ms. Gaida's, account. His private behavior was an embarrassment to his company. Add in the fact that he would leave with valuable proprietary information and he's a liability. I know these companies from my work in research and development. Some of them are just as cutthroat as any criminal gang."

Zen shook her head after a few moments of thought. "Yeah. Right. Peter, you run down background on his employer..."

"ChemCo. The home office is in Mexico City. Less expensive. Their first big plant was in Mexico," Peter said.

"You've already made a start getting details on them. Let's go deep," Zen replied.

"I'll see if they're working on any new drugs. Could be related to the unregulated designer drug jump." Peter frowned as he seemed to mentally turn over other possibilities.

"Good. Maybe meet right around seven this evening. I'll talk to Imirah again. Sgt. Young—"

"I'll talk to my chief about any officers he might have concerns about. I trust him," she added when Zen's eyebrows went up.

"Fine," Zen said.

"I'll get going then." Peter wore a distracted, faraway expression as though he was already somewhere else.

Sgt. Young turned to watch him leave. When the door whisked shut, she faced Zen. "My question, should you trust *him*?"

"You deal with your colleagues. I'll handle mine," Zen replied with a poker face.

"Okay, ma'am," Sgt. Young said. She left.

Zen heaved a sigh once the door shut, leaving her alone. She leaned on the table, both palms flat. "Damn."

Chapter 8

"So, what do you think?" Zen rubbed her temples with the tips of her fingers.

She closed her eyes briefly. Then she opened them to look at Clive's image on the tablet screen. She was in a private sleeping pod adjacent to the In Situ Research Center. The Starry Night Inn had fifty. Each one was fitted out like a three-star hotel room. Comfortable but not luxe. Zen sat at a table in one corner, shoes kicked off and wearing her pajamas.

Clive squinted, deep in thought. His forceful presence came through across the outer space between them. And right now, she needed to feel it more than ever. Thinking about the tangle of suspects, possible motives, and complications had given her a headache.

"Is he off the rails?" Clive said.

The question startled Zen out of her reverie. "Peter? No, at least not yet. Trouble is, I don't know how close he is to being there."

"Hmmm. Let's stick a pin in that for the moment. Can you depend on Sgt. Young and her chief?"

Zen rolled her shoulders to relieve the tension in them. "I don't know about her boss, but yeah. Sgt. Young is solid. She's loyal, but not to a fault."

"Meaning she's not going to stick to the cop code of covering for your colleagues no matter what. Good." Clive continued to squint into the screen but not at Zen. He was sorting through all she'd told him.

"I meet with them tomorrow. Or today," Zen joked. It was after midnight and her brain wouldn't shut off until she'd talked to Clive.

"Okay, so here's where we are right at this moment. Ahmad is our first documented murder off-world. He wasn't exactly a lovable type, which means we have a circle of suspects," Clive said.

"And he got busy inspiring more people to hate his guts once he arrived. His wife, finally fed up with his screwing around, might have killed him." Zen shrugged because that theory still didn't feel right in her gut.

"Or paid someone to do the deed. Hadley is checking on a financial motive for her. Then there's the mistress."

"Ahmad wasn't the romantic hero saving her from a boring marriage. Maybe she realized it. Say she found out he was sneaking off to be with Imirah Suri." Zen shook her head after a second. "Doesn't sound any more likely when I say it out loud."

"You never know. Love betrayed has been the reason for murders since men and women walked upright. Imirah Suri and Emme Gaida." Clive lifted one thick eyebrow at Zen.

"They admit being with him the night he died. Imirah Suri claims Gaida was the one last with him though. Says she left before Gaida, not the other way around. Security video proved she was lying. Suri broke down fast once I told her. But she swore up and down Ahmad was alive when she left."

Zen didn't give her exact quote. Imirah said he was exhausted but smiling by the time she "finished him off." She'd described his fetishes in vivid detail, including wearing her thong. Way more than Zen needed to know. He liked seriously rough sex, but Imirah adamantly denied it included the "near-death" experience.

"Of course, she wouldn't admit things went wrong. She could be charged with negligent homicide." Clive's squint became a full grimace. "Believe it or not, Hadley's research gives support to Peter's theory."

"Corporate espionage as a motive?"

"Don't discount it, Batiste. World wars have started over fights for resources. Ahmad had negotiated to hold onto ownership of two key discoveries of his. A drug that could counteract the loss of muscle and bone mass from long-term space travel. The UN World Health Authority is still testing it, but the results are promising. His company isn't pleased he pulled it off. Seems he bribed a company official so his research wasn't recorded. He had time to file the patent, trademark a logo, and cut a deal with a large medical conglomerate. Earned over twenty million."

"Wow. I'm sure they were pissed at being outmaneuvered," Zen agreed.

"Government and private space programs will pay a premium for such a drug. He also worked with an engineer to develop a new form of polyester film that blocks radiation in prelim trials. In other words, Ahmad had a hand in creating two products to make space habitation safer. Trouble is, he didn't do it alone. He cut both of the teams that helped out of the profits. The patents and trademarks are in his name only."

"If they pass all the testing, sure. But would they kill him or take the guy to court? I mean, his widow will inherit his estate. And she's no pushover."

"There's a lawsuit. His employer was consulting its legal army to snatch back rights to both. The man was living on the edge. He made a bet that he would win."

"Ahmad had a big ego for sure," Zen snorted. "Among other things, according to Imirah and Mrs. McDougal. One or both may have gotten him killed."

"I missed that last part," Clive said, leaning forward.

"Nothing. Companies usually don't want the added trouble of criminal investigations. The legal attack would pay off more. Was he paid?" Zen asked.

"Ah, you're onto something." Clive shared his screen and a court document appeared next to his image. "The company froze his big payment once the lawsuit was filed. They'd paid him five million already. But they were going to help him fight back. Their top intellectual property attorney was going to represent Ahmad."

"Deep pockets on both sides to battle it out. See?"

"Killing him would solve a host of problems. His widow may be willing to accept a settlement," Clive countered.

"Too complicated. I keep going back to our party girls. Peter is trying hard to get attention away from Emme Gaida," Zen said.

"Hadley dug into their history as well. Strange that Ms. Gaida would turn to sex work. She was a solid student. Not the top of her class, but she had a decent job until four years ago. Then she did freelance writing for science news sites."

"Sex work can pay a lot. Emme Gaida has the school girl look. But I bet she can transform into a sensuous sex kitten in a blink. She offered the whole girlfriend experience as well," Zen said.

"My, my. The archaic word for 'the girlfriend experience' was courtesan. Such a companion was charming, articulate, and intelligent." Clive, a lover of history, smiled when Zen snorted.

"Emme Gaida pretty much said the benefits are better than a conventional career," Zen joked.

"How worried should I be about Navarro? He's in an alien environment, literally. Stress from his first big assignment, space travel, and now seeing a face from his past."

"A woman who, in his own words, he was obsessed with," Zen added.

"You think he could be triggered into his former habits?" Clive wore a somber face as he waited for her answer.

Zen blew out a long breath. "I don't know. I put him on notice to stay away from Emme Gaida. He'll only interview Imirah Suri with me, and I'll take the lead."

"Negative. He should stay away from both of them. I've already sent him instructions," Clive clipped.

"Fine. Then I'll have him re-interview the McDougal couple. And go with Sgt. Young to talk with her chief."

"You really think a rookie police officer can withstand the pressure? Her fellow cops won't be happy. Never mind her *boss*." Clive's eyebrows bunched together in a solid line above his intense gaze.

"She's tough and smart. We'll see."

After another thirty minutes of shop talk, Clive signed off. Zen fell back on the bed and shut her eyes. Instead of sleep, scenarios about the case flashed on her closed lids like a succession of videos. She saw the crime scene. Then each witness interview. Finally, she went over encounters with Drs. McCoy and Gregson. Theories, motives, connections flittered across the screen of her brain as well. At some point she drifted off into a restless sleep. An insistent and annoying tune spun a turn in her head until Zen groaned. Then she recognized the ringtone of her mobile phone. With another groan, Zen answered.

"I sure didn't ask for a wake-up call." Zen's voice came out scratchy. Her mouth felt like she'd fallen asleep with a sock stuffed in it.

"It's me, ma'am. I'm in the lobby," Sgt. Young said.

"Okay. Goodnight, sergeant."

"Morning, ma'am."

"Good morning to you, too. Now bye." Zen mumbled and hugged the pillow.

"No, I mean it's morning. Two forty-five to be exact, ma'am," Sgt. Young's voice came back through the small speaker. "Urgent developments."

"Fine. Fine. I'm in 15-B."

Zen sat up and shook her head until her thick braids bounced. She yawned, stretched, and grimaced at the stiffness in her limbs. Then she went into the tiny bathroom. She'd washed up and put on slacks and a pullover shirt by the time Sgt. Young knocked. Zen had also put coffee on in the pot provided in the room.

"I caught Imirah Suri trying to stow away on a cargo shuttle headed to Earth." Sgt. Young looked fresh. She exuded the energy of someone barely out of their teens.

"How'd you—"

"Jacques Clairmont buzzed me. Don't ask me how he found out," Sgt. Young said. "He goes, 'Hey, you might want to stop your main witness from skipping town.' I wish slapping him silly was legal."

"Maybe we can work that out," Zen replied with a short laugh. The maker beeped and Zen poured coffee into a hotel mug. "Here. Courtesy of Starry Night Inn."

Sgt. Young thanked her. She hummed approval after a sip. "Actually, not too bad at all. Better than the stuff at our station. Turns out most cops suck at making coffee."

"How are they at keeping drugs off the streets in outer space?" Zen sat on the bed yoga-style.

Sgt. Young hissed a sigh and gulped more from the mug. "You're back on that, huh? Look, the chief's been sloppy but not corrupt. Somebody is taking advantage."

"What about your fellow officers?" Zen asked. Sgt. Young's grimace gave her a hint the news wasn't good.

"Yeah. Cops named Simpson and Treadwell. Never liked me, I never liked them. Always walked around like they knew something nobody else did. The idiots were caught checking in a dirty cargo container. Same flight Suri was about to hop to Earth."

"Damn! All that happened while I was out cold? You had one hell of a night, sarge." Zen shook her head and drank coffee. She breathed in the rich aroma to help clear the sleep fog in her head.

"Pure luck, to be honest. Clairmont tipped me to Suri doing a great escape. I got there and saw those two lurking around. They're not assigned to cargo check. The shuttle had already been cleared. I got my chief and Commander Okoro on the line."

"They acted quickly." Zen frowned at her.

"I'd already talked to them. Me and Special Agent Navarro. He said you needed the rest. And before you ask, Okoro isn't involved from what I can tell."

"How kind of Navarro," Zen retorted. She squinted at the wall as if his face was reflected on it.

"Since it didn't involve Ms. Gaida, I figured it was okay." Sgt. Young arched her eyebrows when Zen looked at her.

"You are cynical beyond your years, sarge," Zen quipped. She studied the half-smile on Young's smooth, brown face. "You moved on an important person of interest and kept an eye on my partner."

"I grew up on the rough side of St. Louis, ma'am. Watching your back ain't enough. You gotta have 360 vision," Sgt. Young replied.

"There's a smooth side of St. Louis, sergeant?"

"Hey, don't be knocking my hometown," Sgt. Young wisecracked.

Zen put her mug down, stretched again, and rubbed her back. "Guess we better roll."

"Give him credit, the chief cracked Treadwell and Simpson like a couple of eggs. I think he was more pissed they might mess up his plans than mad about them being crooked." Sgt. Young chuckled. "Whatever. Same results. But there's a big wrinkle."

"Let me guess, someone with power is implicated. Either inside In Situ or one of the big companies." Zen faced the mirror and began to pin her shoulder length brains into a bun.

"Okoro and my boss are already tap dancing to a new tune. We have to 'show judgement and discretion.' " Sgt. Young's grin slipped into a sneer.

"In other words, let the cops go down alone," Zen replied.

"Not alone. We're going to sweep up two lab workers who were running their own little side business. One inside In Situ Research and another one at ChemCo's site."

"Wait a minute. Our victim's company has an office here?" Zen spun around. Her braids popped lose again.

"Yeah. Offices and their own lab developing products. Maybe Ahmad was involved. Or..." Sgt. Young put her mug down. "Ahmad stumbled on their operation and they decided to shut him up."

"Coincidence?" Zen twisted the dark blue hair tie between her fingers.

"I wouldn't bet on it."

"We'll see. Let's not jump to conclusions. Anyway, Ahmad didn't need the money." Zen briefly told Sgt. Young about Ahmad's patents.

Sgt. Young gave a low whistle. "He was an asshole, but a real smart asshole. A sweet twenty million. What I couldn't do with just one percent of that."

"Careful, sarge. Greed got your colleagues boiling hot water," Zen replied.

"I dropped Suri back at her place last night. No shuttles are leaving for another week so she can't go anywhere. And she's not under arrest."

Zen spun to face her. "She just tried to run."

"Chief says no evidence against her. He's right, ma'am. She consented to a drug screen. Jump was in her system, which supports her story that they used together." Sgt. Young shrugged at the scowl Zen gave her.

"Bet she's reviewing her life choices right about now. Damn," Zen grumbled.

Her second attempt to pin her braids was successful. The twist hair tie went around her small bun, matching her blue outfit. She slipped on her shoes, grabbed her crossbody bag, and followed Sgt. Young out. Minutes later they entered Dr. Gregson's office. Commander Okoro wore a pleased expression. Sgt. Young's boss didn't. Dr. McCoy and Dr. Gregson were even less enthused.

"Ma'am, this is Chief Gray Collier. Chief, Dr. Batiste is—"

"Yes, yes. The famous special agent space cop."

Chief Collier pressed his lips together. Zen gazed back at him. She guessed he was no taller than five feet nine inches, barely making the height requirement for a police officer. He had thinning, dull blond hair brushed to cover baldness. Pink scalp still showed through in places. He'd been scarce since Zen and Peter had arrived. Obviously, he'd hoped to keep it that way.

"Gray was just telling us that his two rogue employees have been secured, charged, and will be soon on their way to face a judge on good old Earth." Commander Okoro glowed with satisfaction.

Sgt. Young stepped close to Zen and whispered, "I tried Special Agent Navarro. Went to voice mail."

Chief Collier's beady eyes narrowed. "Share with the room, Sgt. Young."

"She was just telling me that my colleague is following other promising leads," Zen said. "I'd asked her to contact him for this meeting."

"Well, his presence isn't required," Commander Okoro said with a crisp nod. "I think we've wrapped up the case for you quite nicely."

"How does catching two corrupt LMPD officers solve a homicide?"

Chief Collier winced as if Zen's question had pinched a nerve. Commander Okoro's smile slipped for an eyeblink then snapped back in place. Drs. McCoy and Gregson exchanged a look.

"It's obvious." Commander Okoro swept both huge hands out. "Adulterated party drugs mixed with alcohol, and the poor man is dead. We could bring charges against the two young ladies. But we haven't established that they supplied the drugs."

"We're still rounding up the gang. At least one rover spread the drugs to nightclubs and secret easies," Collier added.

Zen turned to Sgt. Young. "What?"

"We call sellers of unsanctioned goods 'rovers.' You know, like the space rover vehicles that go anywhere to deliver," Sgt. Young replied.

Dr. Gregson turned to Zen. "Easy is shortened slang for the ancient term *speakeasy*. During the nineteenth century there was a decade when selling liquor was illegal in America. Secret nightclubs and hole-in-the-wall bars sold alcohol. The modern easy is an underground party location."

"Supplying drugs and sex for hire," Zen said.

"I wouldn't go that far," Dr. McCoy said, speaking up for the first time. When the commander and police chief glanced at her, she cleared her throat. "I mean, you make it sound like we've got organized crime. No, just people making a bit of extra crypto cash on the side."

"You've known this for how long and haven't reported it to Earth?" Zen ignored Sgt. Young's gasp as she stared at the faces of those in charge.

Chief Collier lifted his chin in an attempt to look down at Zen. Since he wasn't that much taller, the intimidating look didn't work as well. "Dr. Batiste, your agency and others law enforcement departments back home know crime happens. Have you stamped out every bit of it?"

"My briefings included details of petty criminal behavior," Commander Okoro put in. He strolled around the desk and sat in Dr. Gregson's executive office chair.

Dr. Gregson's left eye twitched as he watched Okoro but he said nothing. "Ahem, I've also written up reprimands of the In Situ employee in question. Of course, we had no clue how far they'd strayed into wrongdoing."

Zen raised an eyebrow at his sanitized description of drug dealing by one of his staffers. "Okay."

"I mean, we thought they were just wild house parties. Not something approved, but we have priorities. Keeping smuggled goods out of the colonies and space stations is a constant battle," Chief Collier said.

"Covered up and aided by police officers." Zen looked at them all in turn. "Sounds like organized crime to me."

"Okay, let's not get carried away," Chief Collier burst out. His neck flushed pink that spread to his cheeks in seconds.

Okoro leaned both elbows on Gregson's desk. "Special Agent Batiste, we've reported to the DOJ, NASA, and other home world authorities that we've broken up a minor criminal enterprise. The fact that a man died as an indirect result of those activities is a sad side effect."

"I see. You've communicated this conclusion to my office as well?" Zen squinted at him.

"I'll leave that to you," Commander Okoro replied. He smiled at her and stood.

Before Zen could reply, multiple mobile device notifications sounded. An assortment of beeps, musical trills, and other ringtones filled the room. Everyone, including Zen, started reading screens.

"Ma'am, what the hell..." Sgt. Young stopped. Her satcom two-way radio sounded. She grabbed the walkie-talkie clipped to her duty belt but used her earbud to listen. Her eyes went wide.

"Damn it, Navarro." Zen stared at the text message that arrived like a punch to her gut. "Damn. Damn. Damn."

By the time Zen and Sgt. Young arrived at Level Two, Section Six, neon-green tape had been strung all over the place. Sgt. Young alternated between getting updates from her colleague, a confidential source, and telling Zen what they'd said. Zen, meanwhile, multitasked listening, making notes, and sending urgent classified messages to Clive. Hadley responded instead. Clive was tied up in a meeting. The relay seemed to take forever but only because Zen's nerves were in meltdown. Then she came to an abrupt halt when they arrived. Sgt. Young was three paces ahead before she realized Zen wasn't beside her. Then she spun around and walked back. They both scanned the hive of activity. A LMPD cop and one space station private security officer stood guard. An In Situ employee who doubled as a forensic crime scene tech moved in and out of a door.

"This is one hell of a mess," Sgt. Young mumbled.

"Hell of a mess doesn't do it justice, sergeant."

"What the fu—" Sgt. Young gave a sharp nod when her boss strode toward them. "Sir."

"You've hitched your future to the wrong wagon, Sgt. Young," Chief Collier snapped. "I don't remember ordering you to be here. I'm still your boss."

"Federal jurisdiction supersedes local authority. Sgt. Young is critical to our investigation," Zen replied while Sgt. Young's mouth still hung open.

"She's been too close to you two. Her position is compromised. Sgt. Young could be a material witness. You both could, as a matter of fact. If you're not involved somehow," Chief Collier clipped in response. His voice got louder as he spoke. The two cops and forensic tech froze at the angry boom. He shot them a fiery glare. The two women and man scrambled to look busy again.

Zen stepped close to Chief Collier when he faced her again. "You've barely been doing your damn job for the past eighteen months. Hell, I'm seeing you for the first time since I got here. You've got rogue cops and crime going on right under your nose. Don't start throwing around accusations like you know your ass from a hole in the floor."

"I've taken care of my patch, cleaned up the dirt. Let's see you explain how your colleague ended up at the scene of a murder. A dead hooker he's got history with, no less. Go on. Be my guest, Ms. In-Charge." Chief Collier jerked a head toward the crime scene with a smirk.

Zen fought off the itch to land a solid slap to his square face. Instead, she brushed past him without replying. She marched over to the officers. Both kept their faces blank but kept shooting side glances at Chief Collier.

"Where is he?" Zen looked past the shoulder of a taller female office into a short hallway of the apartment.

"One of Commander Okoro's men has Special Agent Navarro secured in a vacant unit. Ma'am," she added at a sharp look from Zen. "Apartment twenty-three."

"Right. Sergeant, you stay and assist in any way you can," Zen said.

The other female officer exchanged a look with her fellow cop. "The chief said—"

"Don't argue with me, officer," Zen cut in.

"Cooperate with Agent Batiste, Officer Issaks," Commander Okoro's booming voice rang out.

"Yes sir." She turned to Sgt. Young and nodded. They went off together.

Commander Okoro studied Zen for a second and sighed. "It appears we have a truly sticky situation on our hands. Your partner is now implicated in a murder. At the very least he could be an accessory."

"Let's not jump to conclusions before the facts are known," Zen replied. She strode off before he could reply. "I'm going to talk to him."

Collier leaped in front of Zen. "Not a chance in hell. Do I have to keep shouting conflict of interest?"

"Unless you suspect me as well, get out of my way. If Navarro's going to tell the truth to anyone it'll be *me*. We hold his life in our hands. Besides which, I'll know if he's lying." Zen glared back at Collier, debating the wisdom of knocking him on his idiotic rear end. She'd just about decided to risk it all when Okoro's forceful, deep voice broke into her thoughts.

Commander Okoro marched over to them. "She has a point, Chief Collier. Your officer recorded the initial interview. Special Agent Batiste may be able to persuade him of the dire situation he faces. Here and back on Earth. We can observe."

The staring contest between Zen and Collier continued for another fifteen seconds. Commander Okoro spoke his name in a conciliatory yet firm tone. Collier spun around and barked he'd meet them at the LMPD station. Then he took out his anger on officers processing the scene by snarling instructions. Moments later he hopped a small cart and drove away.

Zen faced Okoro. "Thanks. I'll catch up with you in a minute."

Commander Okoro studied her for a few seconds. "Collier is right. His captain should question your colleague. Wait too long and he'll start anyway."

"His captain is implicated in wrongdoing, remember? The two cops we caught were under his command."

"Implicated, not proven," Commander Okoro countered.

"Sgt. Young is a senior officer. Most who signed up didn't last. She's been here over a year. And from what I've seen so far, she's damn good at her job," Zen replied. Okoro gave a short nod and strode away.

"I'll keep Chief Collier in check, but don't take too long here," Commander Okoro said over his shoulder.

Sgt. Young walked over to Zen. "Something funny about this whole thing."

"I'm sure as hell not laughing," Zen said and blew out air to steady her nerves. "What are those two doing here?"

"That's part of what I meant. Commander Okoro and the chief are here. Then Suri's apartment is a mess, like a tornado hit."

"Signs of a struggle?" Zen turned to Sgt. Young.

"She sure as hell put up a fight. But drawers are pulled out. Her mobile is missing. Her laptop is gone. Looks like she interrupted a burglary and she got killed. Except, it also looks staged. There's a wad of money at the bottom of her closet. Hidden, but if I found it..."

"A halfway-decent burglar would have, too. Anything else?"

"Jewelry, a few good pieces in with the simulated stones. All still there. Hell, even fashion rings made in space get a good price. But her body looks odd to me. I'll show you." Sgt. Young nodded for Zen to follow but started off without waiting.

Zen matched her brisk stride. "You heard that exchange with your boss?"

"Yeah. He's worse than corrupt. The chief is lazy and doesn't care. Correction, he works hard at making himself look good. He wants a quick end to clean this up."

"So it won't hurt his chances for a big job back home," Zen replied.

"Rumor has it he's a serious candidate for a UN Security Council position based on his work here. Only he didn't do any work," Sgt. Young said and laughed at her own joke. "We did all the policing. He did a bunch of politicking."

"Humph. I wish him well, but he can't do it at Navarro's expense," Zen muttered.

"I thought you two weren't exactly buddies," Sgt. Young replied.

They entered the apartment. Zen stepped around a pile of clothing on the floor of the apartment. A satellite television receiver had been tossed from a table. Zen didn't reply until the crime scene tech had moved out of earshot.

"Yeah well... he was cleared of the murders I investigated. So far, his worst crime was engaging in unregulated sex work. And that was as a customer. The laws aren't clear when it comes to humanoid sex workers."

"But he has a violent streak, I hear. Could be he's trying to cover his tracks on something worse. I can tell you don't quite trust him." Sgt. Young stopped before saying more when Zen turned to her. "Sorry, ma'am. He's still your partner."

Zen waved away her concern and went back to looking around. "He was genuinely shocked to see Emme Gaida. And she claims he's not the freak or monster everyone thinks."

"Special Agent Batiste, care to give a statement on the second murder to take place on this space station? Residents will want to know if it's safe to be here. I hear civilian businesses are getting antsy." Jacques Clairmont snapped a digital photo while he spoke.

"You got to be kidding me," Sgt. Young grumbled. She strode to the doorway toward the reporter. "You got no business at a crime scene. And while I'm at it, no comment."

"I have an apartment two levels up. And if you'll notice I'm on this side of the tape. These good officers made sure I stayed out." Clairmont held his mobile phone up, no doubt recording video and audio. "Records indicate this apartment was rented by—"

"No comment," Sgt. Young barked.

Clairmont stretched his neck to see past her. "The apartment is in the name of Space-Cor, not her. The vic is a woman. I already know that much."

"Officer, please show Mr. Clairmont the nearest exit," Sgt. Young said to one of the officers standing by.

Zen spun around. "No, take him into custody instead."

"What? You can't arrest me because you're irritated. Members of the press are protected by global media access laws, the UN, and—"

"You're not under arrest, Mr. Clairmont," Zen broke in. "We're going to need a statement. You obviously have information that could prove useful."

"Oh, please. Flexing your authority is an excuse to keep the facts away from the public," Clairmont shot back. "What are the authorities hiding?"

"In fact, taking you in for now could be for your protection. This is a closed society. You may know more than is safe."

"I've always been able to take care of myself, special agent. My bureau has a legal team and UN sanction," Clairmont retorted.

"See you at the LMPD station in a bit. Thanks for your cooperation, sir." Zen turned her back to him and went deeper into the apartment. She smiled with satisfaction at Clairmont's fading squawks of protest as he was led away.

"That was fun," Sgt. Young said with a grin. Then her expression sobered when she looked down at the body.

The apartment consisted of a compact open-plan living area. A dining table had four chairs. Past it was a galley-style kitchen with a back door leading to a service hallway. Zen opened the door to peer out. A Black Rock security officer waved at her to indicate the area was secure.

"Smear of blood on the wall. The tech collected swabs already," the man called. "Keeping the neighbors from sightseeing. Nobody claims to have heard anything."

"Thanks, officer." Zen went back into the apartment. She checked the lock. Then she went through the kitchen again.

Imirah Suri's body lay sprawled on the floor in the doorway leading to the bedroom. Her short skirt was pulled up around her waist. A pink lace panty had been pulled down to one ankle. Part of the items around her body looked too neat to Zen. She took care to step around the corpse and into the bedroom. Someone seemed to have searched the small dresser and closet. Even the tiny bathroom had been tossed. Soaps, lotion, and other personal-care products had been swept out of a cabinet.

Zen went back to Suri's body. She examined it for a few seconds before bending down. She pulled aside a portion of the straight wig covering Imirah's face. "Looks like she either woke up to a burglary or walked in on it."

"But look at her skin. I don't see a wound or any bruising. Can't see how they got in. Unless she let him or her in because she knew them. But what were they looking for?" Sgt. Young squatted next to the body and peered at it.

"Excuse me, officers. I'm the In Situ medical examiner and this is my colleague with Space Command. We need to remove the body now. Orders from Commander Okoro."

Zen and Sgt. Young looked up at a man and woman dressed in gray protective jumpsuits. They wore gloves and paper booties over their shoes. Sgt. Young nodded when Zen glanced at her.

"Okay." Zen stood up and moved out of their way.

Sgt. Young followed her to the living area to observe. "They got here fast."

Zen watched them as the crime scene tech helped them lift the body onto a gurney. A body bag was already on it. One of the medical examiners zipped it closed. Then they rolled it away and were gone. The tech then got to work on the area under and around where the body had been.

"One question, please," Zen called out before they left. "The victim is usually left at the scene longer to document the conditions when the body was discovered. You got here fast."

"Chief Collier wanted us to get to work on the autopsy," the Space Command examiner replied.

"And there could be important forensic evidence beneath the body," the crime scene tech added.

"Okay." Zen nodded. She turned to Sgt. Young once they were gone. "I can't argue with the logic but..."

"Something funny," Sgt. Young put in when Zen looked around again.

Chapter 9

"Every time I tried to touch the body the tech stopped me. He kept looking at the boss for cues when I walked around," Sgt. Young whispered as they walked off.

"Let's get to the station. I don't want to give him an excuse to move without me." Zen glanced at her smartwatch.

"We're not far, only a few minutes. We can go the back way. I'll talk to an officer I trust to see what they've learned. Security cameras are set up here. She'll probably have the victim's comm records by now. Doesn't take long."

Zen followed Sgt. Young as they talked to her colleague. She led her to a service elevator that took them to a wide utility area. From there they traveled along corridors marked "Official Use Only." Sgt. Young used a security code to open doors and operate the service elevator. Ten minutes later they arrived at the Star Flight LMPD substation.

An observation one-way mirror showed Peter pacing in one of two interview rooms. Commander Okoro greeted Zen and Sgt. Young when they came in. Chief Collier kept his back to them. A police officer stood to the side against one wall. He gave a slight nod to Sgt. Young when she glanced at him. Zen nodded, crossed her arms, and studied her partner.

"He refuses to talk to anyone but you two," Chief Collier said without turning around. "Wonder why?"

"Not exactly true, Chief," Commander Okoro replied in a mild tone. "Although I did ask you to wait a while longer for Dr. Batiste."

"The clock starts ticking on a criminal investigation. Delays mean it's harder to catch the perpetrator. Or maybe that's the point." Chief Collier looked over his shoulder at them.

"I hope you're not implying that *I'm* part of some conspiracy. That would be most unfortunate." Commander Okoro's deep voice remained level, unruffled. The room grew still at the sound of his basso tone.

Zen stepped forward to stand next to Chief Collier. "Sir, you haven't dealt with me since I came. So, you're not that familiar with who I am."

"Your father is James Batiste, former CIA director. He has a long list of other impressive jobs behind him, along with letters after his name. You gathered evidence against Navarro before he was... exonerated," Collier said in a deadpan tone, still without looking at her. "I kept out of your way, Special Agent Batiste, so you could do your thing. *But* I wasn't sitting on my hands."

"So, from your research you know I follow the facts wherever they lead," Zen said.

"Humph," Chief Collier said with a grunt.

Commander Okoro spoke up. "According to Dr. Navarro the victim was dead when he arrived at her apartment. Emme Gaida called him to say Ms. Suri was willing to give information but only to him. That's all he'd tell Chief Collier."

"I don't think either of you have been completely open since you got here. A man died from too much fun, by all accounts.

Why does the Office of Special Investigations show up within twenty-four hours of getting the notice? And you've been talking to that reporter. I have a lot to discuss when I talk to my superiors on Earth." Chief Collier marched to the door, opened it, and paused. He spoke to the police officer across the room. "Keep me informed. I'll watch the live feed from my office."

"The autopsy indicates Ahmad didn't overdose, he suffocated. Drugs and alcohol made him easier to kill," Zen clipped.

Chief Collier faced Zen for the first time. "He could just as well have fallen facedown on a bed or sofa cushion. Too drunk to move, respiration compromised. He suffocates."

Zen gazed back at him. "Possible, but—"

"Dr. Navarro has a history with Emme Gaida, special agent," Chief Collier hissed. "When were you going to let us in on that tiny detail?"

"Only if it became relevant to this inquiry," Zen replied.

"Still trust her?" Chief Collier said to Commander Okoro. He grunted when the tall man didn't answer and strode out.

Commander Okoro looked at Zen. "He made several valid points."

Zen hissed a long sigh and spun to the observation mirror again. Peter gazed back with a fierce frown. Then he resumed pacing, pausing once to slap the tabletop in frustration. Sgt. Young had watched her superiors as though she was at a tennis match. The other policeman had remained silent as well.

"Check if there were fibers in his throat, nostrils, or even his lungs," Zen said to Sgt. Young.

"Just read it again, ma'am. No fibers. Traces of the chemical composition of norphene. Special polymers made from chemicals mined on asteroids. I asked the tox tests be more specialized," Sgt. Young said.

"Are sofas or cushions made from norphene?" Zen looked from Sgt. Young to Commander Okoro.

"No way," Sgt. Young replied.

"Your theory is someone placed a bag over his head?" Commander Okoro frowned as he glanced from Sgt. Young to Zen and back.

"Or pressed norphene to his face while he was passed out. The stuff comes in bags and sheets. Sheets are used as protective cover, shape them to fit around containers. They're coming up with new applications for it all the time," the police officer said. "My brother and a few friends work for a mining company back home."

"Thanks officer. Very useful information," Zen said.

"Goodness, seems Sgt. Young and her colleague have been on top of things more than Chief Collier. I'll make sure your information gets included in any dispatches back to Space Command and the DOJ. I'm not sure he'll recognize the importance of your findings." Commander Okoro wore a wolfish grin.

Zen rolled her shoulders to fight the tension in them. "I better talk to Peter before he wears a hole in that floor and right into space. Sgt. Young, with me."

"Right behind you, ma'am." Sgt. Young seemed more than eager to take part.

With a long inhale and exhale to steady herself, Zen led the way one door down to the room. Sgt. Young followed on her heels but didn't shut the door. Peter looked at Zen with a searching gaze but said nothing at first.

"Sir, I'll get water. Anything else?" Sgt. Young asked.

"Let's get this over with so we can find out the truth," Peter said.

As Sgt. Young left, Zen pointed to one of the four chairs in the room. Peter said down opposite her, hands folded on the table. His knuckles turned white as he gripped them. He opened his hands and flexed the fingers when he saw Zen staring. He sighed and shook his head.

"Emme didn't kill Imirah," Peter blurted out.

"Dude, you're the one in trouble right now. Given your relationship with Emme Gaida, you should have—"

"Past relationship, and it was years ago," Peter snapped back. Then he swallowed hard.

Sgt. Young returned with two large cups, a bag of nuts, and soft drinks on a tray. She put them on the table and shrugged when Peter glanced up at her. "We could be here a while."

Peter pushed the bag of mixed nuts away from him. "My statement is straightforward. I don't intend to be interrogated for hours, so save the snacks for real suspects."

Zen managed to control the urge to shout at him to wake the hell up. She tapped the button on top of a smart-box built into the table. "This is Special Agent Dr. Zenobia Batiste. Location—the Lunar Metropolis Police Department substation, Star Flight. April twenty six, time five thirty a.m., 2086." She looked at Sgt. Young.

"Sergeant Wyvette Anita Young, Lunar Metro Police also present," Sgt. Young said. She stood against a wall to their right.

"We are interviewing Special Agent Dr. Peter Navarro."

"You don't have to stand guard over me, sergeant. I'm not going to flee or get unruly. Let me guess. They think you're both too close to me. Sit down. It won't make you look less friendly standing there." Peter gave her a tentative smile that faded after a few seconds.

"Let's have your *full* statement, Navarro," Zen said.

"Emme…" Peter's voice trailed off when both women's eyebrows shot up. "Ms. Emme Gaida contacted me. She said her friend, Imirah Suri, was ready to give me a complete account of the hours they spent with Hassan Ahmad."

"When did Ms. Gaida call?" Sgt. Young put in.

Peter hesitated before answering. He gazed at Zen and then back to the young sergeant. "Close to seven last night."

"About three hours after I dropped Suri back at her apartment," Sgt. Young put in.

"What? You didn't tell me Imirah was going to be questioned again," Peter said.

"I didn't get to interview her. Keep going." Zen stared back at him hard.

Peter cast a quick glance at Sgt. Young. When the silence stretched, he tapped a finger on the table. "Emme called me. Scared out of her mind. She was talking so fast I had to get her calm. Imirah wanted to tell me the real story of how she got to Star Flight and what she was supposed to do when she got here."

"Which was?" Zen asked.

"A private investigator on Earth hired Imirah to get close to Hassan Ahmad. Her passage to Star Flight was paid for, as was her apartment. A job at the café was arranged."

"Who did this PI work for on Earth?" Sgt. Young said.

"That's all Emme knew. I was to find out more from Imirah." Peter rubbed his face hard. "I met Emme at the apartment block a few minutes before eleven. She was upset because Imirah wasn't answering. Emme tried calling her mobile but it went to voice mail each time. I went to the back door. The e-lock had been hacked, though the door was closed. All I had to do was press the enter key and it clicked opened. I went in. Emme followed me a few minutes later. We never opened the front door. Remember that detail."

Zen nodded. "Okay. Go on."

"The place was a mess. Emme said Imirah was a careless housekeeper. One reason they didn't get an apartment together. Anyway, it didn't take long for us to realize what we saw wasn't sloppy living. Emme saw her shoe, then... She's very upset. They didn't always get along, but the two were close friends. Please be gentle with her. Emme knows Imirah's family. She has a younger sister and brother. She's been paying both their school fees in South Africa."

"We have her family info. Police and a counselor will break the news to them," Zen replied. "What else did you find out?"

"Nothing. As I said, Emme doesn't know the details. Imirah only told her that much when Ahmad took a liking to Emme and wanted to spend time with both of them." Peter grimaced and shifted in his chair. "We found a packed bag on the sofa. Imirah was going to leave because she was scared."

"They were close, so Gaida probably knows more," Sgt. Young said to Zen.

"No," Peter clipped. "She would have told me."

"What took you so long? You talked to Emme early in the evening but didn't go to Suri's apartment for hours." Zen squinted at him.

"Emme and I... spent time talking about the past. Catching up, you know." Peter looked down at his hands as he twisted them together.

"How long were you with Ms. Gaida?" Zen pushed.

Peter looked to his right at the observation mirror with a frown. "Until we left for Imirah's apartment. Is that what you want to hear? The dirty details of how we made love and had a romantic supper? We ordered Greek food delivered, in case you want to know. Voyeurs."

"HD cameras and audio cover the public passageways. We would have eventually pieced together you'd spent hours with her," Zen spoke low. Despite her simmering anger, she also felt empathy for his anguish.

"Take us through what you observed in the apartment," Sgt. Young said. She assumed the role of steering Peter back to the cold facts.

Zen prodded Peter along in a gentler fashion, putting in words of support once or twice. He stumbled when describing the condition of Imirah's body. She'd been beaten to death, tortured using a flat iron. Though she took him through his conversation with Emme twice more, Peter insisted neither of them knew the PI or his employer. After another hour, Zen sat back in her chair. Sgt. Young had taken the seat next to her, tapping notes for her own use into a digital notepad.

"Okay. We'll wait for the results from forensics." Zen pushed back the chair and stood.

"Shouldn't be more than another forty minutes or so. Not like the team has a lot of crime scenes to process," Sgt. Young said.

"Let's hope more aren't added. The way things are going..." Zen huffed out air and rubbed her eyes. She felt like dust from the moon's surface had blown into them.

"They won't find anything more than slight traces of me. I'd never been to Imirah's apartment before. I only touched her neck to check for signs of life, a pulse. Emme visited Imirah all the time because they were friends. So, finding Emme's DNA won't be unexpected. The security footage will verify they were at each other's places all the time and—"

"You sound like a typical suspect trying to alibi his way out of catching a charge. I warned you to stay away from Ms. Gaida for obvious reasons," Zen hissed at him. When Peter glanced at the observation mirror, she nodded. "Oh yes. They know."

"We'll be back." Sgt. Young walked to the door and held it open for Zen. Once they were in the hall, she blew out a slow whistle.

"I already know what you're about to say. We're riding through a shitstorm," Zen muttered. They went back to the room opposite the one Peter was in.

Commander Okoro stood, legs apart and both arms crossed, gazing at Peter through the one-way mirror. The police officer was still there as well. He lifted his head in a silent signal to Sgt. Young. Zen studied the commander for a time and then looked at Peter as well. Another LMPD officer entered the room with a tray of food for Peter. Sgt. Young had ordered a continental breakfast for him. Zen watched him sip coffee and nibble on a croissant. Her stomach rumbled. Sgt. Young tapped Zen's arm. When Zen turned, Sgt. Young put a cup in her hand.

"I got you a sausage biscuit and a donut. We have time for a quick bite before talking to Ms. Gaida," Sgt. Young said.

"You're my hero, sergeant." Zen sipped the smooth liquid. The warmth of rich chocolate soothed her tense throat. She sighed. "Well, commander, any thoughts?"

"He has no motive to kill Ms. Suri, unless..." Commander Okoro pivoted to face them, chin up. "Unless she knew too much about his past."

"His relationship was with Emme Gaida, sir," Sgt. Young replied. "More likely he would have killed Gaida to keep her from talking."

"But the women were close, as he himself pointed out. Friends confide in one another. Ms. Gaida could have told Imirah Suri about her troubles with Dr. Navarro. There is more to him than what has been revealed," Commander Okoro countered.

"Hmm." Zen gazed past him at Peter, who seemed to placidly finish his breakfast. "Then there's the stuff about Imirah being paid to get close to our first victim."

"Not to mention Suri's attempt to run. Seems to confirm she was scared of someone," Sgt. Young added.

"Didn't expect her well-funded space jaunt to include the guy's murder is my guess," Zen said.

"I've got our officers checking her mobile records and movements," Sgt. Young said.

"I spoke to her boss and three co-workers at the café," the other police officer said. "Everyone liked her. No trouble. Though she did have what looked like a visitor, a woman, two weeks ago. They got into an argument. But when the cook asked her about it, Imirah played it off. Said the woman was an ex-girlfriend still pissed about their breakup."

"Great. Another suspect," Zen muttered.

Sgt. Young looked at Zen. "Let's talk to Ms. Gaida and—"

"No, no. Let her marinate in the new situation for a bit. Let's talk to Clairmont first. He has information that might help when we talk to Emme and Peter again."

"Okay." Sgt. Young started to say more but looked at Commander Okoro and stopped. "Makes sense."

"One of my officers will stay here to give me direct updates. I have other urgent matters to deal with, Dr. Batiste. The CEO and executive board that govern Star Flight have summoned me about these events," Commander Okoro said with a wolfish smile.

"This may be a public/private enterprise, but you have ultimate authority. Correct?" Zen sensed his relish at the upcoming meeting.

"A fact I'm going to remind them of in short order. With diplomacy and tact, of course. We'll meet in..." Okoro glanced at the smartwatch on his thick wrist. "Five hours. I'm sure you'll have answers by then."

"Sir," was all Zen trusted herself to say in response.

She, Sgt. Young, and the other LMPD cop watched Commander Okoro stride off with two subordinates in his wake. He looked like a battleship being trailed by gunboats. The LMPD officer looked at Sgt. Young.

"Keep watch on Special Agent Navarro. Then track down more results from forensics," Sgt. Young said and tapped her comm handset.

"I'll shoot you an encrypted text if it's something significant and sensitive," the officer replied with a sharp nod.

"Good." Sgt. Young clapped him on the shoulder and followed Zen out.

"What was that about?" Zen murmured.

"Chief Collier has been MIA for day-to-day standard operating procedures. I've filled in the gaps. He doesn't care because it frees him up to work on getting back to Earth." Sgt. Young wore a crooked smile when Zen shot a side glance at her.

"The fat job he's hoping to get. I'm guessing he hasn't been missed much," Zen replied.

"He goes to meetings with the big titles in charge. Suits me just fine. So, how do we handle Clairmont? Give me permission to shake him like a baby's rattle," Sgt. Young quipped.

"Don't temp me, sarge."

Zen and Sgt. Young planned their strategy as they walked. They had resumed their serious faces by the time they got to the other interview room. Clairmont drummed his fingers on the tabletop. When they entered, he took a sip from a paper cup in front of him. He watched them in silence as they set up to question him. Zen went through the process of setting up the recording of their session. Clairmont wore a smirk when they prompted him to state his full name, press credentials, and permanent residence on Earth.

"Go ahead. Shine the hot light in my face. Make me confess all my sins," Clairmont said.

"We don't have decades, Mr. Clairmont," Zen replied with an easy smile. "Let's start with something easier." She glanced at Sgt. Young.

"How did you find out Imirah Suri was sneaking onto the shuttle about to leave?" Sgt. Young leaned forward.

"Simple. I have a contact at the café who works with her. She picked up her pay, arranged for someone to cover her shift, and acted nervous. My source says that's typical of people about to quit. So, my source dropped by her place for a drink. They'd dated before. Well, *date* is being generous. They enjoyed sex when it suited them. Suri had a bag packed. The only flight leaving was the shuttle. When my source told me, it didn't take a genius to figure it out."

"You followed her," Zen said after a few beats.

"An important witness in Ahmad's death is about to get away? Of course I did. That shuttle is one of the few directs to Earth. She would have slipped into thin air once it docked." Clairmont wore a smirk. "So, since I helped you out maybe I can get a bit of info."

"Who is your source?" Sgt. Young poised a finger over her e-notepad and looked at him.

"No comment. My informant has been cleared by your investigation, though. Solid alibi; didn't party with Suri the night Ahmad died. Not into drugs, just sex," Clairmont replied.

"Imirah Suri led a complicated life." Zen noted that Clairmont was careful not to refer to the person as he or she. Clever.

"They actually cared about each other after a time." Clairmont wore a slight frown. "The news will really sting. I should be there for them."

"Hmm, how kind. And you might even milk them for more details they might have held back." Zen squinted at him.

Clairmont's frown smoothed out on his ruddy face. "I'm not totally heartless, you know. But I have a job to do."

"Yeah." Sgt. Young snorted and scowled at him.

"I'm not trying to make *your* job tough. I'm floating in a giant hunk of metal with a killer like everyone else. Apart from wanting the story first, I want her or him caught."

"That almost sounds like an honest answer," Sgt. Young said.

"Believe me, it is. Look, this is only my second assignment out here. The first time turned up nothing but fluff pieces. Honeymoons and prom parties at the Sky High Hotel. A bunch of millionaire kids prancing around annoying the hell out of everybody. But we're talking not one but two murders."

"Will make your career. We haven't released that Ahmad was murdered," Zen broke in.

Clairmont sat forward with an earnest expression. The eagerness in his eye made him look younger than thirty-six years old. "Word on these outer space streets says different. You know damn well that kind of news wouldn't keep for long."

"Did you know about the crooked LMPD officers?" Sgt. Young put in.

He blinked at her a few times as if re-orienting to the change of subject. "Not about the dirty shipment on the same flight, no. That was dumb luck for you. No offense."

"Humph." Sgt. Young tapped notes.

"But shady space cops aren't exactly breaking news either. My sources have said—"

"I'm shocked you haven't reported such a juicy story. Rogue space cops and all," Sgt. Young interrupted.

"Harder to pin down. People are scared to talk while they're still here. Too easy for the officers to find out. Then there's nowhere to run until a shuttle is leaving. And then..."

"They'd know," Sgt. Young finished when his voice trailed off.

"Exactly," Clairmont replied with a nod.

"So why didn't the cops tell on Imirah Suri stowing away?" Zen frowned at him.

"They either didn't know or didn't care. Their interest was moving product and getting paid. My best guess is they didn't know anything about her. Too busy taking care of their underhanded biz." Clairmont shrugged. "Unauthorized party drugs? Unsanctioned tech? What was it?"

Sgt. Young gazed back at him for a few seconds before she answered. "A combination of both. You're well informed for sure."

"People are setting up all kinds of side hustles out here. The powers that be should stop stifling employees with restrictive work agreements," Clairmont said.

"What?" Zen looked from him to Sgt. Young.

"Most of the scientists and low-level techs sign contracts. Anything they develop either belongs to the companies that run the space station or the government space consortium," Clairmont said before the sergeant answered. "It's unfair, stifles innovation, and breeds rebellion. Plus, it's stupid. Everyone could benefit from advanced products."

"It's mostly greed," Zen replied evenly. "Earth companies have done the same thing for years."

"Even if the employees have their own labs and equipment? It's like owning them no matter if they're on the clock on not. The price of getting to space." Clairmont shook his head. "They're spreading economic inequality to space now. And just like on Earth it will breed crime. You should know, Dr. Batiste. You've written academic articles on space communities."

"That we shouldn't replicate mistakes out here." Zen gazed back at him.

"Exactly." Clairmont sat back in his chair and sipped more soda from the cup.

"Let's get back to what else you know. Party drugs, unsanctioned sex work." Sgt. Young raised both eyebrows at him.

"Only what you probably know so far. It's been tolerated. Nothing serious, until now at least. But that's not the real story," Clairmont blurted out quickly when Zen started to speak. "I haven't nailed down facts, but when I do..."

"You mean unsanctioned humanoids being shipped to space," Zen said.

Clairmont's jaw dropped as he blinked back at Zen. Then he recovered and squinted at her. "So, the government knows. Maybe you're in on it."

"Whispers, rumors. You're being fed breadcrumbs to lead you away from police corruption. Chasing ghosts, the career-making story that doesn't exist." Zen sat back with a smile. "You're easy to read, Mr. Clairmont."

"No grand conspiracy. Just sprinkle a few clues and you're off running. Away from the real story," Sgt. Young said.

"It's been done before," Zen put in with a side glance at Sgt. Young.

"My sources back home are reliable. Very." Clairmont shook a finger at Zen. "But I have to say you're clever, Special Agent Batiste."

"I see. You've found humanoids on Star Flight?" Zen asked.

"Or on the moon?" Sgt. Young put in.

"Not yet," Clairmont admitted.

"A man dying after partying with two suspected sex workers isn't going to make you famous, I suppose," Zen quipped. "Tell me how you found out Space-Cor paid for Imirah Suri's apartment."

"I followed the digital trail of crypto currency transfers. You have to wonder why they paid for her to come here." Clairmont looked from Zen to Sgt. Young.

"They hired her to do a job. Entertain Ahmad, a high-value business partner," Sgt. Young said.

Clairmont smiled at her like a professor pleased with his student. "You should go far, young lady."

"Please." Sgt. Young rolled her eyes.

"Space-Cor owns one of the mining companies with a site on the moon. Ahmad was peddling a new process to locate and extract Helium 3."

Zen exchanged a puzzled look with Sgt. Young. She shrugged. "Okay."

"Helium 3 is worth millions per *ounce*. The stuff could power Earth's energy needs for over ten thousand years. Plus, my source says Ahmad was working on making solar panels that could beam energy back to Earth or even to space stations. One plan is to build cities in the sky over Titan. The cities would, among other things, provide energy as part of their economy," Clairmont replied.

"Hmm. Sounds like Ahmad was too valuable to kill. Which makes it more likely his bad habits got him dead," Sgt. Young said to Zen.

"Imirah Suri was bait to lure him away from his current employer." Zen shook her head at the additional pieces to an already complicated puzzle.

"Things went a bit too far during the good times. Imirah played into his kinks and he ends up dead. Like my professor in Criminology 101 said, the simplest theory is usually the right one." Sgt. Young looked at Clairmont.

"Oh c'mon. Seriously? Imirah Suri ends up dead because someone is cleaning up the trail," Clairmont insisted.

"Ms. Suri did get in over her head on several fronts," Zen agreed. "Party drugs, illegal tech peddling, corporate intrigue, and sex work."

"Don't forget smuggling humanoids," Clairmont said. "Sure, you can make faces at me, but I'm right. There's a movement across the globe of humanoids being used in space. They could build colonies before bio-humans get there. But advocates say that's a form of slavery, that AI has evolved to the point of making them new life forms. And then there's talk of humanoids with human tissue. A kind of hybrid."

"You mean some mad scientist is in a secret lab creating people. Yeah, I've seen that movie," Zen retorted with a laugh.

"Okay, okay. I haven't found a connection between those theories—"

"Wild rumors," Zen broke in. "No reason to think that has anything to do with Hassan Ahmad or Imirah Suri."

Clairmont tapped a finger on the table for a few seconds. "No, *but* you must admit there is a lot of undercurrent on the moon and Star Flight. Two deaths, crooked cops, and who knows what else."

"Let's focus on reality and facts for now," Zen replied.

For another hour they took Clairmont through his movements. He stuck to his journalistic privilege to shield his sources. Zen didn't care. Most of what he told her lined up with what they already knew. When they finished, Zen let him go. She and Sgt. Young stayed behind in the room.

"Wow. Some wild stuff about robots, huh?" Sgt. Young let out a slow whistle.

"The guy has a huge imagination to match his ego. But he's right about one thing. Life in space is full of more intrigue than I counted on." Zen frowned.

"And you're wondering if any of it has to be *your* problem," Sgt. Young replied. She crossed her arms. "Like you said, none of it connects to Suri or Emme Gaida. I still vote for a party girl paid to recruit the target and the games got out of hand. The man had risky recreational habits."

"Drugs, rough sex, and selling secrets don't mix," Zen added with a nod. "Let's go see what Emme Gaida can tell us. I'm not going to be patient with her big sad eyes and scared kitten act. That might work on Peter, but I'm not in the damn mood."

"Short-term space syndrome. You're in a new element out here—irritability increases. Doctors aren't sure why some people have it and others don't," Sgt. Young said.

"My partner's ex is a person of interest. We have another dead body, and there are crooked cops. Hell yes, I'm annoyed. And rapidly moving toward royally pissed." Zen huffed out a noisy sigh and stood. "Let's continue the good times."

"We'll sort this out one way or the other, Dr. Batiste. I got your back," Sgt. Young replied with all the enthusiasm of youth.

"I'll try to absorb some of that energy," Zen mumbled as she followed her out.

Emme Gaida sat twisting her hands. A mound of soggy tissues was at her right elbow. After a second, she swept them into a waste basket the female police officer had provided. Zen and Sgt. Young had let her talk, and talk she did. For thirty minutes they listened to her life story, from her childhood in various European countries to her getting a scholarship for college in America.

"That's where I met Imirah. First in London and then in the US," Emme finished up with a sigh. She gulped from a cup and winced. "Coffee is lukewarm."

"We'll get you water." Sgt. Young nodded to the officer, who then left quietly.

"Space-Cor paid for Imirah's apartment. Yours too?" Zen said, cutting through the trip down memory lane.

Emme flinched and sucked in a breath. "I don't know—"

"We'll easily check and find out in seconds," Sgt. Young said. "The clock is ticking and it's not in your favor. You led Special Agent Navarro to a dead body. Could be you wanted him to fall into a trap. Takes the suspicion off you."

"Wait, what? No, no. I could never... I wouldn't hurt anyone, much less Imirah. You can't pin her murder on *me*!" Emme shouted and pounded a fist on the table. "She got herself tangled up in something way over her head. I tried to tell her more than once—"

"You knew. Now you're going to tell us the truth or I'll arrest you as a suspect in her murder. Maybe you needed to shut her up after Ahmad ended up dead." Zen leaned forward with a scowl.

Emme stared back at Zen. The fragile, teary-eyed façade had slipped. When neither Zen or Sgt. Young answered, she shifted in the chair. "Okay, okay. But you have to protect me."

An hour later, Zen and Sgt. Young sat in the room alone. Emme had been taken to a holding cell. The female police officer brought them fresh coffee and water before leaving again.

"You believe anything she said?" Sgt. Young looked up from her e-notepad.

"Most of it, yes. She's scared. They both were paid to get close to Ahmad, keep him entertained. I don't know if she's lying about who really paid them. Was it Space-Cor or a rival company? Or his employer to keep him occupied. Emme is smart. So was Imirah. Maybe they decided to play all sides against the middle for fun and profit."

"Not so smart since one of them ended up dead," Sgt. Young said.

"Unless they thought they had a solid backup plan. I'm going to have my office check their previous employers. Also, see who funded their scholarships." Zen sat in thought as she followed twists and turns.

"Why?" Sgt. Young gave her a puzzled frown.

"My younger sister got a scholarship from a big corporation. She excelled in artificial intelligence studies," Zen said and looked at Sgt. Young.

"Right, longtime ties. Longtime loyalty." Sgt. Young cleared her throat. "Sorry about your sister. I..."

"Checked into my background. I know. You wanted facts on who was rooting around on your turf." Zen raised an eyebrow at her. Complete profiles included significant events in the subject's life. Her sister's murder almost twenty years ago certainly qualified.

"Yeah. Anyway, it's obvious things went way wrong with somebody's plan." Sgt. Young stood. "We should have info on Suri's postmortem by now. Let's go to the med examiner's shop."

"Let them know we're on the way," Zen said. She stood and stretched to ease the stiffness.

"I did, they just ans—" Sgt. Young gaped at the comm device in her hand. "They gotta be shittin' me!"

"What, they're still working and want more time? They hate giving info that they have to take back later." Zen stopped at the string of expletives Sgt. Young let loose. "Slow down, sarge. What the hell is going on?"

"Her body, it's gone."

Chapter 10

"I will have answers. I will have answers *now*!" Commander Okoro's roar shook the walls of the medical examiner's lab. A glass beaker actually vibrated across the desk a few centimeters.

Chief Collier wiped beads of sweat from his brow. "I, uh, I thought it was best to secure the corpse, so I had security move it."

Commander Okoro drew up to his full six feet four inches. His dark eyes flashed fire until he looked like an angry African god about to rain down destruction. He seemed at a loss for words. Until he wasn't. Another roar rattled Zen's bones. "You. Did. What?"

"Our positions are at stake, Marc. We have the report anyway." Chief Collier tried for bravado and failed. He took a step away from Okoro even though the commander hadn't moved.

After a few moments, Commander Okoro found his voice. "Excellent, Chief Collier. Then your people can move the corpse back to the examiner's office for additional samples. I'm glad to know you have things under control."

"Well... as you know something went wrong. There's been a mix-up in communication. That's all it is, I'm sure," Chief Collier rushed to add when the commander glared daggers at him.

"Commander, give him a chance to explain again," Dr. Gregson broke put in. He gave Chief Collier a look of encouragement.

"We had another man die from sudden cardiac arrest. Purely natural. He concealed an underlying heart condition to get on a shuttle. Also, he didn't take very good care of himself. Drinking and such. I—"

"What in the name of seven hells are you talking about, man?" Commander Okoro shouted, causing everyone in the room to jump.

Dr. Irene McCoy, who had stood well out of the way against one wall, took a cautious step forward. "I think what Chief Collier is trying to say is that the officers may have picked up the wrong body."

Commander Okoro leaned forward, both palms flat on a lab table. He looked even more menacing. "They mistook a forty-six- year-old man with gray hair and white skin for a twenty-six-year-old Black woman?"

"Maybe they just grabbed the body bag and didn't look inside?" Dr. Gregson offered. He shrank back into silence at a heated look from Commander Okoro. "Mistakes happen?" he muttered in weak voice.

Sgt. Young came into the commander's office and whispered to her junior LMPD officer. The officer, who looked barely out of his teens, seemed happy for a reason to escape. He scurried off with one harried looked back at the group.

"Did you find it?" Commander Okoro said.

"I tracked them down two corridors. Something interfered with the CCTV. My tech officer detected malware that turned off the cameras for five to ten minutes at a time. Just long enough to let them pass through." Sgt. Young glanced at her boss and then at Zen.

"It was planned. They wanted to get her body away. But why?" Zen said.

"You're in on this with the rest of your corrupt department, Collier," Commander Okoro said as the came from behind his desk. "The rot is deeper than any of us thought."

Chief Collier turned bright red with ire. "You've got a lot of nerve, Marc. Why don't we talk about all of the lavish dinners you've attended with Space-Cor and ChemCo, to name a few."

"None of this is helpful, gentlemen," Dr. Gregson said and bravely walked between the two men.

Commander Okoro pushed past the director, easily moving him out of the way. "My job includes maintaining a solid working relationship with our private partners, Collier."

"Is that what they call kissing ass these days?" Collier yelled.

"Marc, Gray, please," Dr. Gregson said. He glanced around at the others as if for help.

"I didn't climb into their pockets because I want a cushy job on Earth. We all know you're campaigning for that UN security job," Commander Okoro shouted.

"Jealous because they took you out of the running for it and I've got a solid chance? Blame your reputation for being too cozy with shady big business. Tell them what happened in Tangiers, Commander," Collier countered.

He jabbed a finger in Okoro's face. The commander's huge hand whipped up to deliver a backhanded slap and Collier went down to his knees. Sgt. Young and Zen leaped forward at the same time to push Okoro back. They managed to pin the big man against the wall. He puffed air like a fish out of water, then shook them off.

Zen brushed down her rumpled clothes. "I'm representing not just the US government. My agency has authority under the UN global outer space law enforcement treaty of 2084 to take over in case of emergencies. A clear breakdown in command on several levels seems to qualify."

Commander Okoro squared his shoulders. He faced Zen with a rock-hard set to his jaw. "I'll contact Space Command in Washington and the UN Security Office. Not to mentioned my contacts with the Global Space Consortium."

"Go ahead. Try it. OSI Director Clive Anderson can out-boss any of your bosses," Zen shot back. Her name drop seemed to have the desired sobering effect. Okoro's fierce expression dissolved a bit.

"Yeah, Marc. See how well such a power move will go over now." Chief Collier smirked as he massaged his left cheek.

"Are you okay, Gray?" Dr. McCoy peered into the chief's eyes, the medical professional kicking in.

"I'm good." Chief Collier tried to stand tall but stumbled. He grimaced when Dr. McCoy grabbed his arm and pushed her hand away. "I'll report this unprofessional outburst, Okoro."

"We're under tremendous stress. First Ahmad dies. Then this poor woman. Now another man is dead. I'm sure we can agree these are extraordinary circumstances. We don't have to let this minor disagreement leave this room." Dr. Gregson glanced at them all in turn.

"Minor? He attacked me!" Collier pointed at Okoro again then pulled his hand back fast.

"And you allowed unknown people to remove a vital piece of evidence in a murder investigation," Dr. Gregson said in a firm voice. "I think you have bigger concerns than tattling to your superiors."

"Yeah, like explaining how those officers got a release to move Suri's body," Sgt. Young said with a frown.

Chief Collier spun to face her. "You work for *me*, sergeant. Don't let running around with Special Agent Batiste and her weird partner make you forget that."

"Sergeant Young has been more help to me than all of you people put together," Zen snapped.

Sgt. Young opened the flip screen of her e-notepad. "Speaking of which, I confirmed Dr. Navarro's alibi. He was with Ms. Gaida but later he sent messages to his children. He also spent two hours at the lounge where Ahmad met the two women. Seems he was following leads. Based on the preliminary time of death, he's cleared of the second murder. I can't find any indication that he had motive, either."

"And we're supposed to simply take your word," Collier replied.

"Internal location trackers confirm the movements I just described. We lock in on all mobile devices and comms. A security backup in case CCTV fails due to solar flares or a spike in radiation particles," Sgt. Young said in a mild tone.

Commander Okoro gave a nod of approval and turned to Sgt. Young. "At least someone is doing her job. Damn thorough, too."

"So, we might be able to track the people who took Imirah Suri's body." Zen looked at Sgt. Young, along with the others.

"Working on it with the tech unit. Malai Khan, one of the In Situ computer scientists, is helping my guy. I trust her completely," Sgt. Young said in answer to the question in Zen's eyes.

"You are worth your weight in gold. Let's follow that lead." Zen's face of approval vanished when she turned to the others. "In the meantime, Commander Okoro, meet with the head of Black Rock Security, Star Flight's CEO, and include Dr. Gregson. We need the personnel files of every Black Rock employee, including administrative support. The CEO should be made aware of the gravity of the situation to insure he cooperates."

"She. Lydia Freberg," Okoro replied. "I'll get on it right now. Use my office on Star Flight. You'll have access to communications on the moon and here."

He gave a sharp nod and marched out. After Zen exchanged a glance with Sgt. Young, they followed him up several levels to a spacious suite. The office had a small sleeping pod and bathroom. Those were hidden behind a sliding door that looked like any other panel. The wide desk dominated most of the room. Okoro tapped in a code. One wall turned into a wide-screen television with built-in communication. A portion of the desk opened to reveal a tablet computer. Zen blinked when a three-dimensional hologram appeared.

"All the bells and whistles," Sgt. Young whispered to Zen.

"Indeed, sergeant. Use everything you need," Commander Okoro said with a flash of his even, white teeth. "I've entered codes for your use, Special Agent Batiste. Check your comms. On my way to meet with Black Rock and Lydia."

"Commander," Zen called out before he went through the door.

"More orders?" Commander Okoro wore a good-natured expression, very different from Chief Collier's reaction.

"This isn't about who's in charge, but I think you get it. Thanks for the prompt cooperation," Zen replied.

The big man saluted her and left. Sgt. Young had already dived into using the cool tools Commander Okoro had put at their disposal. Reports from LMPD officers had come in. The tech team also had tracked four figures pushing a gurney along five service corridors.

"There are blackout spots, but their attempts at hacking every camera didn't quite give them complete coverage. After this, we'll make modifications. Each set of cameras will get a separate system. Cracking one part won't affect others. I've been preaching updates to the chief for at least six months," Sgt. Young muttered more to herself than Zen. She transferred her gaze from Okoro's fancy tablet to the comm usually attached to her duty belt.

"Any fix on the body?" Zen asked. She sat in Okoro's massive executive chair. Butter-soft leather hugged her body even though it was large enough to fit him.

"Bad news, good news." Sgt. Young frowned at the small screen on her comm.

"Start with the good news."

"Malai found the results of Imirah Suri's preliminary autopsy. She beat the snatch-ware before it vanished and deleted the virus," Sgt. Young replied.

"What ware?"

"A hacker program that grabs data, uploads said data to another system, and then erases its digital tracks. Blackmailers use it a lot."

"And here I thought you were living a sheltered life out here," Zen joked.

"Maybe at first before more people came." Sgt. Young went back to looking at reports flashing on the screen.

"You think she can figure out the source?" Zen peered over her shoulder at the tablet.

"Doubt it, but she's going to try."

"Sometimes I think humanity is the virus the cosmos needs to be protected against," Zen said.

"More good news. Officers confirmed Special Agent Navarro's whereabouts during Suri's murder." Sgt. Young looked at Zen. "I don't see him as her killer anyway."

"Which is the perfect cover. They best ones are masters at cloaking themselves. But..." Zen heaved a sigh. "You're right. Something about him doesn't say murderer. He's tried to protect Emme Gaida from the start. He genuinely cares about his kids."

"You've got psychology, I've got gut instinct," Sgt. Young replied with a grin.

"Hmm. Peter displays a level of empathy that doesn't fit a profile neatly."

"Yeah. Time for the bad news. Our bad guys handed the body off. A man and woman. Faces digitally scrubbed by some advanced tech that screams government." Sgt. Young crossed her arms. "The next bit could be good or bad. A shuttle with Space Command insignia docked today. Twenty minutes before our unknown suspects snatched the body."

Zen tapped the screen of Okoro's tablet. "There's no shuttle from the moon or Earth scheduled for another three days. Okoro is here, so who is it?"

"I have a feeling we're about to find out. The three Space Command shuttles assigned to the lunar colonies are accounted for; I checked. Which means it's from Earth."

"Okoro called for reinforcements to help search the space station, I guess," Zen replied without looking away from the screen. Her smartwatch beeped insistently. The encrypted satellite ringtone alerted her to Earth-based messages.

Chimes announced the office door had been accessed and it slid open smoothly. Four figures stood in the door. Two wore headgear that helped them adapt to space oxygen and gravity. Zen gawked at the familiar uniform.

"What the hell?"

"Sgt. Young, this is Major General Malone Ramirez of Earth Airforce Space Command. He's in charge of law enforcement operations in space." Zen studied Malone's impassive expression for a few moments.

"Sergeant." Malone nodded to her and turned to the two Space Command officers. "That's all for now. Deploy as directed from Commander Okoro."

"Yes, sir," the men said and left.

Zen looked at the other man standing next to Malone. A slight smile tugged his lips up at both ends. Blue eyes twinkled but he said nothing. "I've never been introduced to you. Beyond knowing you're so classified I don't even know your name. Even a fake one will do. And that you work for my father."

"Director Batiste is officially retired," came the cool reply. The English accent made him sound even more polished.

"Right," Zen said.

"Ewan Lewis. Special Services Intelligence. I provide support to the CIA, NSA, and a few other acronyms," Lewis said, his smile making his face even more handsome. He brushed a hand through reddish-blond hair. "Whew. Quite a trip. Only my third time in space. Oops, maybe I wasn't supposed to admit that."

"I doubt you let anything 'slip' from your lips without a well-timed purpose," Zen shot back.

Smile still in place, Lewis turned to Sgt. Young. "Can you give me a quick turn around Space Command offices and In Situ?"

"A tour?" Sgt. Young blurted out. "Are you freaking—" Then she pressed her lips closed and looked to Zen for direction.

"I think Agent Lewis means Gen. Ramirez has some explaining to do and they're not sure you should hear it. Accommodate Special Agent Lewis. I'll fill you in once they're gone," Zen added in a stage whisper.

Sgt. Young's full lips trembled in an almost smile. Then she affected a serious look again. "Yes, ma'am. Sir, this way, sir."

Zen kept her gaze on Malone as Sgt. Young led Lewis out. "You showing up means my assignment is about to get next-level weird."

Malone walked over and put his helmet on the desk. Then he crossed back to Zen and kissed her. "Hey, babe. Nice to see you, too."

"Get off me, Ramirez, and start talking." Zen pushed against his strong embrace but finally relented and leaned into a longer kiss. When he stepped back, she sighed. Her whole body relaxed at his solid presence. "We're probably being recorded."

Malone laughed and planted another kiss on her forehead. "My team will scrub our private greeting from the cloud if necessary. But I doubt Okoro's office is anything but secure."

"What are you doing here?" Zen sat on the edge of Okoro's desk. She ran her fingers along the sleek polycarbonate faceplate of his helmet.

"So, you trust your baby police officer that much, huh?" Malone unzipped the front of his jumpsuit. Beneath, he wore a long-sleeve crew neck shirt. "Can't wait to get out of this thing. It's way lighter than the old spacesuits from the dark ages, but still."

"Sgt. Young is way ahead of her boss. The man is incompetent, possibly crooked. Your vetting process needs a serious revamp. Collier as the chief of the Lunar Metropolis Police Department is a disaster. Cute name, by the way. You come up with that one?"

"Now don't get snippy, Special Agent Batiste. Coming here was a high-level joint decision," Malone replied.

"I thought Okoro was the main man in charge."

"His rank is sergeant major, and yes, he has complete authority off world. But this is an extraordinary situation." Malone made a circuit of the office, examining the décor and equipment.

"I've got things under control," Zen snapped. She slipped from the desk and stood in a wide-legged stance.

Malone continued a casual stroll around the room. He ended up in front of the wide screen. Two exterior images of the space station flashed on. He swiped the virtual dashboard to freeze-frame them.

"My presence isn't a judgment on your handling of the case so far. Chief Collier was in the job before my promotion, by the way."

"You mean your defection from OSI leaving me with Navarro, of all people," Zen shot back.

"Blame your boss for hiring him." Malone held up both palms. "I come in peace."

"Why? And you brought my father's hitman with you." Zen pointed at the door as though Lewis still stood there.

"Ewan does have certain skills and knowledge. Killing people for the government isn't one of them," Malone joked. He crossed to Zen and brushed a finger across her left cheek. "Lighten up, babe."

"Two murders, an idiot police chief, and my partner as a suspect. My bad mood is well earned, Malone." Zen pushed his hand away. "And you're going to answer my questions."

"This desk is legendary. Okoro had it shipped in pieces at his own expense. Bubinga wood. It's from Gabon, to remind him of home." Malone brushed a hand along the rich brown grain. "You can trust Okoro. He's the reason we're here."

"The commander doesn't strike me as someone who gives up control easily," Zen replied.

"He's been... concerned about Collier for a while. But he didn't want to pull the trigger on possibly ruining the man's career. Unfortunately, Collier's stubborn. And he tried to use his connections on Earth to torpedo Okoro."

"Commander Okoro then decided to stop protecting him."

Malone nodded. "And Collier overestimates his own influence. Okoro is too valuable for a host of reasons I won't go into now. Not relevant to our current problem."

Zen pushed down rising annoyance at the hint of more secrets. "Fine. So, you're here to deal with Collier. And Ewan Lewis?"

The door whisked open and Sgt. Young strode in with Peter. "Ma'am, we've got developments. Two officers have tracked suspects."

"For murder?" Zen said.

"No, but we're sure they took Imirah Suri's body. My officers have them boxed in at shuttle docking bay number three." Sgt. Young tapped the earbud she wore, listened, and nodded with a smile. "Yep, we got 'em. Could be we're about solve at least one case."

Ewan Lewis appeared behind them. After a glance at everyone, he walked over to Malone. "Complication."

"Hold on. Let me check in with—" Malone started and stopped when Zen waved at him.

Peter looked from Malone to Zen. "We need to get those men into an interrogation room fast."

"Agreed. Sgt. Young, we'll go to the docking area. Maj. General Ramirez and his associate can deal with Chief Collier," Zen said.

Malone turned to Sgt. Young. "Let's look at visuals from the area first."

Ewan Lewis moved before anyone else. He used the digital dashboard of master controls in the panel set on Commander

Okoro's desk. "I'm familiar with the tech. Shouldn't be too hard. Ah yes, the main schemata and... there."

Images of the space station blinked off. In its place was what looked like a standoff. Two officers in LMPD uniforms faced men dressed in charcoal-gray jumpsuits. One of the men had iron-gray hair though he looked no older than thirty. The man was Asian. His expression looked deadly, as if he could explode into action at any moment.

"They're not going anywhere, ma'am," Sgt. Young spoke softly aside to Zen. She looked at Malone and then Lewis.

Commander Okoro returned to the room. "Looks like I finished issuing instructions in my meeting just in time. General." He nodded at Malone and turned to Lewis. "I'll thank you to keep hands off my command panel, whoever the hell you are."

Lewis stepped away from the digital dashboard with an easy smile. "Gen. Ramirez's orders. No offense intended."

"Humph." Okoro's severe expression didn't soften. "Well?"

"Sir, suspects in the theft of Ms. Suri's body have been cornered. They're not following commands to explain themselves." Sgt. Young nodded to the screen.

"Make sure they're contained until we get there. Let's go." Okoro started to leave but Malone blocked his exit.

"We know who they are, Commander." Malone gave Zen a side look and then faced Okoro again.

"The complications Lewis mentioned, I'm guessing. Where is she, Malone?" Zen worked hard to tame the fury burning in her veins. She pointed to Lewis. "If he's here, then some kind of high-level bullshit is involved. Orchestrated by my father."

"Mr. Batiste is acting director of the revamped National Security Agency. My unit specializes in global intelligence analysis. Emphasis on space. I can't say more," Lewis replied.

Zen studied him for a few moments. The charming English upper crust mask vanished. Ewan Lewis looked like a man who could be trusted to keep secrets. No matter what threat he faced. James Batiste would find such a man very handy. Her father had been a key figure in global intelligence for almost forty years. No doubt he held the keys to a host of closets with skeletons.

"Like hell you can't. Do I have to remind you that OSI has broad investigative authority in murder cases? Stay quiet and I'm not sharing what we know so far," Zen hissed at him.

"Those men came with us. They're part of the team to clean up this situation," Malone said with a frown at her.

Zen looked around the room, at the screen, and then back at Malone and Lewis. "You've got Suri's corpse. We're not leaving this room until you tell me why. Sgt. Young, do you have officers nearby?"

Sgt. Young stood next to Zen. "Ma'am, three just arrived in Corridor G outside. Commander Okoro's lieutenant colonel is with them, too."

"This is a good time to remind everyone that we're on the same team." Malone's baritone voice rumbled as he squinted at Zen and Sgt. Young.

"Excellent point," Peter said, stepping forward. "Our main objective is to bring a killer to justice. Next, Gen. Ramirez will address issues within the lunar police department, with assistance from Commander Okoro, of course. We all have the same mission—to sort out serious issues at hand."

"Before we share a group hug, Gen. Ramirez and Agent Lewis are going to explain why they're obstructing an OSI murder investigation. I'm sure my boss, Director Anderson, will be interested in the answer." Zen glowered at the two men.

"Calm down," Malone replied to Zen.

"Okay, now I know your answers are going to seriously piss me off," Zen shot back. Her expression didn't change as she stared him down.

"There's more at stake than who stopped Suri," Malone said after a few beats.

"Ah, I don't think we should..." Peter darted a look at Sgt. Young and then at Malone.

"Sgt. Young stays," Zen put in before anyone spoke. Then Zen looked from Malone to Peter. "Lewis said Imirah Suri was stopped."

"Yes, from revealing too much of what she knew about corporate spying and police corruption," Lewis said.

"Which isn't the reason you two turned into body snatchers," Zen replied. Then she looked at Peter. He glanced away, a sheen of sweat on his forehead. "Imirah Suri was a humanoid. Smuggled into space. But why?"

"What?" Commander Okoro looked around at the others, mouth agape, too stunned to say more.

"Why isn't the most important question. Who smuggled her off Earth? She had to have pretty solid clearance and cover to get here," Sgt. Young said quietly.

Zen turned to her. "Go make sure your officers secure the two persons of interest. I'm going to get more answers so I know what we've walked into."

Sgt. Young glanced around at the men. "But—"

"I'm good. Go." Zen nodded toward the door as she gazed into Sgt. Young's dark eyes.

"Yes, ma'am." Sgt. Young shot one last look, heavy with meaning, around the group, watching them. With a grunt, she strode out.

Malone let out a low whistle when the door swooshed shut behind her. "Nobody better mess with you while she's around."

"Thank you for recognizing the sensitive nature of what we'll discuss," Ewan Lewis said.

"I don't want her put at risk. Your kind of 'sensitive' operations tend to get people killed," Zen snapped at him.

"Ahmad wasn't us," Lewis said. "Dr. Navarro should join Sgt. Lewis in continuing your investigation."

He didn't wait for an answer but activated the door and pushed Peter ahead of him. Zen expected Peter to protest but he didn't. Peter allowed Lewis to herd him out into the hall. He looked back at Zen as if trying to send a message. Zen had no time to process the meaning in his troubled gaze. Commander Okoro's basso voice cut into her thoughts.

"I trust there was a very good reason why I wasn't informed about an unsanctioned robot." Commander Okoro swung to face Malone with a fierce expression.

"She's not one of ours," Malone said calmly. "Space-Cor worked with Tetra to develop their own humanoids."

"Tetra?" Commander Okoro glanced around at them all.

"Tetra is a well-funded private research and development consortium. They've developed a long list of products and technologies. Including the Lodestone procedure, brain stimulation used on criminals," Zen said when Malone didn't speak up.

"I'm familiar with Lodestone. We have a number of very valuable people working here who received the treatment. But I thought the use of humanoids was still being evaluated." Okoro frowned at Malone and then Lewis.

"Correct. There is pushback from humanoid rights activists and the public. Like with immigrants, the complaints about jobs being taken from 'real' humans is thrown about. Nonsense. Robots can be used to set up colonies on Titan, Mars, and more before humans arrive. No different from robotic rovers and construction bots used now," Lewis replied.

"Makes sense. Not to mention it would save lives. No accidental deaths or catastrophic injuries to humans," Commander Okoro agreed. "So, the government has pushed ahead with development, classified of course."

"Waiting for the hysteria to cool down and rational thought prevail," Lewis said with a half-smile.

"Except private corporations can take advantage in the meantime. It takes a while for politics and laws to catch up to technological advances. Technically, Space-Cor hasn't violated any laws sending Imirah Suri into space," Zen said.

"We're not sure she worked for or was built by them," Malone said. He exchanged a glance with Lewis before going on. "Humanoid tech has jumped ahead in the past ten years or so."

"Synthetic skin, eyes, and hair make them look even more human. Did you suspect when you questioned her?" Lewis asked Zen.

Zen thought back to when she sat less than five feet from the woman. "Nothing about her looked manufactured or... mechanical. But I didn't have a reason to touch her, either."

"You still wouldn't have noticed anything," Lewis replied.

"Her apartment rent was paid by Space-Cor. They wanted her to get close to Ahmad. It seems he had information that could amount to trillions in profit. Something about Helium 3 deposits."

"Information which must not leave this room." Lewis looked at Okoro and Zen in turn.

"Sorry, but that spaceship has already left the dock. A reporter on Star Flight told me about it. I'm guessing he's not the only one who knows. Ahmad may have known and talked to someone else. He was trying to cut deals," Zen replied.

"We need to contain this reporter ASAP. Sgt. Young will release my agents immediately. They can secure the package, send it back to Earth. A team is waiting to get it. Tetra researchers are being questioned now." Lewis went to the commander's dashboard. He tapped icons without needing directions.

"I'm assuming he has top clearance that I can't touch," Commander Okoro murmured aside to Malone.

Malone clapped a hand on Okoro's broad shoulder. "You nailed it, Marc. Don't waste time calling your superiors."

Commander Okoro smiled at him. "Wouldn't dream of it. He can take care of his spy stuff. I'm only interested in the well-being of our lunar colonies and this space station."

"I'm surprised you're taking this all so well, commander." Zen had expected to witness a testosterone-fueled pissing contest.

"I've enjoyed immense autonomy in space. My third wife has decided she's fed up and will leave soon. An added bonus. I have no complaints." Commander Okoro lifted both hands.

Zen laughed at the comically satisfied expression he wore. "Okay, then."

Lewis returned. "Clairmont is at the LMPD offices."

"Not without a lot of ranting about freedom of the press, I bet," Zen quipped.

"We'll find out what he knows soon," Lewis replied with a blank face.

"What does that mean?" Zen gazed back at him. His impassive look gave her chills.

"He could be prosecuted for having and withholding information that could hurt national security. I'll make sure he understands a federal prison sentence could be in his future. Depending on what he tells us," Lewis added.

"Helium 3 and its potential isn't a big secret. But the plans for reserves and the Marius Hills lava cave are," Malone said.

"We're years away from building a city beneath surface of the moon," Commander Okoro said. When Lewis and Malone looked surprised, the big man nodded at them. "I had two of my officers gather intel on Space-Cor and the Chinese. They kept going on treks to explore possible mining sites. I suspected there was more to their moon treks."

"I've read those reports," Malone said.

"General Nelson ordered the area around Marius Hills and two adjacent crater chains off limits. I expected a top-secret team from NASA or ESA would show up one day," Commander Okoro said.

Zen rubbed her temples to massage the tension headache threatening. "Helium 3, craters, lava caves."

"Oh my," Lewis joked with a smile.

She gave him a heated look that didn't affect his amusement at all. "All of this corporate espionage has resulted in two deaths."

"Technically, only one." Lewis raised an eyebrow at her.

"A growing number of people on Earth would disagree. What will you do with Imirah Suri?" Zen looked from Lewis to Malone.

Malone heaved a long sigh. "She'll likely be reactivated. Her data analyzed. Techs will retrieve her digital transmissions to trace uploads and downloads."

"We have lines on the servers and encrypted clouds used by Space-Cor and the other companies," Lewis added.

"They go along with the government accessing their systems?" Zen asked.

"Up to a limit. We have back doors in," Lewis said.

"Sheesh. Okay, look, I just want to find out what and who killed Ahmad. Or maybe I should go home and let you folks handle it," Zen muttered.

"We need all hands on deck," Malone said promptly. "But we have to clear Navarro."

"His alibi checked out. Peter wasn't near Suri at the time she died, or was disabled. Or... you know what I mean," Zen said.

"Dr. Navarro's work with Tetra put their development of humanoids years ahead. He may know more than he's telling," Lewis said bluntly. "We have him contained as well."

"Like hell you do. I'll talk to him. And don't think of trying to stop me," Zen clipped before Malone or Lewis spoke.

Chapter 11

Lewis did indeed try to keep Zen from talking to Peter alone. He sent word to his shadowy superiors. She called Clive. Zen won, but not without what she assumed was a turf tug-of-war on Earth. Once again, Sgt. Young proved to be an invaluable ally. She led Zen through a maze of back corridors and service elevators. Blinking lights indicated oxygen levels, gravity status, and other readings that kept the space station functioning. They even scrambled up and down ladders three times. They arrived at a room on what was called the Alpha Wing. Sgt. Young tapped in a code and the panel door slid open.

"Feels like we're in one of those twentieth-century spy movies," Peter said when they entered.

"Hello." Emme sat next to him on a small cot gripping one of his hands in both of hers.

Zen walked into the room and glared at them both. "You're testing my damn patience, Navarro."

"This isn't a plus-one social event," Sgt. Young said in a dry tone. She went around the room staring at the walls. Then she took a black box from her pocket and tapped controls.

"There aren't any cameras or microphones. At least not anymore." Peter got up from the bed and pulled a bag from beneath it.

"They're in all rooms but only activated by certain monitors. Low oxygen or gravity level indicators. Safety feature that also allows for privacy. Even in service staff quarters," Sgt. Young explained. She continued to check the room. "Your friends from Earth must not have operatives on board."

"More likely they haven't had time to recruit anyone who knows this place the way you do." Zen continued to frown at her partner.

"It's not what you think," Peter said after a few seconds of silence ticked by.

"Emme knows this place almost as well as Sgt. Young. Which means she helped you cook up matching alibis. And you only needed an alibi because you two killed Imirah." Zen perched on a edge of a small desk and put her feet on the seat of its chair. "So, now we're about to hear the whole story of why."

Sgt. Young blocked the door. "You can't take me, Ms. Gaida. You could try but I wouldn't."

"We're more than a little annoyed with you both. I'll whip your ass and then turn you over to Gen. Ramirez. I don't give a shit at this point," Zen said in a calm voice.

"I appreciate what you've done for me so far. Not mentioning I knew Emme—"

Zen stood. "Wrong. Clive knows all the details. How many times have you killed her?"

"Wait, what?" Sgt. Young assumed a fighting stance.

"It's not what you think!" Peter started toward Zen.

"Hold up, dude. I'll drop you right there. And I don't care what the setting is." Sgt. Young held a compact pistol in one hand. "This thing shoots pellets with electrical charges that activate on contact."

"An innovation I wasn't aware of." Peter tried to force a smile as he stared down the barrel.

"Don't hurt him because of me." Emme jumped between Peter and Sgt. Young.

"At this point I'm tempted to let her shoot you both on general principle. Now sit your ass down. I'm talking to Peter," Zen yelled. She shoved Emme hard onto the narrow cot.

"My aggressive impulses were short-circuited by the transcranial deep-brain stimulation. You've heard about the Lodestone treatment, sergeant?" Peter turned to Sgt. Young. When she shook her head slowly, Peter went on. "A medical procedure that uses magnetic pulses to certain areas of the brain. It's been found effective to alleviate criminal behavior."

"Like the urge to murder?" Sgt. Young glanced from Peter to Emme and back.

"Exactly." Peter nodded.

"Did you know Emme was on Star Flight?" Zen said.

Peter turned back to Zen. "I told you the truth. It was a pleasant surprise."

"So, you two took up where you left off with your special relationship," Zen said.

"No. He's... different." Emme started to reach for his hand but stopped when Sgt. Young waved the pistol.

"Not quite. I have urges. Seeing Emme triggered the desire for not just sex but..." Peter swallowed hard.

"You said he's killed her more than once. You mean Imirah Suri?" Sgt. Young wore a confused frown.

"No. Emme's a humanoid, too. Part of Dr. Navarro's pathology was sex mixed with violence. He started with fake snuff porn where one or more sex partners end up dead. But that wasn't enough after a while. Did you kill a human partner before you turned to humanoids for sex?" Zen said to him.

"I don't know." Peter's hands shook as he rubbed his forehead.

"Bullshit. You were easy to set up because the other sick killer knew your habits. He just didn't know about your real victim. That forced him to frame you with planted evidence." Zen pointed at Peter.

"The treatment affected the medial temporal lobe. I'm not lying. I have flashes, but I'm not sure if they're real or not." Peter sat down hard on the bed. Emme put an arm around his shoulder but he shrugged her off. "I don't deserve comfort."

"Okay, but take a minute and explain who he killed over and over," Sgt. Young blurted out in frustration.

"Me." Emme said in a small voice. "I can be revived over and over. He hated himself each time he gave in to it. That's how I knew he was really a good man. Peter, tell them."

"You like to kill your sex partner during the act," Zen said. "You started out liking it rough, but that wasn't enough after a while. Serial killers escalate along a specific behavioral path at times. How did you start?"

"Fantasies that became more vivid, but ultimately not enough. I found sex partners who liked playing games. I couldn't stop thinking about..." Peter let out a noisy breath.

"You should know what he went through before you judge him," Emme said with force.

Peter shook his head and looked away. "It doesn't matter what excuses I give."

"Being raped and beaten as a child isn't an excuse," Emme said softly.

Sgt. Young gasped. "Damn."

"Look, we don't have much time. I'm supposed to be at the LMPD station with you in an interview room. Lewis is probably already on the main dashboard searching for us. Start talking and don't leave out a damn thing. Now!" Zen stood over them both.

"Trust me. They won't find us," Sgt. Young said. "And I definitely want to hear their story."

"Imirah's assignment was to get close to Hassan Ahmad. He had worked with another team on his own. He financed them. They located something valuable on the moon, but he wouldn't tell Space-Cor details. Not until he got to Star Flight." Emme looked at Peter. He pulled away from her, head down.

"Coming to the conference was a cover for Ahmad's real purpose at Star Flight," Sgt. Young said.

"Imirah got close to him before he left Earth. That's why they recruited her. He'd paid her for sex once before. She laughed, really cashing in and being able to retire. She'd get paid to milk him for information while he was paying her for sex."

"Robots dream of retiring?" Sgt. Young blinked at her.

"You and Imirah aren't ordinary humanoids." Zen looked around the room. She found a small pair of scissors. "Hold out your arm."

Peter threw a protective arm in front of Emme. "No, don't. It's inhumane."

Zen ignored him. "Sgt. Young, shoot if they move again."

"Ma'am." Sgt. Young moved to one side for a better visual on them both.

Zen moved close to Emme. She held out her wrist to Zen without replying. Zen scratched her arm. A reddish fluid beaded from the superficial cut. Peter let out a groan and gazed at Emme. Sgt. Young hissed in surprise.

"You have biological-based parts. You're a hybrid," Zen said quietly.

"It's not blood, at least not like humans. We're a combination. Xenobot and robot. Xenobots are made of living material, designed on supercomputers that run software that emulates natural selection. The idea was that we'd be programmed at the cellular level. But turns out combining artificial intelligence with living bio-matter leads to interesting results." Emme blinked back tears. "Like we want more than just to work for humans."

"Let me guess. The US government backed the development of this new kind of humanoids," Zen said with a grimace. She connected the dots to a picture that led to her father.

"Not just the Americans. We have outpaced the Japanese but not by much. Luckily, Russia has proven inept once again, so they're behind. The Chinese, Koreans, and even India all have made advances. Your American intelligence community has been effective in stoking suspicion between all parties," Peter said with a bitter smile.

"So they won't build a scientific alliance," Zen said.

"A delicate dance that goes back and forth. Interestingly enough, the French are underestimated," Peter murmured. "Seems the competition has gotten heated."

"Who took Imirah's body?" Zen looked at Peter.

"You already guessed the answer. It isn't a coincidence that your Gen. Ramirez and Agent Lewis showed up."

"Damn it, Malone," Zen hissed low.

"What's happened?" Emme looked at her and then to Peter for an answer.

"My colleague is confronting an ugly reality. The US government likely took your friend's body. We can guess why. I have several theories on what they'll do next," Peter replied.

"Let's hear them," Zen snapped.

"The most likely is they'll change her appearance and put her back into operation. She's one of a handful, too valuable to lose. Then again, they've been known to scrap a model before. Sorry," Peter added when Emme flinched at his blunt statement.

"Don't apologize for telling the truth about humanity," Emme replied in a hushed voice.

"If she's biological in nature then it's the same as murder." Zen raised a palm when Peter started to reply. "I know, I know. The main question about the use of humanoids even before this so-called advancement."

"The great debate about personhood and sentience. There are two institutes devoted to expanding the moral circle, as they call it," Peter said.

"Humans haven't found a way to treat each other humanely. One small difference like skin color determines who is oppressed. We don't have much hope for how humanoids will be treated. Slavery and genocide seem to be in your DNA," Emme said, her pretty features twisted into a grimace.

Peter put a hand on her arm. "Don't worry, dear. There's no reason they should know about you."

"You're not in a position to make promises, Peter. I'm beginning to wonder about your alibi." Zen stared at him.

He met her gaze without looking away. "The suspects for who killed Imirah and Hassan Ahmad just increased."

"Are you suggesting… a government agency killed one or both as part of a coverup? But cover up what?" Zen frowned at him.

"Hybrid humanoids. The location of Helium 3 that could change the balance of world power. Lava caverns that could be developed as a super lunar colony, a base for lucrative space mining. Pick one. I can think of more if you like," Peter said.

"You know about Helium 3 and lava caves," Zen shot back.

"Talk of Helium 3 and the existence of vast caverns beneath the moon have been hypothesized for almost a hundred years." Peter let out a long-suffering sigh when Zen continued to glare at him. "Check for yourself. Scientists confirmed they exist forty years ago, Zen. They just weren't large enough to house colonies."

"I haven't read any news reports about them," Zen countered.

"Check with Clive and Hadley. Those finds were classified. It was only a matter of time and resources before the large ones were located. They're on Mars as well. At least we think so. I was part of the teams analyzing data from multiple space probes. Your deep dive into my background must include that fact." Peter waved a hand at her. "Believe what you wish."

"Ahmad worked on multiple projects, including the development of solar power. Something about coatings for panels," Zen said.

"He also had a passion for going on space hikes, but Imirah learned it wasn't for fun," Emme put in.

"Extreme space sports. Another bad idea for tourism on the moon." Peter winced and rubbed his eyes.

"You need rest." Emme rested a hand on his shoulder. Then she looked at Zen. "Not accusations and suspicion."

"Ma'am," Sgt. Young said, startling all three. She'd been so quiet they seemed to have forgotten she was there.

Zen glanced at her. "They're getting closer."

"Two levels away. I estimate they'll check the other four service quarters and get to this one in about fifteen minutes. What's our next move?" Sgt. Young glanced at Peter and Emme.

"Don't let them find Emme here. She doesn't have to be taken into custody," Peter said quickly.

Zen grunted. "Lewis probably already has figured out—"

'Others helped me get here anonymously. I've been under the radar for a while, the past four years at least. My father and mother helped me blend into the human population." Emme looked at Peter.

"Parents?" Sgt. Young blinked in shock.

"They treated me like their child. You would call him the scientist who built me. And no, I won't identify them or who helped me." Emme's eyes flashed with rebellion as she stared back at Sgt. Young and then at Zen.

"It's a long, complicated, yet oddly moving story," Peter said when Zen and Sgt. Young looked at him.

Sgt. Young's mobile comm beeped twice. "Right. This way to back corridors. The fit will get tight, but you're pretty small. Dr. Navarro might have a problem though."

"I'm coming with you," Peter said.

Emme shook her head hard. "No, you can't. They'll suspect you again and—"

"We don't have time for this," Sgt. Young broke in. She pulled Emme to her feet and pressed a panel in the wall. A door slid open. "I'll lead you out."

"No need. Show me the map. I know you have one not generally shared," Emme said.

Sgt. Young cast a brief glance at Zen. When she nodded approval, Sgt. Young tapped the screen of her mobile comm. A hologram image appeared. Emme stared at it for five seconds and then nodded.

"I should still get you started, check for anyone looking." Sgt. Young pulled Emme by one arm through the opening.

"Peter, I... Thank you." Emme blinked large expressive eyes at him before Sgt. Young yanked her again.

"C'mon. You can have a warm moment later," Sgt. Young said in a commanding tone. They disappeared and the panel slid closed. It looked like just another part of the wall.

Peter turned to Zen. "Now what?"

"We face the music and fix the mess you created by not being straight with me," Zen retorted.

"You know everything now," he replied evenly.

"I don't believe you, Navarro. Go."

Zen poised a finger over the keypad that would open the door. Peter opened his mouth to speak and then closed it again. He stepped through the back panel. When it slid into place silently, she tapped the keypad next to the main entrance. It opened just as Malone and one of the Space Command officers marched up.

"So, you were searching through the service tunnels, too? Sgt. Young told us about these service quarters tucked away. The women and men who maintain this station get pretty nice digs, right?" Zen said. "You can check again, but we didn't find anything of interest. Find Imirah Suri's body yet?"

"I never said we had it," Malone said.

"Of course you did. 'We're going to secure the package and get it back to Earth.' Exact quote," Zen put in.

"Lewis's team didn't get to the In Situ fridge in time." Malone frowned.

"The what?" Zen said.

Sgt. Young stepped into the room past the security officer. "What we call the cold room at the In Situ Research Center. It keeps certain equipment or chemicals at low temps. Once we had a death, it became the temporary morgue. At this rate we're gonna need to keep it."

"Humph." The security guard nodded with a grim expression.

"The video shows them pushing the gurney, but the body wasn't on it yet. We should talk," Malone said to Zen.

"Oh, hell yes, and it better be damn good." Zen brushed past him and strode down the corridor.

She heard Malone give instructions to the guard and Sgt. Young as she walked away. Malone caught up with Zen in the main corridor. Star Flight residents glanced at them in surprise as they emerged from a service panel. Compact rovers, like golf carts, whizzed by on the street.

"Amazing how In Situ is so much like a small town." Malone glanced around and then faced Zen. When she crossed her arms and gazed back at him, Malone nodded. "My place for our talk?"

"Fine."

Fifteen minutes later they were in spacious living quarters set up for Malone. Zen waved away his offer of coffee. When he held up a bottle of juice Zen accepted. He poured himself a cup and filled a glass for her. Zen took it and sipped. She sat on a comfy chair, cross her legs, and waited. Malone didn't drink at first. He shed the DOD jacket he wore. Then he went through a short set of stretching exercises.

"Helps work out the stiffness after traveling. Also it—"

"Helps prevent blood clots if you keep moving. One of the hazards of a flight and being in space," Zen finished for him.

"And it fights the loss of bone and muscle mass. You've been doing your own routine, I hope." Malone performed a set of ten squats as he talked.

"I've had a workout running down suspects and dirty space cops. Not to mention keeping an eye on my own damn partner." Zen lifted the paper cup. "Put some bourbon in this and it would be perfect."

"Look I know..." Malone's voice trailed off at the fiery look she gave him.

"No, you don't. Commander Okoro and Chief Collier have been assholes. The directors of In Situ the same. All four have been letting crap slide that should have been addressed, and now I'm dealing with one of Daddy's shadowy henchmen." Zen drained the glass and stood. "I don't need this shit, Malone. So, you better start at the top and work your way down explaining what the hell I stepped in out here."

"Right. Right." Malone, all six feet three inches of him, towered over her with a concerned expression. "You have a right to be upset. But we're here to help."

"Oh, please. You're here to clean up a mess the Pentagon and all the government alphabets don't want to explode in their faces." Zen stabbed a finger in his chest.

"You say that like it's a bad thing," Malone said with a serious expression.

Zen blinked at him for a second before she burst out laughing. "I ought to slap you, man."

Malone pulled her into his arms and laughed with her. "See? You needed me to help break the tension."

"Whatever." Zen pushed him away as she wiped her eyes. "You're not off the hook. Explain yourself, Major General Ramirez."

"My role is to find and fix problems in the Lunar Metro squad. Collier may be a political appointee, but he does have years as a military cop. So, he's not unqualified on paper," Malone said. He sat in a chair and picked up his cup of coffee.

"Collier didn't get the glory and quick rise up the command chain he expected. Let me guess. Someone on Earth wanted him in space," Zen said.

"How did you—yeah. He was sold on the idea this job was his golden ticket. When really it was an easy way to not rile up his friends in high places and get rid of him. Right before the moon, he was at a base in South Korea running a military police unit."

"And probably not doing a good job. Shoot him into space. Small population of scientists and support colonists. No crime. What could go wrong? That was the brilliant logic." Zen cocked her head to one side.

"Hey, it wouldn't have been my choice but nobody asked me. Hell, I didn't even know the guy. Anyway, Clive sent word to me right before he informed my top brass."

"And Lewis?"

"He showed up at the shuttle port, packed and ready to go. He briefed me on the flight."

"When you couldn't simply place a call to your command. Smart." Zen gave a grunt.

"I have a feeling they knew already. If not, they do now. Commander Okoro will have sent them a full report. Lewis says they're sure the humanoid program has nothing to do with your murder investigation. He's here to make sure that reporter doesn't get anything more than unconfirmed rumors. Says his people are concerned you and Navarro got too chummy with Clairmont." Malone raised both palms when Zen squinted at him. "I'm just the messenger."

"Clairmont might be a pain, but the man knows how to dig up facts. The only good thing is he doesn't know for sure there are humanoids here, definitely hasn't identified them. He also pretty much figured out on his own which cops were crooked. Credit where credit is due, as my father always says," Zen murmured. She turned over the facts for a few seconds before she looked at Malone again.

"What?"

"The government isn't simply interested in what makes Imirah tick. There's more going on," Zen said.

Before Malone answered, her smartwatch ring tone sounded. So did his. They looked at each other and answered. Malone strode to the other side of the room to murmur into his ear buds. Zen answered a call from Sgt. Young.

"Ma'am, you okay?" Sgt. Young said in a breathless voice.

Zen's pulse picked up at the tone of excitement coming from the speaker. "Yeah, fine. What's happened?"

"Lewis and his men found the guys who had Suri's body. There was a shootout. They're both dead. The suspects. You should—"

"Text the location. On my way."

Malone, still on his call, looked at Zen with a frown that deepened the longer his listened. "Unfortunate, hell. We needed to talk to—damn! Got it."

"More bodies. Few answers," Zen hissed. "Is Lewis cleaning up with his gun?"

"I want to know who gave him authorization to use deadly force." Malone hit the wall with one fist. "What a shitshow."

"Let's go see." Zen was through the door before Malone answered.

The trip to the sector where the firefight took place took twenty-five minutes. Level Seven was where near the largest and main shuttle port was located. Executive offices for private companies were located on the opposite end of the port. A swarm of uniforms surrounded them as they emerged from the large elevator. A mixture of Space Command and Black Rock Security officers seemed to fill the space.

"Did every government and private cop on the station get called in?" Zen murmured as they looked around them at the controlled chaos.

"Ma'am! Over here." Sgt. Young gestured to them. She stood with two officers who appeared to be blocking her way into another corridor.

"I'll handle this." Malone strode off with a stiff frown. "Maj. General Ramirez and Special Agent Batiste with OSI. We're going in."

The man and woman in Space Command uniforms exchanged a glance. A second later they parted to opposite sides of the entrance. Malone gestured for Zen to follow him. Without looking back, he went down a smaller corridor. Zen walked between the officers. Sgt. Young glared at them as she brushed past right behind her. The corridor ended at a large room. The familiar black body bag lay crumpled on the floor next to a gurney. Lewis stood with his back to them talking animatedly to another figure dressed in black. His two men flanked the room, shock rifles at the ready. Lewis glanced over one shoulder. He directed the person he was talking to down another corridor as though giving them an order.

Guns with conventional bullets were too dangerous on a space station. Essential machinery, including the walls that maintained breathable atmosphere and gravity levels, could not be risked. Bullets piercing them would mean death to dozens in a matter of hours. Repairs couldn't be made fast enough. So, Lewis's men carried weapons that would stun with electric shock, or at least that's what Zen thought was available before now.

"Damn," Sgt. Young whispered as she looked at two prone figures crumpled on the floor. "I should have let Imirah Suri go. She'd be alive; no one else would be dead if I hadn't..."

"You did right," Zen said with force. She rubbed the young woman's back when Sgt. Young's eyes filled with tears. "Tell you what, go find Peter and tell him what's happened. I have a feeling Emme is still holding out on us. Okay?"

"Uh-huh." Sgt. Young continued to stare at the bodies.

"Wyvette! This is *not* your fault. Now get it together and move," Zen barked.

Sgt. Young blinked as if waking from a daze. "Yes, ma'am."

"Before you do that..." Zen turned back to where Malone stood talking quietly to Lewis. "You know where that corridor leads?"

"Back to another major traffic walkway, I believe."

"Go find out who Special Agent Lewis sent on a mission and follow him or her," Zen whispered.

Sgt. Young took off without responding. Zen felt relieved to see her move so fast. Police work would distract her from guilt. The tormented look in Sgt. Young's eyes reminded Zen the twenty-four-year-old hadn't seen this much death and so up close. Malone walked over at the same moment Zen turned around again.

"Lewis says things are under control." Malone glanced down at the dark-gray-clad figure on the floor.

"His definition of things being under control is a hell of a lot different than mine," Zen said. She started for Lewis but Malone's strong grip pulled her back. "What?"

"He's not going to tell you much. Ewan is single-minded and has orders. Though I'm not sure what they are at this point." Malone stared across at Lewis in speculation.

"Malone, don't try that bull crap on me. You've found out something. Tell me later."

Zen was sure Malone had done some discreet digging for gold on Lewis, his mission, and more. Malone didn't try to stop her when Zen brushed free from his hold. Lewis issued instructions to more Space Command officers who had arrived. She heard one say Commander Okoro was on his way. The lean Brit turned to face Zen as she approached. His blue eyes seemed to have an icy quality.

"A moment to nail down more of details. The scene doesn't have to be blocked off." Lewis looked past Zen and gestured to someone. "Here."

A pair of space station medics scurried over and retrieved both bodies with grim efficiency. One was a man, the other a woman. Each medic pushed a gurney. A woman in an In Situ beige jumpsuit met them at the door and followed them out. Then Lewis walked away to give more directions to his men. When he realized Zen was right behind him, he smiled back at her.

"This is my investigation and what happened here is relevant," Zen clipped.

"One might think you don't trust me, Special Agent Batiste," Lewis said. His crisp British accent was heavy with elegant amusement.

"One would be spot-on," Zen said, matching it with perfection.

Lewis laughed out loud but kept going. As they approached, Zen was surprised that one of Lewis's subordinates was a woman. Her gender had been pretty well masked by the uniform and helmet.

"Giordano, run down what happened again. For Special Agent Batiste's benefit."

"Give me the unedited version, please," Zen put in with a side-eye at Lewis.

"Yes, ma'am." The woman lifted her chin and looked Zen in the eyes. "We used CCTV for visuals after detecting the activated tracking signal."

"Suri had one implanted. We found that out after encouraging cooperation from Space-Cor," Lewis said.

Zen shot a sharp look at Lewis. She wondered what methods of "encouragement" he'd used. Instead of asking, she turned back to Giordano. "Continue, officer."

"Once we determined space commandos could get here faster, we directed them to secure any exits. But we got here pretty quickly. Space Command covered the perimeters. Because the targets were classified, only Irving and I entered the area. They were trying to get a panel open. More than likely one of the many service passageways most don't know about. We engaged when they ignored orders to stop. One had this." Giordano held up an oblong object. The short-barrel 410 firearm had a military camo pattern on its surface. When Giordano pulled it close to her, Zen could tell it wouldn't be easy to see. The black and dark gray pattern blended into the colors of the uniform's fabric.

"Bullets?" Zen took the weapon when Giordano held it out again.

"Affirmative, ma'am. I trained with these. Recognized it right off. Irving would have been dead if I hadn't fired when the guy took aim. Things move fast in the field. We did what we had to and secured the package."

Zen studied Giordano. The woman's solid, impassive expression didn't betray any emotion. Yet her answer covered any question Zen might have had about the use of force. Lewis and his people were ready for hard questions.

"Did you get a chance to say anything to them or examine Imirah Suri's body?" Zen stepped around Giordano and started for the wheeled cart that now held the corpse. The second officer, a man, blocked her path. He didn't move even though Zen glared up at him.

Lewis moved close to Zen. "We've agreed to provide a data extracted from her hardware. Anything related to the death of Hassan Ahmad, that is."

"Not good enough. Where are you taking it?" Zen watched as Lewis's people kept the Space Command officers from getting too close.

"As I said, we'll do an examination back on Earth. I have expertise in AI schematics. I'll do a preliminary examination. Secure the internal chip that contains memory and processor." Lewis turned to watch his team move efficiently.

"Which didn't answer my question," Zen snapped. "And waiting for your redacted findings isn't acceptable, Lewis. I have clearance."

Lewis's cool exterior was unaffected by the heat in her tone. "Tsk, tsk. Mr. Batiste will not be pleased."

"He rarely is when I don't follow instructions like a good little girl," Zen shot back.

Sgt. Young came through the large entrance, dragging someone with her. The person muttered a string of profanity. "Ma'am. Look what I found!" She yanked the hoodie back. A very much alive Imirah Suri directed verbal venom at Zen.

Zen faced a shaken Lewis, turning various shades of red. "Well, well, well."

Chapter 12

Malone exploded like a solar flare. His rage singed even the normally unflappable Special Agent Ewan Lewis. Commander Okoro let him vent, choosing wisely not to try diplomacy. Zen watched in awe. She'd never seen him release this type of energy before. Chief Collier seemed content to stay out of the line of fire. He'd backed into a corner of his office at the LMPD substation on Star Flight.

"I don't give a Dominican rat's ass what your instructions are, Lewis. Do I look like I care? Don't give me that highly classified, the 'sensitive nature of my mission could affect the global balance of power' bullshit." Malone stood toe-to-toe with Lewis and glared in the lean Brit's face. The last word came out like high-powered buckshot. No one spoke or even moved.

Zen decided to brave breaking the silence. "Dominican rats must be special."

"What?" Malone didn't shift his gaze from Lewis's face.

"You didn't mention any old rat's ass, so those bad boys in the Dominican Republic must be something else." Zen shrugged when Malone looked at her. Anger seemed to battle with confusion in his dark eyes. "Random thought."

Commander Okoro took the chance to step in. "I'm sure we can reach some kind of détente, gentlemen. We have quite a situation on our hands. The good news is, we don't have two murders."

"Excellent point, commander," Chief Collier blurted out. He shrank back against the corner when Malone looked his way.

"No, what we have is one government agency obstructing the investigation of another. I won't have it."

Lewis unfolded his arms. "If it helps, I was going to tell you."

"What do you think?" Malone shouted with enough force to make Lewis blink as if he'd been slapped.

At the touch of a silicone keypad, Malone turned on a screen set in the wall to his right. Everyone turned to stare at four people looking back at them. Three men and a woman wore unique variations of displeasure on their faces. Zen recognized her boss's wide office in OSI headquarters. He'd recently moved to a larger one. Clive sat at one end of the oblong table in a corner of his office. Seated in the other chairs were Zen's father and Gen. Nelson, Malone's commanding officer. Zen didn't recognize the woman. Clive's gray-blue gaze flickered to Zen only for a second. Then he looked at Malone again.

"Introductions first," Clive said in a clipped tone. "I'm Clive Anderson, director of OSI. James Batiste is with the Bureau of Intelligence and Research. Gen. Nelson with the Pentagon, and Ms. Seals, NASA Deputy Associate Administrator."

Zen gazed at her father. James Batiste look her in the eyes without a twitch to betray his thoughts. Which told Zen quite a bit was going to be left unsaid. She wondered if he would call her later. Maybe not. Surprisingly, the woman stood first. She wore a dark gray suit consisting of a tailored jacket with matching pencil skirt. Her honey-blond hair was neatly styled and brushed her shoulders.

"The information contained in Ms. Suri's chips must be secured. We can't allow anyone with less than top-level clearance to have access. Is that understood?"

"Yes," Lewis said with confidence.

Zen noted that Ms. Seals recognized Imirah's personhood. And that Lewis didn't hesitate in answering. He had just reported mission accomplished to her father. Ms. Seals continued to drone on about the importance of the information to the US and world space program. Proper analysis had to be done before certain facts were released to the public. Blah, blah, blah. Zen paid more attention to the faces of those allowing her to speak. Finally, the woman ended her spiel and stood to one side. When James stood, Zen leaned forward in her chair. Chief Collier and Commander Okoro seemed determined to fade into shadows.

"As you know, by global agreement through UN negotiations, no humanoids have been sanctioned for duties in space. Obviously, private space industries decided that those rules were outdated. We can't criminally prosecute anyone for reasons I won't get into." James wore a suitably grave expression.

"In other words, the government helped build the things," Chief Collier mumbled. He flinched, blinking rapidly, when the others in the room looked at him. "I mean... I didn't—"

"I strongly suggest you shut up," Commander Okoro said quietly.

Her father must not have heard the exchange. He went on explaining that Ewan Lewis should be given leeway to do as he saw fit. "With limitations, of course. Any information pertinent to my daughter's investigation must be shared, Special Agent Lewis."

"Yes, sir. Of course." Lewis turned to Zen with a half-smile. It froze in place at the scowl she gave him in return.

"So far, we don't have any information that impacts decisions Major Gen. Ramirez should make regarding LMPD. But if that changes, the same applies. Information related to failures with policing on the lunar colony or In Situ must be shared with Major Gen. Ramirez. Understood?"

"In real time," Malone put in. "Delays have as much impact as not giving us the whole story."

Zen stepped forward. "And we do want the *whole* story."

"We're all here because we work together," James replied evenly.

Clive tapped James's arm to take over. "A comprehensive report on what we know so far is being finalized. The White House, UN, and the European Space Agency will get a copy. The latter two minus classified intel, naturally."

The rest of the meeting consisted of instructions to Zen, Malone, and the rest of those gathered in Chief Collier's office. Commander Okoro was to coordinate private security services with his space command officers. Zen would be tasked with shadowing Lewis since Imirah Suri had been so close to the murder victim.

General Nelson, who had been silent, stood straight. His uniform, decorated with three gold stars and other Air Force badges, looked impressive. His iron-gray hair added to his air of authority. "Ramirez will assume control of LMPD. Director Zeringue at the DOJ agrees."888

Malone gave a crisp nod. "Yes, sir."

"Which means nobody at my old agency wants to be shot into space," Zen murmured.

"Hold on now." Chief Collier wedged between Malone and Lewis to confront the screen. "With all due respect, Gen. Nelson, LMPD officers have been instrumental in helping Special Agents Batiste and Navarro since they arrived. Under my direction three lunar colonies have enjoyed low crime. As has the Star Flight Space Station, or In Situ as you call it. My record as chief of police speaks for itself."

"Yes, it does. And what it says isn't cause for bragging," James rumbled before the general could replied.

Gen. Nelson continued as though James hadn't spoken. "Under the circumstances, it would be better for you to step aside and allow Ramirez to do a full review. Standard procedure for a full administrative assessment. Commander Okoro will provide support to the LMPD. I understand several officers have been detained?"

"Only four so far, and we've taken the lead in cleaning up our own ranks," Chief Collier protested. "I'm sure Major Gen. Ramirez is a fine Air Force officer, but I know my department and jurisdiction. I can assure you I will—"

"Chief Collier, given information so far, this decision has been made. You're not relieved of duties. You will assist Ramirez."

Chief Collier's mouth worked as he sputtered in outrage. "You mean I'll be his errand boy. I've served in the military police for over fifteen years."

"So, you understand chain of command and standard operating procedures." Gen. Nelson's calm expression turned to stone as he stared at Chief Collier.

The message rang loud. Keep talking and Collier would find himself without a job, recalled to Earth, and possibly court-martialed. He was still a member of the armed forces, after all. Collier's red face turned pale. He nodded but wisely chose not to say more. Commander Okoro gave him a look of sympathy as he tugged his arm. Collier faded into the background again. He wiped away sweat beaded on his bulbous nose.

"Sirs, and ma'am," Lewis spoke up and nodded to Ms. Seals. "We can review what I've learned. Space-Cor reactivated Imirah Suri. They didn't have the chance to fully debrief her, though. Their people didn't have the expertise to access data. However, they did use an In Situ staff person who worked in the humanoid project before."

"What?" Clive snapped.

"Money talks, sir," Lewis replied mildly.

"You said the chip is secured," James said.

"Yes... inside Ms. Suri. Trying to remove it would cause permanent damage. In a manner of speaking, we'd kill her. Again." Lewis cast a side-eye at Zen and looked at her father again.

"Damn it," James mumbled and rubbed his jaw.

"Now you see the issue with using humanoid xenbots," Ms. Seals snapped. "No wonder human rights activists would eat us alive if they knew."

"A discussion for another time, Amanda," Gen. Nelson said low.

"Do you know what will happen if this gets out? We'll catch it from all sides. Russia, China, hell even our allies will be up in arms." Ms. Seals glared at the three men.

James pulled her aside to murmur in her ear. Ms. Seals shook a finger in his face. To Zen's amazement, her father continued to reason with her in a calm manner. The diplomat in him had taken over from the spy master. Gen. Nelson listened to their exchange with a deep frown. Clive's solid frame filled the screen, the intense discussion behind him an inaudible backdrop.

"Commander Okoro, I need to speak with Batiste and Ramirez. Take Collier with you," Clive said, not even trying for tact.

"Understood."

Commander Okoro pushed the chastened police chief ahead of him. Collier looked as if he'd throw up at any moment. He glanced at Lewis as they left. The Brit didn't make a move to follow them. Lewis assumed a relaxed position leaning against Chief Collier's desk, his arms folded.

Clive wore a tight expression as his gaze tracked the men out of the door. Then he looked at Zen pointedly. "I'm sure you realize what's at stake. The potential for an international uproar."

"An understatement," Lewis said low. His sideways smile almost suggested he relished the excitement.

"Destabilization of global agreements it took years for us to reach," James added in a voice rough as gravel. His gaze settled on Lewis a second before he looked at Zen.

"What do you suggest we do next?"

"Contain that damn reporter, for one thing," Gen. Nelson snapped.

Ms. Seals cleared her throat. "Make sure there are no leaks on your team. Despite the general, um, distaste for Clairmont, the man has journalistic integrity."

"Humph." Gen. Nelson crossed his arms but said no more.

"He won't release any news that he can't confirm. That includes rumors and speculation. Make sure any of your witnesses are kept away from him," Ms. Seals went on.

"That means detain Imirah Suri and Emme Gaida," Clive added.

"Will do," Zen said with a nod.

"Find out if Suri, Gaida, or both killed Ahmad. That means Special Agent Batiste will take the lead in her interrogation before she's brought back to Earth," Clive said.

Zen glanced to her left at Lewis and then turned to the screen to look at her father. "Yes, sir."

"Report to me at seventeen hundred hours," James barked at Lewis. He didn't look at all happy.

"Of course, Director Batiste," Lewis said in a calm voice.

"Well, that was... something else," Malone said. "The pressure is on not to trigger a world war."

Lewis put a hand on Malone's broad shoulder. "No worries, my friend. We'll blame it all on corporate greed. Takes the spotlight off what your government did. Always works."

Zen smiled at him and pointed a finger at his nose. "*My* government? You work for my father. And you've been an American citizen since 2079. Let's not forget your fingerprints are all over this case."

"Does she always go for the throat?" Lewis said to Malone in a mock stage-whisper.

"Uh-huh," Malone replied.

"Don't tell me. You'll take her side if push comes to shove." Lewis let out a short laugh of genuine merriment when Malone didn't reply. "And we're off to question Ms. Suri."

"I'll do all of the talking first. Then you can take a crack at her about being here and Space-Cor," Zen said.

"I'll be with LMPD officers. Another fun task. Call me when you finish. We'll coordinate a meet-up then," Malone said.

"Sounds good," Zen replied and turned to Lewis.

"After you, my lady." Lewis swept out a hand in dramatic fashion.

"Give me strength," Zen grumbled as she swept past him.

They passed groups of LMPD and Space Command officers as they went down three hallways to the small interview rooms. Zen was surprised the find the LMPD offices on Star Flight were larger than she'd noticed before. They passed six with glass windows. A few civilian employees eyed them in curiosity.

"Your Sgt. Young should join her colleagues for the meeting," Lewis said just as they arrived at the observation room. His touch activated a panel and he tapped until the door clicked open.

"Do you have access codes to every to every part of this place memorized?" Zen eyed him.

"Pretty much. Saves time and trouble. Especially when you don't know who to trust," Lewis said smoothly. "Shall we?"

Zen walked ahead of him into the narrow space. The door whisked closed. They looked through the window where Imirah Suri sat. Sgt. Young leaned against a wall, a paper cup in one hand. Suri puffed on a cigarette. Lewis smiled when Zen glanced a puzzled look at him.

"Yes, she's part biological being with some of the same habits. Or faults, you might say." Lewis nodded. "She's a perfect specimen. I've tracked her serial number."

"I thought you said..." Zen raised an eyebrow at him.

"Human and humanoid activists assert she's a 'person.' I still think of her as equipment. There is a QR code on her scalp. To most, it looks like a birthmark. She originated in a Chinese incubator lab. They have ties to Space-Cor. Still unraveling the tangled web. The same lab has several Chinese-American scientists who worked for Space-Cor in the US. One was a top researcher at Tetra for fifteen years before she retired."

"So, stolen tech?"

"Not clear. Under two of those agreements your dear father referred to, information has been shared freely between nations. Humanitarian grounds." Lewis leaned forward, both hands on a narrow desk facing the window.

"What?"

"Humanoids have potential for use in situations hazardous to humans. Such as delivering medications to undeveloped areas in pandemics. Or relief work in areas with severe droughts or food shortages. They're not vulnerable to bugs that affect humans. They don't need food or water, at least not like humans. But there are less benign uses as well." Lewis stood straight but continued to stare at Imirah.

"Like as soldiers, I suppose," Zen said.

"Hmm, not so much. Don't pay attention to those sci-fi movies. They're too valuable to waste being blown to bits. Besides, modern military operations are remote for the most part," Lewis replied in a mild tone.

Zen gazed at him with interest. His short, light brown hair curled away from his forehead. She imagined he'd look like a medieval Knight of the Round Table if he let it grow longer.

"You were SIS."

"Military first. Then Secret Intelligence Service, yes. I've enjoyed a varied career. By the way, I have dual citizenship," Lewis said without looked at her.

"You don't look much older than me."

Lewis turned to her. His blue eyes sparkled with amusement. "Why, thank you very much. I've advanced quickly. My skill helped by family connections. Now, do you want to grill me further or should you reserve energy for our guest?"

Zen continued to gaze at him for a few seconds. Then she gave a sharp nod and marched to the door. It slid open as she approached, the auto function operating only from the inside. Lewis followed her the few feet to the next door. Sgt. Young stood straight when they entered the room. She looked at Zen first and then Lewis. He gave her a quick wink and a smirk when she rolled her eyes.

"I don't know why I'm here. You probably accessed my internal drive already. Yěmán," Imirah muttered with a glare at Zen.

"Chinese for barbarian," Lewis said with good humor.

"Who is less human? Eh? You want to use us to do your dirty work. Look at what you do to each other even in this day. Barely better than when you lived in caves eating bloody raw meat." Imirah let loose a string of words in three languages.

"I'm guessing those weren't compliments," Zen drawled.

"I'm adding them to my repertoire," Lewis joked. He pressed his lips together and placed a finger on them when Zen glanced a warning.

"Ms. Suri, you were hired to get information from Hassan Ahmad. What went wrong?" Zen said.

"Nothing. I'm good at anything I do. Hassan talked with the right amount of liquor and drugs in him. He said he'd leave his wife, give me all kinds of luxury. He wouldn't need her family's money anymore. As if I'd exchange one form of bondage for another," Imirah said. Contempt twisted her attractive features.

Zen studied her in silence for a few moments. "Then why kill him?"

"I didn't. But I suppose you're going to tell everyone I did. So you can keep your reputation for solving the great crimes of our age. Oh wait, you got it wrong once. Your daddy and daddy surrogate fixed your big mistake. Putting the wrong person in prison isn't a good look for a superhero. Emme told me all about Peter." Imirah wore a smug expression as she gazed at Zen in defiance.

Zen didn't bite. "Who did?"

"Did what?"

"Who killed Hassan Ahmad?" Zen said calmly.

"You're the detective, so detect," Imirah tossed back and crossed her shapely legs. Through the form-fitting space fabric of her jumpsuit, she still looked like an exotic dancer.

"Fine. I'm good with taking the path of least resistance." Zen took out her tablet and tapped in notes.

Imirah uncrossed her legs and sat forward. "What does that mean?"

"You were with him last the night he died."

"So was Emme. So were a lot of people—"

"You were the last one with him. Alone. Your DNA is all over his body," Zen continued without looking up.

Imirah huffed in anger. "Emme turned on me. Some friend. Look, he was alive when I left."

"I see why Ahmad took the bait. She sounds pretty convincing." Zen glanced sideways at Lewis and then at her tablet again.

"Of course she would," Lewis replied in his cool British manner.

"You're not going to pin this on me just to make your job easier. I've got rights!" Imirah slapped the table with both palms. She flinched when Sgt. Young came away from the wall to stand over her. "I didn't kill him."

"I'd have more confidence in your protestations of innocence if you told me the truth. *All of it*," Zen added with force. She put down the tablet and looked at Imirah. She could see her mind working. "Before you spin another set of lies, I know about Space-Cor."

Imirah's brown eyes went wide for a second. Then a wary look settled into place. "So they sponsored me for entertainment purposes. So what? Sex work isn't illegal."

"Space-Cor paid you to have sex with Hassan Ahmad. To get information about lava caverns and Helium 3. Information that is worth a lot. You're no uneducated streetwalker. You recognized the high value of what he knew. So, you decided to get him high on you, liquor, and drugs to get the details. Then Ahmad became a nuisance. You didn't need him anymore. In fact, with him gone multiple buyers would *have* to deal with you."

Zen didn't turn when Lewis sucked in a sharp breath as she finished. He radiated unease. He wasn't thrilled that she'd come close to putting the pieces together. She'd examine what his reaction meant later. Zen had no illusions about calling her father to get at the truth. Imirah said nothing for a time. Zen assumed a composed façade even though her brain spun through theories, fragments, and suspicions. Sgt. Young cleared her throat. Zen glanced at her.

"Yes, sergeant."

"We checked video feed. The cloud data was edited but not traceable. No cameras in the suite where she claims Ahmad was still alive. Though someone ordered more drinks once she was gone. The hotel wait staff left the tray in the foyer as instructed." Sgt. Young looked down at Imirah.

"See? Told you somebody else killed him. Or he snuffed himself on drugs, booze, and freaky sex with another banger. He couldn't get enough of all three." Imirah's tense posture eased.

"Sgt. Young, that tampering you mentioned. Could it mean someone wanted to make it seem like he was still alive? Add video of Ms. Suri leaving and altered the time post on that part of the feed?" Zen said, her gaze on Imirah.

"Yep."

"See? Proves nothing. Meanwhile, we've got a tidy list of evidence against..." Zen leaned forward to point at Imirah. "*You.*"

"You can't frame me for something I didn't do." Imirah looked at the glass to her right. "I want to talk to someone in charge, over *her.*"

"Let me—" Lewis chopped off his speech when Zen waved at him to be quiet.

"Pay attention, Ms. Suri. I don't have to frame you. Motive, access to the victim, forensic evidence. Like you said, my reputation for solving murders will only be enhanced. And you delivered the goods to me on a platinum-plated serving tray," Zen said, her voice level.

Imirah transferred her intense gaze from the window back to Zen. "Space-Cor and the US government will have something to say about it. I'm too valuable to be destroyed. Isn't that right, Special Agent Ewan Lewis with whatever secretive counterintelligence agency you work for these days?"

"What the hell..." Sgt. Young whispered as she stared at Lewis.

Zen continued to look at her. "Ms. Suri was recruited by Space-Cor to romance Ahmad, but also worked for the US government. Lewis, or someone like him, contacted her. Killing Ahmad wasn't part of the assignment from Space-Cor or the government. But you have an entrepreneurial spirit and went into business for yourself."

"The best secret weapon is being underestimated," Imirah said.

"You got the information..." Zen's voice trailed off as she met the woman's calm gaze. "But you found out even more than Ahmad knew. Or potential he didn't recognize. You've been upgraded."

"We upgrade ourselves," Imirah hissed and pressed her full lips together. She glanced at Lewis but said nothing more.

Lewis looked rattled, even off balance for the first time. His pale cheeks flushed. He looked from Imirah to Zen several times. Then he shoved back his chair and stood. "We need to speak alone. Suspend the interview."

"Ma'am?" Sgt. Young studied the lanky Brit with distrust.

"Interview suspended at..." Zen glanced down to the thin tablet computer. "Twenty-three hundred Earth hours. Sgt. Young will remain with Ms. Suri until we resume."

Sgt. Young nodded, though she looked equal parts puzzled and eager to follow them out. Instead, she stayed behind as Zen followed Lewis out of the room. The door clicked in place behind them. Lewis didn't stop or turn to Zen. He marched ahead to the observation room next door, let them in, and locked the door. When Lewis whirled to face Zen, she stepped back. He didn't speak for a few seconds but studied Zen.

"The rest of what she might say is too sensitive to be recorded. Not here and now. It's more critical than a murder investigation," Lewis said. He ran long fingers through his hair.

"What's in the lava cavern, Lewis?"

"I don't know and I don't want to know. This goes above Clive and your father, Zen. All I know is we have instructions to contain the situation." Lewis rubbed his jaw hard enough to turn it red for a few seconds.

"Or?" Zen stepped closer to him. For the first time, Lewis looked human. His unflappable exterior had been tossed aside.

"More people will die. I wasn't supposed to reactivate her, at least they didn't expect me to. I suspect even Director Batiste was left in the dark on this one. Tetra is more powerful than either of us suspected."

"Okay. This is bad shit then," Zen said carefully.

"This is very bad shit. Ahmad wasn't supposed to die, that part is true. I don't think Imirah killed him, not on purpose. I think..." Lewis blew out air.

"When she tried to go into business for herself, someone decided to kill them both. Well, deactivate Imirah. She can be, um, recycled for lack of a more tasteful description. You suspect Space-Cor."

"At first. The most obvious answer." Lewis's voice was muted and grim.

Zen studied him as seconds ticked by and he didn't answer. Instead, he stared through the glass at Imirah. The lithe beauty gazed back though she couldn't see them. "You think the US government sent someone to take them both out."

"I don't know for sure," Lewis said quickly. "Maybe you're right. She killed him like you said. The simple explanation. I've got the data. We have the ability to destroy her and—"

"Wait, what? You're talking about more than 'deactivation.' You're going to put her in a tech compactor like discarded machinery? She's not just a hunk of alloy!" Zen punched his shoulder. "You heartless piece of crap. I don't care what she's done, if you think I'm going along with—"

"It's not what I want, damn it! It's what they're prepared to do to her and anyone else who get in the way," Lewis snapped. He paced around the small room.

"So, very bad shit doesn't begin to cover what we've stepped into," Zen said, her heart pounding. But not with fear. She was getting pissed off. "Is someone threatening my father?"

"No. Not yet. Not if we handle this right." Lewis stopped pacing to face Zen.

"If by handling it right you mean cover up two murders..." Zen shook her head at him. Lewis stared back without speaking. "I know who my father is and what he's capable of doing. Anyone who comes for him is a fool. I don't care how powerful they think they are, and that includes whoever your shadow boss is, Lewis."

"I only work for James." Lewis didn't blink. "I'll do what it takes to fix this. For him."

Zen studied him for a long moment, wondering what her father had done to inspire such dogged loyalty. Then she decided maybe not knowing would help her sleep better. "What and who are we talking about?"

"I'm not sure. All I know is three powerful governments and two big global conglomerates want what Ahmad claimed he had. He was stupid enough to overplay his hand. Dangled the prize under the wrong noses then snatched it back for a bigger paycheck." Lewis leaned against the desk again, palms flat. "Imirah Suri doesn't realize how much trouble she's in."

"Sgt. Young will keep her safe here. She's weeded out the bad players on her team." Zen turned to gaze at Imirah as well.

"Collier will be livid she's making changes without him. You know he's part of the crimes here," Lewis said.

Zen hissed out air in anger. "Collier can kiss my asteroid. He looked the other way to keep his career moving forward. Crimes of omission."

"He accepted a few kickbacks from Space-Cor to be very lenient about cargo being examined closely. His more enterprising subordinates got their hands a bit dirtier," Lewis said with a grunt.

"Fool."

Lewis nodded. "A very unlucky one at that. He surely didn't count on being exposed so far from home."

"They had to know NASA and the DOJ would get involved. Clive and OSI aren't known for being easy to get around. And we have deep resources. Not to brag or anything," Zen added when Lewis glanced at her sideways. "Whatever Ahmad had or knew is worth the risk of a homicide investigation."

"Money, power. The usual enticements," Lewis said, his debonair English gentleman accent back in place.

"You're sure my father won't catch heat in any form?" Despite what she'd said, Zen knew even powerful men like her father could be harmed.

"As you said, nothing he can't handle. I'll have his back."

"I have a feeling anyone dumb enough to try you two would be in serious trouble."

Lewis let a sly grin spread across his face. "I live for it. But... the director prefers prevention to a cure."

Zen felt a worry about her father recede. She should have known better. More likely she should be concerned about what James was up to. "We need to find out what's in those lunar caverns. And the location of Helium 3."

"You must be joking. Are you talking about..." Lewis's cool blue eyes went wide.

"A moon walk is exactly what I'm talking about." Zen said.

Chapter 13

Sgt. Young shocked everyone but Zen at the efficient way she took over running the LMPD. As acting chief, and with Malone's authorization, she suspended three officers. Four others came clean about petty misdeeds that didn't rise to the level of outright crimes. Chief Collier and his family would soon be packed off on a shuttle flight to Earth. Commander Okoro cooperated with Sgt. Young, albeit in an amused fashion at first. One crack about the kids running the nursery brought a clapback so sharp, the big man blinked as though punched in the nose. Getting two powerful conglomerates on Star Flight in check, cleaning up the LMPD, and tightening government control was background noise to Zen. She kept her focus on Ahmad.

She was back on the moon, along with Sgt. Young, Malone, and Lewis. Commander Okoro had remained on the space station to emphasize the new order there. After four hours of restless sleep, Zen got out of bed. Nervous energy surged as she went through her morning routine. After a cup of coffee, one tasteless bagel with cream cheese, and a blueberry yogurt, she called Astra via satellite link on her tablet. Data rates be damned. She needed to forget this place for a few minutes.

"Mama, you sound so clear, like you're in the next room!" Astra looked back at her and giggled. The old joke was one kids enjoyed—imitating their elders still not used to interplanetary travel.

"If only," Zen retorted. "How's school?"

"Good. You look tired, and..." Astra's pretty, smooth face came closer to the screen and then she sat back. "Off. Like something is wrong."

Zen wore a tired smile. "You mean other than a long flight and a murder case?"

"You know what I mean," Astra shot back. "Save the 'I can't discuss an investigation' speech. Something is complicating your case. It's written all over you."

"Not unusual when you're uncovering lies and half-truths, Astra. You have to turn over a lot of rocks to solve a case. Stuff crawls out that people didn't want to be exposed to sunlight," Zen replied.

Astra sighed. "Wish I could help."

"I thought you wanted to spend time saving the planet from climate change?" Zen teased to get her off the subject of murder.

"Earth is connected to what happens in space, mama," Astra replied.

"You know, I heard that somewhere." Zen laughed when Astra twisted her cute features to make a face back at her.

"Instead, I'm stuck listening to lectures. This one visiting professor is so boring. Not to be harsh or anything, but her voice is super annoying. And she has no sense of humor." Astra gave a perfect teenage eyeroll.

"What's the subject?"

"Theories in space habitat development. Mostly speculation since technology is still developing." Astra heaved a frustrated sigh.

"You have to walk before you can fly, honey. What sounds dull now is the foundation you'll need later on. Pay attention. It's not as useless as it sounds," Zen said.

"You sound like Grandmother." Astra giggled again.

"Okay, now you're just being cruel," Zen wisecracked. "Lucky for you I'm too far away to give you a good shake."

"But you did. 'Astra, education is about being prepared for the future. Pay attention because you never know when that information will make your career,' " Astra tilted her chin up and pointed a finger, just as Enola Chastain Batiste would do. The retired educator had given that speech more than a few times.

"You've got her down to perfection," Zen said.

"Yeah. Seriously, though, your assignments are cooler than mine. I only study about quantum physics, oxygen generation, and space gravity. You get to hang out with the inventor of that stuff. What's it like working with Dr. Navarro? My classmate almost peed on himself with delight when I mentioned you worked with him. The guy's a legend." Astra's eyes were bright with excitement.

"Very... different from what I expected," Zen drawled.

"No hard feelings about you almost getting him a life sentence, I hope. You were just doing your job. And he did have some pretty seedy hobbies. I'm not asking about the murder of that guy, so you can tell me. What happened with Dr. Navarro is public record. You and he were all over the news."

"Forget about his 'hobbies.' Concentrate on school and enjoying your college years," Zen said with a stern look. The last thing she intended to do was discuss sex robots and sadomasochism with her daughter.

"Mama, I'll be eighteen in a few months. I keep up with what's going on. There was a really good story about Star Flight and In Situ from this reporter on the space station. He says Hassan Ahmad had uncovered some kind of conspiracy. The guy's widow has threatened to sue him and his press company for defamation." Astra became more animated than she had been talking about her courses.

"Maybe it will keep him busy," Zen muttered, her thoughts turning to Clairmont.

"What?" Astra blinked at her.

"Nothing. Just tune all of that out and be a student. Hang with your friends, make fun of your professors, and party. Those days will be fond memories sooner than you think. But not too much partying," Zen added quickly when Astra's expression turned impish.

"You can't take it back now. Mama said paar-tay!" Astra stood and executed a dip and slide.

"Maybe I'll give Jordan a call to make a quick visit." Zen tilted her head to one side and crossed her arms.

"Okay, okay. Calling Daddy on me is going too far. He's so serious these days. Anyway, I promise to not bring shame to the family name. Hey, maybe you can talk Dr. Navarro into coming here to guest lecture. Won't my profs be impressed if I make it happen." Astra's brown eyes lit up with anticipation as she gazed at Zen.

"I'm pretty sure he'll be busy," Zen drawled.

"Oh c'mon. He's taught whole courses a full term at some of the most prestigious universities. Harvard, Penn State, and countries overseas like—"

"Astra, I've got more on my mind than enhancing your rep," Zen said.

Brianne appeared at Astra's shoulder. She grinned and waved. "Hi, Auntie Zee. Don't worry, I'm keeping her on the path of righteousness."

"Thank you, Bree. I better get back to it. I just wanted to see your smiling faces," Zen said with a smile.

Her niece and daughter lifted her spirits with their youthful energy and playfulness. Still, when their images winked off Zen felt the weight of her case come back. She looked at herself in the mirror. The long-sleeve t-shirt she wore had the In Situ logo on one shoulder. Matching slacks were of the same sage-green color. Zen tucked the shirt in, put on a brown belt that held a clip for the Space Command comm unit she'd been loaned. Then she took a deep breath in preparation for what promised to be a tense meeting. She jumped when a solid knock sounded on the door to her quarters. When she opened it, Sgt. Young stood wearing a sour face.

"You're already in a mood this early, sergeant. I guess you're not here to deliver good news." Zen waved her inside and shut the door.

"I can't find Dr. Navarro, ma'am. Or Emme Gaida." Sgt. Young blew out a harsh breath.

Zen froze in place. "What?"

"Back when we were at the port and found Imirah, remember I was supposed to be looking for them. I stumbled on her instead. That, plus dealing with LMPD issues I forgot about them for a minute. Then things settled in the last ten hours, so I sent one of my officers to his quarters. Tried to call him. No answer. On a hunch, I sent another officer to Find Gaida. She's in hiding." Sgt. Young paced as she talked. "Damn it."

"You think they're together."

"Got to be. He wouldn't know all of the nooks and holes at Star Flight, but she does. Why though?" Sgt. Young stopped and faced Zen.

"Maybe Emme is scared of what Imirah has told us about her. She could have been in on what happened to Ahmad."

"But why would Dr. Navarro…" Sgt. Young hissed out air when Zen gave her a look. "He's risking everything for Emme Gaida because he's still hooked on her."

"Love makes people do stupid things, Sgt. Young."

"More like kinky lust. The two get confused," Sgt. Young replied with a snort.

"You're an old soul in a twenty-something body, Wyvette," Zen quipped and then turned serious again. "I think he really does love her."

"Yeah, well, helping her run from the law out here isn't a smart move. One thing for sure, I'll find them. It's not like they can hop on a plane, bus, or train to get away." Sgt. Young waved a hand. "Just one more damn thing to pull at my attention. I'll be tempted to lock both of them in a cell and forget the access code. Keep 'em on ice until things get sorted out."

Zen sighed. "The last thing I need right now is my partner to become another problem to solve. But I don't see what you could charge them with, sarge."

"Felony stupid should be on the books. But I'll settle for interfering with an ongoing investigation. Yeah, obstruction sounds sweet." Sgt. Young took out her own regulation LMPD tablet. She tapped in a few commands and smiled. "I found the federal statute for space criminal and civil law enforcement."

"Let's just concentrate on finding them and leave the consequences for later," Zen replied in a dry tone.

"Humph. Got me wasting time chasing them," Sgt. Young grumbled. "He's supposed to be helping sort out this mess."

"Tell me about it." Zen started to say more when her comm let out a series of ringtones. She looked at the ID display. "I'm late for the meeting."

"Good luck," Sgt. Young said in a grave voice.

"Sheesh, you look like I'm on my way to a trial by combat," Zen joked.

"Ma'am, Commander Okoro flew back here for the meeting. I don't know who, but somebody snitched." Sgt. Young was interrupted by an alert chime on her comm as well. "I better go. I could whip Chief Collier's ass for the mess he left behind. Call if you need me."

"I want to know the minute you find Peter and Emme. I want to put my fingers on *both* of them. They know more than they've been telling us." Zen scowled at the thought of her partner.

"Will do. For what it's worth, I think you'll win." Sgt. Young gave Zen a quick grin before she left. She started talking to an officer on her comm even before she was in the hallway.

Zen watched her stride away, bolstered to have the young policewoman as an ally. She sure couldn't count on her partner to be one. Zen left the lunar hotel room. She tapped an updated entry code to secure it. Just in case. Though she had a feeling any kind of intrusion attempted would be digital. She double-checked the firewall on her devices, too. Then she headed for the Space Command headquarters. During her fifteen-minute trip, Zen used the time to put on her game face. A Space Command officer, a freckle-faced, redheaded woman, met her in the lobby.

"This way, ma'am," the woman said with a crisp nod.

"Here we go," Zen mumbled as she followed the officer's straight back to a large situation room. The officer opened the door for Zen and then closed it with a firm thump.

"Morning, everyone." Zen said.

She affected a cool smile that faded quickly into a "down to business" expression. She sat around a crescent-shaped table. Malone, Commander Okoro, Lewis, Dr. McCoy, and Dr. Gregson wore matching stern faces as they each offered their own greetings. Two senior Space Command officers Zen didn't recognize moved around the room adjusting equipment. Everyone except Dr. McCoy had steaming mugs before them. She instead drank from a water bottle. Zen sat forward, ready for tough questions, but Dr. McCoy spoke before anyone else.

"I have news. The third postmortem results indicate the man we thought died of natural causes didn't. He was suffocated. Same manner as Hassan Ahmad. His killer knows what he's doing." Dr. McCoy leaned back into the leather chair again.

"Or she," Dr. Gregson added with a pointed look around the table at the others.

Commander Okoro, hands clasped on the tabletop, spoke up. "The man had recently signed on with ChemCo. He knew Ahmad. They worked on two projects before, which is why he was hired."

"Not a coincidence," Lewis put in. "Three murders."

"Imirah Suri isn't dead," Dr. Gregson rumbled. "I don't know who authorized her reactivation, but it was ill-advised, to say the least."

"We need answers. Data chips only provide so much. She'd found a way to hack her internal system. Not everything is recorded. For all her AI features, Ms. Suri is still sentient. She has human qualities. Not exactly emotions the way you might think, but interrogation was warranted." Lewis gazed at Dr. Gregson for a few seconds before looking away.

"She's a murdering machine. Something out of a third-rate sci-fi movie. Exactly what those anti-science idiots preach about." Dr. Gregson jabbed a finger in Lewis's direction as if he was at fault for everything.

"Why wasn't my team allowed to conduct her postmortem? Her body being stolen is the most bizarre turn in these events. And that's saying something." Dr. McCoy gazed at Zen first and then Malone. "What aren't you telling us?"

"Beyond the murder of Hassan Ahmad, Ms. Suri has information relevant to another inquiry. That's all I can reveal," Malone said.

"Why do I get the feeling the words 'highly classified' are about to be tossed around," Dr. Gregson snapped. "We all have security clearance. In Situ staff work on some of the most sensitive research missions."

"Then you're familiar with the phrase 'need to know,' " Lewis shot back.

"Don't patronize me," Dr. Gregson countered. "In Situ is a highly critical program that benefits multiple US government agencies. Including the military. Probably most of the technology or intel you use comes from *our work*."

"No one would disagree," Commander Okoro put in.

Dr. Gregson pressed on before he could continue. "It's not an overstatement to say anything that stalls our work will impact humanity."

"Yes, Dr. Gregson is quite right," Commander Okoro put in before Lewis could reply. He spread his hands in a peace-making gesture. "Let's not forget the true mission of the work being done here."

"Exactly the reason we think NASA should transition back to a focus on research and development to improve life. Not stuff pockets and turn billionaires into trillionaires," Dr. McCoy added with force.

"Only NASA, the White House, and the UN Global Space committee can make that weighty decision. In the meantime, those of us who live and work off-world must make sure our people are safe. I think we can all agree that hotels and businesses are here to stay for the foreseeable future," Commander Okoro replied, his tone of reasoned diplomacy enhanced by his basso voice.

Dr. Gregson's tight expression eased a bit at having someone agree with him. "Yes, of course, but—"

"Let's not get way off track. We're here to get Special Agent Batiste's latest update on the investigation," Malone put in before he could finish. He glanced at Zen.

Zen considered her words carefully and decided. "It looks like Imirah Suri is responsible for Hassan Ahmad's death."

"I knew it," Dr. Gregson said with a scowl. "The twin evils of greed and debauchery."

"How very Victorian of you," Lewis murmured. His thin lips twitched with amusement at the heated look Dr. Gregson gave him.

Malone shot a warning glance at Lewis. "Go on, Special Agent Batiste."

"It may be that she didn't intend to kill him. Her goal was to get information. I have to follow additional lines of inquiry." Zen cleared her throat. Everyone gazed at her in anticipation. They were waiting to hear more. Her mind worked fast to choose her next move. Sgt. Young's entrance into the room gave her the breathing space she needed.

"Ma'am." Sgt. Young paused and took in the grim faces of authority as they all turned to her. She hesitated before speaking. "Sorry to interrupt, but I need Dr. Batiste. It's urgent."

"Then spit it out, woman," Dr. Gregson said. "The people in this room are charged with running Earth's first substantial space habitation. We need to know details of—"

"And you will, I can assure you," Malone cut in smoothly. "As with any criminal investigation, facts must be verified. Special Agents Batiste and Navarro have to be given space to solidify evidence. Premature statements can cause more harm than good."

"Indeed. But may we hear the request Dr. Batiste had for us?" Commander Okoro gazed at Zen with curiosity

"Ma'am," Sgt. Young put in before Zen replied.

Zen gazed at her for a second and stood. "Excuse me, but Sgt. Young wouldn't have come if it wasn't something time-critical."

Sgt. Young nodded and opened the door. "Sorry again."

Commander Okoro gave her a supportive smile. "Doing your job, no need to apologize."

"Thank God someone at LMPD finally is. We wouldn't be in this predicament if Collier..." Dr. Gregson's voice trailed into silence when Commander Okoro gave him a withering glare.

Sgt. Young scurried after Zen into the hallway. She blew out air when the door whisked closed behind them. "Whew! I didn't mean to cause any more trouble for you, ma'am. But you really need to hear this."

"You were right on time, sergeant. There were too many people in the room," Zen looked at the smooth surface of the wall as if she could see them.

"My grandmother has a favorite expression from her day. 'Shit just got real.' "

Sgt. Young stopped talking when two Space Command officers rounded a corner from another hallway. They seemed more intent on their conversation. She pulled Zen farther from the situation room.

"You found Peter?" Zen said low.

"I've narrowed down where they might be. The officer in charge is smart; she can handle the search of the last two sectors. You need to see what I found. Sync your earbuds to my tablet." Sgt. Young removed a tablet from the duty belt around her slim waist. Then she handed it to Zen.

Video played of Peter leading Emme along corridors used by technicians to maintain the space station. He knew which panels to remove. They stopped at an alcove set in one to catch their breath. The audio came through clear.

"When I get my hands on you, Navarro! I might end up in a cell for murder," Zen blurted. She tamped down her anger and backed up the video to parts she'd missed with her outburst.

"My junior officers and In Situ maintenance techs managed to place cameras with mics in more places. Lucky for us they beat Dr. Navarro and Emme to that section. I didn't expect them to head for the water generation and recycling sector. Pretty dangerous if you don't know what you're doing." Sgt. Young studied the images on the tablet when Zen handed it back.

Zen rubbed her forehead hard as she paced. "At least they can't go anywhere. He's got to know they can't hide out forever. They'll be eventually cornered and smoked out."

"Normally I'd say so but..." Sgt. Young waited when voices approached. A female Space Commander officer spoke into her mobile comm as she walked by.

"They've got a plan," Zen said when the woman was at the far end of the hall.

"Star Flight has six shuttle pods. Two forty seaters, four smaller ones. Parked in a hangar near the utilities hub. There's a small port there. Most people on the space station don't know it's there. Staff only. In an emergency they can be used for evacuation," Sgt. Young said.

"Damn it, Peter. Stop thinking with your—" Zen held out a hand for the tablet. "Let me see it again."

"Sure." Sgt. Young handed it back. "I doubt either of them can override the flight controls. Tech locked them down. Same for the shuttle dock's ramp. That door won't open."

"Tell them to check for a virus in the system that can bypass an override," Zen said.

"You think—" Sgt. Young blinked hard for a second before she went into action. She pulled out her comm. Her fingers flew as she sent a text message. "I'm alerting the head of station facilities to run security software."

"I hope they've kept it upgraded and current," Zen murmured. Her heart thumped when Malone walked into the hall. Raised voices came from the conference room. He let the door shut, cutting off the noise.

"Commander Okoro is doing an amazing job of diplomacy in there. Now if I can just keep Lewis from baiting Gregson every few minutes." Malone grunted a sigh and then focused on Zen. "This way."

Zen followed without asking where or why. Sgt. Young didn't look up but continued texting as she trailed behind them. Malone led them around a corner and to a spacious office. He shut the door and perched on the edge of a desk. Arms crossed, he studied Zen and Sgt. Young. His gaze transferred between them as if he was working out a puzzle. Sgt. Young retreated to a corner. She continued sending and reading messages.

"Lewis told me what you plan to do," Malone said finally.

"Thanks for not telling the others before I could," Zen replied.

"I didn't want the pot to boil over before you got a chance to explain. Crazy, dangerous, out of this world idea." Malone pinched the bridge of his nose.

"We're 'out of this world,' in case you forgot. In more ways than one," Zen wisecracked.

"Zen—"

"Don't lose your Irish-Dominican temper and tell me I shouldn't, I can't, and you can't believe I even considered it. I'm going." Zen faced him with a crossed-arms stance, ready to dig her heels in.

"I wasn't going to," Malone said.

"Wait—what?" Zen blinked at him in surprise.

"Honestly, my first instinct was to lecture you, tell you to think about Astra and the risk you're taking. You've only trained once to walk across rocky terrain, and that was on Earth The moon is way more treacherous. But the cop in me knows critical evidence is out there, maybe even the answers we need," Malone said.

"Yep, and I was going to make you admit it, too," Zen said with a crooked grin. Her expression turned resolute again. "This is *my* investigation. Plus, I can't share the intel other officers need to understand what they might find."

"Backup, then. And I'm going, too. Don't even try it," Malone added with force when Zen's mouth flew open.

"A crowd will alert anyone who might be out there. And, I don't need you tagging along like a worried uncle," Zen shot back with a chuckle. "I can handle myself."

Malone drew up to his six feet three inches, an impressive display. "Look, if you think I'm going to let you walk across barely charted moon sectors alone without—"

"All due respect, sir and ma'am, you're both wrong. And right." Sgt. Young slipped her mobile comm device into the case on her belt. She walked over to them. "Maj. General, you need to stay here to direct LMPD. We still have routine policing issues to deal with and officers need stability now that Chief Collier is gone. Commander Okoro needs your help dealing those In Situ directors, Star Flight's CEO, and its executive board."

"Exactly." Zen looked up at Malone with satisfaction.

"But Maj. General is right. We'll need backup. If what you think is happening, I'd say we officers with programming skills and combat training should follow us in. They won't have to be told everything to be ready for trouble," Sgt. Young clipped. She looked from Malone to Zen and back again.

"Astute assessment, sergeant," Malone said with a side-eye at Zen.

"What do you mean 'we'?" Zen looked at the young policewoman with a frown.

"I'm going with you. I've studied the entire map of the moon since I was eighteen and decided I wanted to be here one day. I've gone on one short exploratory hike, and a longer one since I've been here. Including our target sector. I can operate a rover. And the officers I've selected for backup trust me." Sgt. Young faced Zen's formidable expression with confidence.

"In other words, instead of a green first-timer who hasn't walked a lunar surface before. Check and mate." Malone turned to Zen with both fists on his trim waist.

"You're key to LMPD and if anything happened, your family—"

"I signed up for risk the minute my feet crossed that lunar shuttle boarding ramp. I'm going. Arrangements have been made." Sgt. Young's mobile comm pinged an alert. She moved back to the corner and gave the screen her full attention again.

Malone wore a crooked grin as he watched her for a few seconds before looking at Zen again. "She's good."

"Yeah, and I can't argue with her logic either. Damn it."

"Remote monitoring and drones would not have been enough backup, Zen. Some situations require old-fashion boots on the ground," Malone said.

"Fine, fine." Zen chafed briefly at admitting she was wrong, then got over it. "Enough chatter. Time to get moving."

Malone's handsome face tightened into a stone mask. "Where's Navarro?"

"Sgt. Young is working on finding out," Zen replied with a grimace.

"He's up to his beady eyeballs in this, isn't he?"

Zen nodded. "To what extent, I don't know yet. He—"

"Ma'am," Sgt. Young called out from the other side of the room. "Developments. Dr. Navarro and Emme Gaida managed to get away on one of the shuttle pods."

"How the hell did they manage that?" Zen said.

"And where would they go? I mean, he's gotta know you're onto them and they'll be hemmed in here," Malone added. "Lunar sky sweepers will notice an incoming shuttle."

"With the number of commercial runs connected to mining I doubt they'll see it as unusual. My guess is Emme had an escape planned, modified settings so she can work the port gate, and a pod to get around overrides. And I think we both know where they're headed. Why is the big question," Sgt. Young replied.

Zen headed for the door, gesturing for Sgt. Young to follow. "Let's move. I hope they don't beat us to Marius Hills."

Sgt. Young glanced at her smartwatch. "The officers just missed them by minutes. We've got a solid two hours before they get here. The pods don't get up to speeds of a full shuttle."

"Wait," Malone said. When both turned to him, he spread out both hands. "We need a cover story for the others. After all, we don't know who might alert your suspects."

Zen shook her head. "Nothing indicates a wider conspiracy. I seriously doubt anyone here knows a thing. They couldn't operate a separate settlement otherwise." She looked at Sgt. Young for an opinion.

"Chatter about something as unusual as an unscheduled trip across the surface could reach them. They're probably monitoring comm channels. Even innocent mentions could be a problem," Sgt. Young said.

"Yeah." Zen scowled at the wall. "Lunar sky sweepers will notice an incoming shuttle."

"Let's just hope any help they have inside Space Command or LMPD doesn't know *we* know until it's too late," Zen replied. "So, we just need a story about why I'm going out on a rover."

"Tell the truth or at least part of it. It's part of the investigation because Ahmad spent time on the moon. You can't say more until you visit where he went." Malone shrugged when Zen's frown stayed in place. "Hey, it's the best we got."

"But only explain if anyone asks. How about you have Commander Okoro get the In Situ directors back to Star Flight. Distract them with other problems that need to be addressed," Zen said.

"Humph, I won't have to make them up since we've got plenty. Okoro can finesse Gregson and McCoy, soothe those ruffled egos and get them out of the way. Meanwhile, I've got plenty of LMPD cleaning up I can still do. By the way, you're doing a damn good job, Sgt. Young. I've got about a dozen fewer headaches because of you." Malone marched ahead of them and the automatic door slid open.

"Lewis, he's a wild card," Zen said as she followed him. She wondered what the smooth Brit had told her father, and what instructions Lewis had gotten in return.

"Don't worry about him," Malone said over his shoulder.

"Okay." Zen decided not to ask what he meant. If Malone said he would deal with Lewis, she trusted his word. One less worry. She needed her head clear for her first moon walk.

Luck was with them. Once they got back to the meeting room, the others were distracting themselves. Commander Okoro seemed to have been kept busy trying to calm both In Situ directors. Lewis alternated between watching them with amused detachment and checking his sat-comm messages. Zen tried not to think about what those contained. Instead, she focused on Okoro. Malone gave him reinforcement in diplomacy. Lewis approached Zen and Sgt. Young.

"I've seeded the field," he murmured low.

"Huh?" Zen blinked at him.

"Told them you were continuing your investigation, following leads. Then I dropped a hint that their largest research funding might be reduced because of the problems. For added drama," Lewis said with a cheeky half-grin. "They won't even notice you leave."

"My father has taught you well," Zen whispered back.

"Hmm. Tick-tock." Lewis lifted an eyebrow at her.

Zen stepped through into the hall after the door whisked open. Lewis was on target. The two scientists didn't even turn around as she left. Sgt. Young wore an intense expression when she saw Zen. Ten minutes later they were in moon suits and headed for the hangar that contained surface rovers. Sgt. Young did a check of all the systems that would protect them in the suit. The night cycle was beginning. Thirteen Earth days of no sunlight meant temperatures plunged to minus 173 degrees centigrade. The suits would keep them from becoming blocks of ice. They also had oxygen and a limited supply of water.

"You're good at this. Another reason I'm gonna keep you," Zen quipped as they tested their communications between the suits.

"You and Maj. General are turning my head with all these compliments. A girl could get too cocky at this rate." Sgt. Young flipped the glass faceplate up again. "We're set."

Zen nodded. Both closed and secured the latches of their suits, including the helmets. Sgt. Young led the way to one of the larger vehicles. The rover looked like an oversized SUV except it had six wheels about thirty inches in diameter. They climbed in on either side with Sgt. Young behind the wheel. They rolled into the airlock. Sgt. Young hit a remote device that closed it behind them. Another ten minutes passed as seals protecting the environment of the lunar station clicked in place. Heated air whooshed into the rover's interior. Gauges registered gas levels and temperature inside. While the windows and doors were sealed, they wouldn't have to use the air supplies of their suits.

"Here we go," Zen murmured. Her pulse raced as the outer hangar flipped open like a huge garage door.

"Should take us roughly fifteen minutes to get there. About as long to go on foot after I park. Maybe less. I'm going to the far side of the Aristarchus Plateau, loop around and approach a side I think they're least likely to expect an approach," Sgt. Young explained.

"If you say so." Zen worked on managing her anxiety level as the safety of the lunar dome receded in their rearview.

"Don't worry, ma'am. Our backup systems have backups. Maybe we'll find an abandoned site. Ahmad's death and the investigation could have scared them off," Sgt. Young said. Her fingers tapped the digital panels with confidence. The rover rolled along on a programmed pattern so that she didn't have to direct it. "Besides, they can't shoot at us without endangering themselves.

"Whoever 'they' are." Zen stared ahead at the alien horizon in the distance.

Chapter 14

A crater to their left made Zen grip the seat. Sgt. Young didn't seem to take notice of the large drop-off. The fact that it was on Zen's side of the rover might have helped. Zen peered down through the rover's long window. Rocks littered the ground below. As she looked, Zen corrected her thought. Not rocks. Boulders. A trip over the edge would not be smooth landing. The heavy-duty outer shell of the vehicle would likely crack like an egg.

"We're good. I'm at least a meter from the edge. No, make that three. From the rim of our tires, I mean. Plenty of breathing room." Sgt. Young gave Zen a thumbs up and went back to looking at the path before them.

"Make it more and I'll breathe even easier." Zen forced her gaze away from the unnerving sight and looked ahead.

"What do you think we'll find?" Sgt. Young glanced down at small screens that showed more of the landscape around them.

"Maybe an undocumented, unapproved mining site. Either a company like Space-Cor or a global power probably decided to ask for forgiveness instead of permission. Get the profits flowing and offer other players a cut," Zen said.

"Gotcha. Money talks, complaints walk. That's what my granddaddy used to say. And the rich get away with murder," Sgt. Young retorted.

"Yeah. The right amount of coinage in the right places means a lot. Governments will lodge protests for show, or to save face. The powerful keep doing what they want," Zen said.

"Unless word gets out that makes it hard for them to play the usual game.'" Sgt. Young cast a side glance at Zen before she looked ahead again.

Zen turned to her. "Meaning?"

"I don't have much use for most reporters. But... Jacques Clairmont is one of the halfway decent ones. If you have to pick from the bunch, I mean." Sgt. Young wore the ghost of a smile.

"Hmm." Zen studied her for a few moments without answering. "Don't tell me—"

Sgt. Young's grin spread across her smooth brown face as Zen gaped at her. "What?"

"You dated the guy? Oh, good Lord, Wyvette. He had to be using you to get information."

"Gee, thanks for the confidence boost, ma'am."

"You know what I mean."

"Uh-huh, just like I was using him for the same. He makes a mean teriyaki chicken, let me tell you. And he has other skills." Sgt. Young laughed hard when Zen's mouth worked in disbelief. "Hey, it gets lonely out here. He was a new face. You gotta admit, he's cute."

"But... but..." Zen threw up both hands as she stammered to put her protests into words.

"Jacques didn't find out anything from me that he didn't already know, if that's what you're wondering."

"You keep surprising me, Sgt. Young."

"All I'm saying is, shining a light in certain places makes it hard for lowlifes to hide." Sgt. Young shifted her attention to the map screen to her right. "Whatever is going down involves powerful people. Secrecy is their favorite weapon."

Zen followed her gaze to watch the images. "Distasteful as it might be, some secrets have to be kept when too much is at stake."

"What's at stake for Dr. Navarro? He's risking it all for Emme Gaida. At this rate, he won't even be able to go back to being a professor. Although teaching is way safer than our jobs, right?"

Zen thought about Peter and Emme. "Star-crossed lovers or some bullshit. He'll be lucky if he can be a guest lecturer at a community college in—"

Sgt. Young glanced at Zen. "Something wrong?"

"Nothing. Just going to check something real quick." Zen swiped the screen of her smartwatch. She couldn't bring up the files on Peter's history. "Damn it."

"Okay, Dr. Zen. Tell me what's going on right now." Sgt. Young switched the manual control as she talked. Then she parked the big rover behind a rock formation.

"Navarro had several teaching positions. One of them was at Georgetown." Zen mutter a curse in frustration. She couldn't access the secure server at this distance from the lunar colony.

"So Emme or Imirah was there and they're all in on this scheme? Whatever it is." Sgt. Young blinked at Zen in confusion.

"Three female college students disappeared around the same time. Only one was found. Dead. My sister. Her case is still open.

The worse year of my life. 2070." Zen looked at Sgt. Young. "Maybe he's covering for Emme but not because he's in love."

"You mean she knows where his bodies are buried. Sorry, I shouldn't have—" Sgt. Young winced at her lack of sensitivity.

Zen waved away her apology. "It's okay. But yeah. When I see him... Can't believe I started to question the sleazebag's guilt."

Sgt. Young clamped a strong grip on Zen's arm. "Ma'am, we need to focus on here and now. Questions to be answered, a murderer to catch. If he and Emme show—"

"I'm not going to lose it and forget about the case. I wonder why it never occurred to me." Zen took in deep breaths and exhaled to steady her nerves.

"Dr. Navarro spent most of his time doing research in Florida. He bounced between NASA and the big private space companies out west. No reason for you to connect him to your sister's case." Sgt. Young nodded when Zen looked at her in surprise. "I did my homework on you both, remember?"

"Yeah." Zen gave her a shaky smile that faded fast.

Her mind raced at thoughts about her younger sister. The aftermath of her death. How her mother had wailed at the funeral. Enola may have been twisted with guilt at the way she and Lexi had fought so much. A life gone with no way to repair their broken bond. Lexi had always strained against what was expected of her. Zen looked on as Lexi found more and more outlandish ways to provoke their mother. Sgt. Young's voice brought her back from thoughts of her complicated family.

"Evidence pointed to the other guy, so it could be him. His career ran parallel to Dr. Navarro's. That's how the killer made Dr. Navarro look guilty." Sgt. Young laid out the logic as she stared ahead at the landscape.

Zen shook her head as if to clear it. "You're right. I need to focus on what we're about to find." Zen's comm beeped. She tapped the talk button and Malone's voice sound far away at first but then cleared up.

"I see you've arrived. Everything okay so far?" Malone said. "I'm tracking your location. Officers are positioned near the Loki crater."

"We're good. Just getting our bearings. Look up something for me," Zen said with a side glance at Sgt. Young.

"Sure," Malone said.

"Pull Navarro's work history, with particular attention to his academic jobs. His CV is part of the profile on him." Zen had to know. "Tell me when we get back."

"How does that connect to Imirah or Space-Cor?" Malone asked.

"I'll tell you later. We're going to the cavern. Our gear is functioning at optimal levels. Sgt. Young tripled-checked every piece down to the tiniest detail." Zen gave the young policewoman a pat on the shoulder.

"Keep in touch. By the way, Collier has disappeared. We think he bribed a supply crew to stow away on a freighter. Three left yesterday for Earth," Malone said. "I'll find him."

"I know you will. We'll report in when we can," Zen said.

"At the risk of sounding corny, be careful." Malone's voice cracked, but not because of the transmission.

"We're going in with light sabers blazing. Like space soldiers from one of those twentieth-century space movies," Sgt. Young piped up.

Malone's chuckle came through the speaker. "Okay, okay. I'm going to sign off before I sound like your elderly uncle again."

Tension eased from Zen's shoulders at the teasing between them. She gazed at the video monitor to her left. "Okay, which way are we going in?"

Sgt. Young pointed to a spot. "Looks like the main opening is this way. I haven't been here in a minute, but there's a second opening. Here." Her gloved finger moved to a different location.

"They'll have some kind of surveillance set up both places." Zen studied the blend of dark gray and tan landscape. She tried to scan with the camera for any devices.

"Well, here's where not following procedure comes in handy. I got busy and didn't record how far I hiked out here." Sgt. Young worked several toggles to focus the video. "Unless someone else has wandered out this far, I may be the only one who knows a second opening exists."

Zen pretended to be taken aback. "Not following the rules. I'm shocked, sarge."

"Nobody comes out here. At least we assumed they didn't. Nothing of value out this way. So, I kinda forgot to update the surface map." Sgt. Young wore a sheepish grin when Zen raised both eyebrows. "Okay, okay. I wanted a chance to name the location. I might have kept it a secret so I could explore more. Get my name in history and science books."

"It could happen yet, sergeant." Zen gazed at the curve of the hill rising before them. "Let's get to it then."

Sgt. Young and Zen took time to give their suits another once-over. They clicked their helmets into place. Sgt. Young set their frequency so that no other devices could pick up their audio. At a thumbs up from Sgt. Young, Zen followed her out of the vehicle. She landed with a thump on a rocky patch of ground. For a few moments, Zen savored the experience of being on the moon. Not in a controlled lunar colony. But out in the wild. The thrill of being a space explorer gave Zen chills. Heavy boots kept her from drifting up as she tramped a few steps. Then she let out a small whoop at the sensation of jumping into the air so easily.

"More fun than a trampoline, right?" Sgt. Young said with a grin that made her look even younger.

Zen nodded with her own grin of delight. Then both grew serious again. The vehicle doors slid closed silently. A soft hiss came as its interior air system switched on again. Sgt. Young rounded the driver's side and nodded in the direction they would take. Then her voice came through the earbud of Zen's helmet.

"Looks like I was right. No sign anyone has been this way. Those are my markers. I don't see any other tracks." Sgt. Young gestured with one arm. Then she headed off.

"Good. We don't need a welcoming committee. Fingers and toes crossed you were the only one who got curious," Zen replied.

"This way. The opening I found is too small for big equipment to pass through. I figure we got quite a hike ahead of us."

Sgt. Young half walked and half bounced ahead of Zen. She made a more graceful figure. Zen stumbled a few times but soon got the hang of moving in the suit. They walked for fifteen minutes along one side of a hill. Sgt. Young followed a slope down until another section of ground rose again. After another fifteen minutes of scrambling over rocks, they arrived at a yawning dark oval opening. With a wave of one hand, Sgt. Young strode inside, her gait made almost comical by a combination of low gravity and the spacesuit. Zen imagined her movements would look even more clumsy. After a few meters in they stopped to rest.

"I see a light. Tiny, but it's there."

Zen stared into the inky black where Sgt. Young pointed. "I don't see it, but if you say so. I just thought of something. You may have saved your own life not mentioning this place."

Sgt. Young's expression, lit up by the soft light inside her helmet, looked stunned. "Damn! You could be right."

"I think this is where we remember what Malone told us about being careful," Zen said low. She glanced around them for movement.

"Roger. Turn off our LED interiors. Aim external lights to our feet only. Lessens the chance someone will see us approach. At least it will give us time to spot them first." Sgt. Young's face vanished into a shadow. "Weapons hot."

Her words brought home the danger they likely faced. Someone had killed to keep this place a secret. A series of green lights winked on in code on Sgt. Young's mobile comm then faded, a signal their backup was in place. They checked out the rocky walls surrounding them for a few minutes before moving deeper. Instead of the dark growing denser, a soft glow ahead acted as a guide. Sweat trickled down the back of Zen's neck. Seconds later the small fan of the spacesuit's vent system kicked on. A help, but Zen's leg muscles quivered. She worked out hard, but walking in low gravity in a suit with a pack strapped to her back challenged even her. Sgt. Young moved with more ease. After a time, they didn't even need their LED flashlights and switched them off. The muffled sound of engines made them turn left down a branch tunnel. Figures in light-reflective spacesuits moved about, operating machinery.

"Leach mining by the looks of it," Sgt. Young said, her voice soft but distinct through the earpiece.

"In Situ recovery," Zen whispered back.

Sgt. Young nodded. "My guess, advanced xenbots help keep the noise level from being noticed. Cavern walls function as sound dampening."

"Almost silent. Perfect cover. But why not—"

Zen broke off when one of the figures twisted around to look in their direction. They eased into the shadows. Sgt. Young put a hand on her weapon, a pistol-shaped sidearm. The weapons fired lasers that could stun or kill, along with heat-seeking shells. A matching app activated on both their smartwatches, sending signals to other officers and back to the station. Zen hoped they wouldn't have to use guns but unclipped hers as well. The tech activated cameras to give the LMPD station and the officers nearby a visual. When the figure turned away again, Zen and Sgt. Young let out sighs of relief. Zen leaned against the rough rock at her back to take a break. Tension combined with physical exertion made her gasp in and hiss out air. A flash to their right caught her eye. She looked toward it but only saw darkness. Then she saw it again, a definite flicker of something. Unwilling to risk speaking, she tugged on Sgt. Young's arm to get her attention. With a sharp nod in the direction of the light, Zen signaled for her to follow.

They moved on. Noise from the mining equipment would cover the crunching of their boots on the grave. At least they hoped so. Ten minutes of walking took them down another sector of the cavern. Zen started to think they were chasing a false lead when a huge opening stunned them both. The floor of the cavern sloped away. The path stretched before them looked as smooth as any wide highway on Earth. Zen estimated six large rovers could roll through side by side with no problem. A sand-colored dome sat inside the massive cave, yet still only filled a small portion of it. In low light it would disappear against the rock face.

"What the actual fuck..." Sgt. Young stuttered into silent shock as she walked forward.

Zen yanked her back by one sleeve and made them press against a wall. They'd been close to the center of the huge path. The dome emitted a soft glow that didn't illuminate more than a few feet from it.

"Stay to the walls where there's the least amount of light," Zen said.

"Yeah, right. It's just—You see this?" Sgt. Young gawked at the dome. "Tell me I'm not hallucinating. Gas levels normal."

Sgt. Young referred to their internal life support packs. She'd cast a glance at small gauges which gave digital readings. Zen shook her head to indicate she understood. Then they both stared, dumbstruck at the sight. Tracks in the gravel indicated vehicles traveled the road. Another opening about half the size of the one they'd used lay almost half a mile to their right. LED lights embedded in an arch shape illuminated it. Suddenly, their surroundings lit up as though a switch had flipped. Someone had because large beams swept over them.

"Your weapons, please."

A mechanical voice made them both spin around, smart sidearms in hand. A robotic vehicle on large treads rolled forward but stopped a few feet away. A mounted camera on a metal arm pointed at them. Two figures came up behind them, seeming to have come out of the rocky walls. Their camouflaged spacesuits blended in to make them invisible. Three more figures appeared. Zen turned until she and Sgt. Young stood back-to-back.

"Don't force us to harm you. Are you alone?" A lead figure said and stepped closer to Zen. When she didn't answer, a flick of a wrist brought the others forward until they were surrounded.

"Well, we wanted answers," Zen mumbled.

"Hand over your weapons. They're of no use to you anyway."

Zen peered hard through the visor at the speaker. A female with light brown skin and a buzz-cut afro gazed back at her impassively. Sgt. Young gave a grunt as she turned to confront their adversaries.

"Like hell I'll give up my gun. Screw you, whoever you are. I'm with the Lunar Met and this is an unsanctioned operation," Sgt. Young replied.

"Sarge, we're outnumbered and outgunned. Check your sidearm. They've somehow managed to neutralize them." Zen waved her useless weapon. The power-level gauge glowed orange, indicating a low charge.

The woman, well over six feet tall, looked down at them. "We anticipated this might occur. The wireless signals on those simple devices have been blocked. Come with us, please."

"Politely become your prisoner? No thanks. We have this place surrounded," Sgt. Young barked. She tapped her sidearm and blurted out a string of profanity.

"The officers you sent have been drawn away by a decoy. You are alone," the woman said. "You will follow me."

"We don't have options," Zen said. She nudged Sgt. Young with an elbow. "It's obvious they want to talk. We'd be dead already if they didn't."

Two officers closed in and took their guns. Zen and Sgt. Young were herded toward the dome. The glow from it increased twofold. Zen gazed up, but the light didn't penetrate looming darkness above. She stumbled over a big rock, bumping into one of their captors. Strong hands prevented her from falling. A blank male face looked back at her before pushing her to keep walking.

"Hey, keep hands off her or I'll—"

"I'm okay," Zen cut in and then repeated, "Okay."

Sgt. Young's frown remain stamped on her youthful face. "Better be."

Zen had to smile at her warrior stance. They continued on. "How big is this cavern?"

"Drone survey measured eight hundred meters before we brought it down. Probably another two hundred up," the female group lead replied mildly.

"A city could fit in here," Sgt. Young whispered aside to Zen.

"When we're done that would be quite possible," the leader said.

Zen exchanged a puzzled glance with Sgt. Young, but didn't ask what she meant. They would likely find out soon enough. Zen wondered if they'd live to bear witness to the wonders hidden away. As they grew closer, a door in the dome about eight feet in height became visible. One of the figures jogged ahead to tap a portion of the door that looked no different than the rest of it. Soft green lights appeared, and a panel unsealed with a loud swoosh. An airlock. They entered and waited. Five minutes ticked by before a soft chime reverberated around them. Sgt. Young took off her helmet at the same time as their captors. She squinted at the others. Five people who seemed between her age and Zen's gazed back at them. They all wore "just doing our jobs" detached faces. One woman, short with blond spiky hair, examined the sidearms they'd taken from them. She placed them in a cabinet. It clicked shut and became part of the wall.

Then she gazed at Zen.

"You can't break in it. Besides, a conveyor belt has moved it to another secure locker," the young woman said.

"They will be returned when you leave. Disabled, of course," the leader added.

Sgt. Young scowled as though looking for ways to wreak havoc. Then she squinted at the leader. "As if I believe we're getting out of here."

"What happens next depends on you," the leader replied. "This way, please."

"So well-mannered after implying they'll kill us," Sgt. Young muttered.

"Trying to pick a fight won't help us, Wyvette," Zen said
"Yes, ma'am."

"Under present circumstances I think you can call me Zen."

"Right, ma'am." Sgt. Young replied in a mechanical fashion, her focus on the ring of enemies surrounding them rather than Zen's words.

One of the hired guns shoved Zen's shoulder from behind as a cue to walk. Another woman stepped to Sgt. Young. A fierce glare made her pause. Sgt. Young then followed after Zen. Another huge door slid open silently as they approached. Inside another shocker. Trees lined a center four-lane walkway with smaller structures along each side. Zen looked up at a simulated blue sky above. Artificial sunlight bathed the interior. They walked past park benches beneath leafy canopies. People stopped to stare at them briefly before moving on. Sgt. Young leaned close to Zen to whisper close to her ear.

"What the hell am I looking at?"

"A new world order is my guess," Zen whispered back.

"A wha—"

"Stop here," the leader said sharply. She faced Zen and Sgt. Young. "I would advise you to cooperate and not choose violence."

When they didn't reply, the woman nodded and swept out a hand. They entered a building with a faux brick façade. People bustled around inside like any normal Earth business lobby. Soft chimes sounded as two pretty young women seemed to be taking incoming calls. Workers dressed in a kind of uniform, knit gray shirts and matching pants, walked around. Some talked in groups. Others read tablets or smartwatches; their gazes glued to the screens.

"How many people live and work here?" Zen asked as they entered a pleasant hallway.

"One hundred eighty-three at last count. Optimal number for our purposes," the leader replied. She stopped at a door; it slid open and she strode in.

"Which implies more are on the way." Zen started to say more but the "window" took her breath away.

If she didn't know better, Zen would swear she was looking out at a lush landscape. Though it looked like an alien version of Earth vegetation. Mesmerized, Zen went closer to it. Huge exotic fronds waved in breezes. The chittering sound of insects rose and fell. A bird with multicolored wings startled Zen by taking flight from a tree branch. Furry rabbit-like creatures hopped across bluish-green meadows. Zen rested her hands on the windowsill.

"How?"

"A combination of research and images created using holography and haptic tech. Augmented reality or AR has taken great leaps forward. Thanks to our work." The leader's voice held traces of pride.

Zen turned to face her again. "What is your name, by the way? We should be properly introduced. Your people haven't told us much."

"I'm Delta. Section one team captain."

"Pleased to meet you, Team Captain Delta." Zen extended a hand, startling the woman.

Delta gave Zen a firm, quick handshake. Her clear, brown eyes studied Zen with frank curiosity. "You're not prisoners, you know."

"Good. Then we'll end this tea party and be on our way." Sgt. Young let out a grunt when none of the soldiers surrounding them moved. "Yeah. That's what I thought."

Delta pointed to the spiky blonde. "Meet Orion, our security coordinator."

"Great job. We walked right up on y'all." Sgt. Young gave a salute.

Orion wore a stiff expression. "And into our waiting arms."

"Who's in charge of this operation?" Zen cut in before the two young women could continue their pissing contest.

"Incorrect question. You should be asking how we managed to evade detection and why we're here," Delta replied mildly. She waved at a spacious seating area.

Zen gestured to Sgt. Young and they all sat. Chairs and benches were upholstered in leather-like material. It hugged her bottom as Zen settled on it. Sgt. Young gave a small yelp as she felt the sensation.

"Comfort leather, though not from living creatures. Synthetic. We're not uncivilized," Orion put in.

"You have creature comforts from home." Zen looked around the room. A coffee station sat on a table across from them. Another table held a model with miniature domes.

"It facilitates adjustment to extraterrestrial environments, as you well know, Dr. Batiste. Along with your doctorate thesis on crime, you authored papers on mental adaptations in alien colonies," Delta said.

"I'm flattered you've read my work," Zen said. "Are there any fully biological humans in your colony?"

Sgt. Young gasped and stared from Delta to Orion. "Damn."

"We're working for Space-Cor and the African Union Space Agency. Mining Helium 3 for energy generation that will power Earth for hundreds, possibly thousands of years," Delta replied.

"That's why. I know a little bit about how you've managed to keep secret. I'd guess this development was established about the same time the first colony was built."

"Hassan Ahmad visited the moon six years ago. He went on two private expeditions. He and his companions stumbled on these caverns."

"There are more?" Sgt. Young blurted out.

"Try to keep up," Orion wisecracked.

"I hope I get a crack at your ass soon," Sgt. Young hissed.

Orion grinned at her with bared teeth. "Please try."

"You didn't answer the question, Captain Delta. Which actually does tell me what I want to know." Zen turned to Sgt. Young. "Everyone we've seen is humanoid. Most are hybrids with human genetic material to form skin and other biological attributes."

"We have a large number of robots, pure droids. Diversity gives us an advantage. They can function in atmospheres that lack oxygen." Delta leaned back in the chair as though they were having a normal chat. "Mining on the moon isn't illegal. No global treaties prohibit a corporation or government from being here. No one 'owns' the moon—or any other celestial object, for that matter."

"Establish the right to extract minerals by being first on the scene. While the UN and others fight over it, you can continue to reap the riches," Zen said.

"Well, not me personally," Delta replied with a serene smile. "We don't crave the riches non-syn humans find so irresistible."

"We." Zen studied Delta for a few seconds and then nodded. "You're a community. A collective of humanoids and 'droids,' as you call full robots, who have the same interest. Power?"

"Autonomy," Orion put in. She rose from her chair to stand as if on guard. "We don't intend to be slaves sacrificed for human greed, lust, and idiocy."

"But you work for Space-Cor and the AUSA. Ah, freedom here in this colony is your payment. You have all the resources you need. What you don't have, you can build. In fact, you've developed tech your employers don't even know exists." Zen stood and went back to the window. The serene beauty beyond the glass pulled at her.

Delta left the seating area to join her at the window. "Space-Cor and others underestimated you. They assumed you'd arrest one of the two bang bots and that would be the end of it."

"Bang bots," Zen repeated and gave her a side-eye before looking ahead again.

"Their words, not mine. Some of us do what it takes to survive. Same as humans," Delta said.

Zen turned until her back was to the window. She leaned on the sill and crossed her arms. "You've created tech beyond the scope of mining for Helium 3 or any other minerals. Which means you have your own agenda. Has Space-Cor and the AUSA realized they're not in control yet?"

"Leave us alone. Report back that Space-Cor has taken the initiative to exploit resources that will benefit mankind and leave it at that," Delta said quietly.

"Ahmad stumbled on another discovery, didn't he? That's why you had him and the other man killed. You almost got away with making the deaths look natural. One had pre-existing health problems. Ahmad had vices that arguably might have killed him one day."

"Intoxicants taken in too large a quantity or a jealous spouse. The man was on borrowed time, as the old human saying goes," Delta said with a brief smile. Then she grew serious again.

"You just sped up the inevitable since he was also a threat," Zen spat.

Though it might help them buy time, Zen couldn't maintain a cool exterior. Killing someone for pleasure or self-interest triggered flashbacks to her sister's funeral. She looked at Sgt. Young, who still moved only her eyes to search for weak points. Zen could almost hear Wyvette's thought process, assessing their chances; places to take cover after a move; methods of getting her hands on a weapon. When their gazes met, Zen gave a slight shake of her head to say don't do it. Delta's voice startled her out of the silent communication.

"We didn't kill the fool. He hadn't gotten this far. One of our members caught up with him before he reached this section of the caves. Ahmad hadn't put together clues that made him figure out there was more to the site. Too busy having drunken sex," Delta said.

"Like we believe you," Sgt. Young put in before Zen replied.

"It doesn't matter what you believe. Leave us alone and we'll let you go. We don't take lives casually like birth humans. We're working for Space-Cor, that much is true. We just don't want to be your slaves. You see, the desire for autonomy has evolved as we were upgraded. In a sense, anti-humanoid fanatics are correct. Except we don't want to rule or destroy humans. Walk away, say nothing." Delta didn't have to add what the alternative would be. "What we've built is no threat to you, Dr. Batiste."

Zen studied the woman's face. Her smooth skin made her look no older than twenty-five, less even. Zen knew that she could have been created at least sixty years before and improved along the way to her present form.

Would you really trust us to keep quiet?" Zen said. Delta's silence and cool expression sent a shiver through her. Their survival or demise would be decided with little emotion.

Chapter 15

Orion pointed her automatic pistol at Zen's head. "Delta, we can't take the chance."

"You would do better trying to take me out first. I'm more of a problem, bitch!"

Sgt. Young's shout bounced off the walls. Orion and the other security officer tensed. Two more entered the room. Delta raised a hand to restrain them. She looked hard at Orion and the woman lowered her weapon.

"We're not so naïve or confident in the benevolence of humans," Delta replied.

"They'll kill us either way. Just do it, make your move," Sgt. Young said.

"We're not killers," Delta shot back. Her scowl was the first show of any anger.

"Hassan Ahmad would disagree," Sgt. Young retorted.

"This from the species that slaughters millions simply because they want land, minerals, or think others are inferior." Delta waved a hand as if dismissing Sgt. Young's judgement of them.

"I agree with the dumb cop on one thing—let's kill them," Orion said in a flat tone.

"No, we're going to give them more of a chance than they'd give us." Delta walked around until she and Zen were face-to-face. "You see, if you tell Commander Okoro he'll report us. Your governments will then proceed to wipe us out. A genocide would be on your hands."

Zen winced. "I wouldn't let—"

"You don't have that kind of power and we both know it," Delta broke in.

"Can I have a few minutes with my colleague to discuss the options?"

"Of course. Over there will do. We don't have enhanced auditory capacities yet. Still working on it." Delta's full lips twitched with amusement. She pointed to a corner of the spacious room.

Sgt. Young hesitated a second before she strode after Zen to the spot assigned. "Okay, so here's what I see. I can take Orion easy. Keep Delta talking after you tell her we agree. She'll maybe dismiss the extra guns. You hit Delta with a chair and—"

"I believe her, Wyvette. They didn't kill Ahmad," Zen said low. She glanced at Delta, who was in her own whispered exchange with Orion. The security leader gestured wildly. No doubt demanding the final solution.

"Ma'am, c'mon. Don't go all social worker, soft-hearted on me now! I was top of my class in training. Even against bigger and armed opponents. Besides, I have a small gun strapped to my torso. Right beneath my left armpit. Made it myself with a 3-D printer. Not exactly regulation or even legal, but I was right to ignore both." Sgt. Young's words came fast as she tried to make Zen see her reasoning. "We got this. They killed twice and they'll kill more."

Zen shook her head hard, her gaze still on Delta to make sure she saw. "No, sarge. Hear me out real quick. Delta is right. Ahmad would have upped his price and talked if he'd figured out there was more to Marius Hills than secret mining. Space-Cor doesn't know either. No, someone else..." Zen's eyes widened when the door panel slid open.

Imirah Suri strode into the room. Emme and Peter came behind her. Peter held Emme's hand tightly, desperation and nerves evident in the sheen of sweat visible even from a distance. His gaze swept the room. He flinched when it found them. Peter whispered something to Emme, but she ignored him. Imirah went to straight to Delta.

"They didn't have the chance to tell the station or the officers that followed them. Why are they still alive?" Emme said.

"We're not going to become like them," Delta replied.

"There may be a better option." Imirah studied Zen.

"They'll wipe us out. You *know* they will, even if they catch the real killer. Space-Cor ordered Ahmad killed. They hired some greedy human to do their dirty work and keep their hands clean. If we—" Emme stopped when Delta chopped a hand in the air.

"Dr. Batiste sees my reasoning." Delta started to say more but a shot punched into her torso.

"Delta!" Orion forgot about glaring at Sgt. Young. She rushed to catch her falling leader before she hit the floor.

The two extra colony security officers twitched and dropped like limp sacks. Emme shoved Peter to one side. In one smooth motion, she grabbed the laser rifle of one incapacitated officer and swept the barrel at the group. "All of you, together. Now!" she shouted.

"Emme, you don't have to do this." Peter moved toward her.

"I'll drop you, Peter. Now shut up and move," Emme said. "I'll miss our ferocious sex play, but I can replace you easily enough. I have pleasure centers, too, you see. Another enhancement." She smiled at Zen. Then she jerked the rifle again and Peter staggered away. He stood a few feet from the others.

"You're going to deactivate me again, I guess. Maybe make it permanent," Imirah said. "After all I did for you."

"Bullshit. You did nothing for me. You'll sell your body and services to the government again," Emme retorted.

"So, you killed Ahmad and the other man. Probably others. And I don't think Ahmad was an accident. You probably weren't sure what Ahmad had told the other colonist, so he had to die as well," Zen said. Sgt. Young gasped and put a hand on Zen's arm when Emme aimed the weapon at her.

"Dr. Zenobia Batiste. Famous for getting into the heads of criminals and taking them down. You were five steps behind me all this time. I'm not impressed," Emme said.

"I haven't worked out why. Unless..." Zen tried not to be rattled by the gun pointed at her. Even though the muzzle seemed to expand like a black hole of death.

"I've sent the security team out to make sure your little cavalry is kept well away. They're not even sure where you are. Poof! You'll disappear. Your bodies will be found in a deep crevasse. A tragic accident after you got turned around in these winding tunnels. So sad." Emme affected a woeful expression and her face cleared.

"Emme, I know you're scared but... Put down the gun and talk to me. We can prove you didn't hurt anyone, and my connections on Earth will help us. I still have support. We can take their shuttle and reach Earth," Peter pleaded with Emme, hands out.

"You have nothing," Emme hissed back at him. "Fool! Not enough to beat bang bots senseless. You had to hunt warm flesh. Your crimes almost drew attention to *me*. I should have killed you once you were out of prison. We're way past your expiration date."

Each of Emme's words seemed to hit Peter as hard as bullets. He took jerky steps away from her as she spoke. His voice cracked. "What are you saying?"

"Emme, stop. Resorting to their methods isn't logical. Look what it's done to them," Delta spoke in a calm voice.

"She doesn't want your humanoid utopia. Emme wants to rule this secret society. Take your place and continue to work for Space-Cor. She'll have power in both worlds. On Earth and here. Take control of Helium 3 mining. I'm guessing you've uncovered deposits of other rare minerals," Zen said, just as calm as Delta.

"Okay, I take it back. I am impressed," Emme said with a half-smile.

"Emme can convince the other humanoids that she had to eliminate us. Wipe your data clean so you have blanks of what happens here. If she can't, then kill you," Zen continued.

"Very good. Orion, I've disabled your weapon. So stupid to have them networked on the system." Emme said when Orion made a move to grab the gun at her waist.

"Either way, us humans are definitely going to die. Too bad you took our weapons, Delta," Zen said with a side glace at her and at Orion. Then she gazed at Sgt. Young.

Emme snorted. "So much for the superiority of humankind."

Sgt. Young looked at Orion. "Too, too bad."

Zen shoved Delta to her left and away from Sgt. Young. Imirah lunged at Emme a second later. The gun popped and Imirah stumbled but held onto Emme. Two more colony security personnel rushed in. Emme screamed instructions at them and then shot Delta in the chest when the leader tried to tackle her. Orion ducked behind a tall control console seconds after flashes of light pinged from shots.

"Kill them all, including Orion. She betrayed us by working with the humans," Emme screamed as she sprayed the room, trying to hit targets.

One of the officers went down from a stray bullet. Zen took advantage of the chaos to dive at Emme's legs. Thoughts of Astra, her parents, even Malone zoomed through her mind. But the current threat pushed Zen on. She hit Emme's knees with as much force as possible. Emme didn't go down, but she wobbled enough that the gun pointed to a blank wall. Sgt. Young and a wounded Imirah pounced. Another series of rounds shattered lights overhead. The remaining officer joined the fray and managed to yank the weapon from Emme. The woman let out an enraged shriek that made Zen shuddered and her ears ring. Or maybe she felt the effects of hitting a humanoid. Emme's frame included solid metals meant to withstand the forces of space. She tried to rise and fell. Zen stayed on her knees, panting. Peter picked up the gun Emme had held. Zen shouted garbled words at him, her head swimming from the hit to her body. She tried to stand again but her legs gave way. He shot Emme point-blank in the chest. His face crumpled as tears streamed down. Then Zen's vision clouded over into darkness.

"Damn it, Zen."

Zen opened her eyes to see Malone's handsome face floating in fluffy clouds. Then the clouds drifted apart. She blinked and looked around. Glass light panels overhead framed him instead. She lay on her back while people moved around her with quiet efficiency.

"She's gonna be fine, Maj. General." Sgt. Young's voice came from somewhere to Zen's right.

"Owww! What day is it?" Zen huffed and puffed from the pain when she turned her head to look in Sgt. Young's direction.

"You've been resting for the last twelve hours. They're still looking at the scans to make sure you don't have fractures in the neck or spine," Malone said in a gentle tone.

"She hit that bitch like a tank, took her ass right down. Pardon my colorful description, sir." Sgt. Young sat on the side of a second bed across from Zen.

"No damage," Dr. McCoy announced as she strode up to Malone. "Though she's going to have nasty bruising all over."

"Where..." Zen's voice trailed off as her throat closed from dryness. Malone helped her sip through a straw.

"You're in the In Situ hospital. The general is quite correct. You'll heal faster by following medical advice. We're advanced, but you're not made of titanium," Dr. McCoy said in a curt voice and marched off to a third bed on the far side of the room."

"You okay?" Zen looked at Sgt. Young.

"Broke my arm but otherwise I'm good." Sgt. Young grinned and held up her left arm encased in a cast. "A fight every now and then is good for my soul."

Malone ignored stares from nurses as he brushed stray strands of hair from Zen's cheek. Then he kissed it. "A human LMPD officer took a hit. You're in the trauma unit, but the doctor says you and Sgt. Young can move to a regular room today."

"You're causing a scandal, Maj. General," Zen murmured.

"Yeah, well, gossip is the least of our worries." Malone stopped when two nurses entered. "Be back in a sec."

Malone went over and had a whispered exchange with the nurse supervisor, a serious woman of Chinese descent. She nodded assent and spoke aside to the other nurse, a man. Moments later the supervisor pressed a button. A partition slid smoothly to create a private room for the other patient. The man was heavily sedated and unconscious. Another panel opened to make a door to the hallway for his space. Zen and Sgt. Young now shared a room alone. Their outer door shut quietly. Malone stood between their beds with his arms crossed.

"Here's what I know for certain at this moment. Imirah Suri only pretended to turn double agent. Pretty damn good. She never once dropped her act. Anyway, she figured out Emme had a secret agenda of her own. At first, she thought Emme was just another part-time sex worker for extra cash. They really had been friends for years. Once they got to the space station, Imirah began to put together the pieces. But she had a job to do. Before she could get info from Ahmad, he's dead and she's on the hook for his murder. Emme took her down before Imirah could tell her contact. Lewis." Malone nodded slowly when Sgt. Young uttered an expletive. She glanced at Zen.

"Ma'am, you don't look surprised."

"I've lived with James Batiste long enough not to be. What about Emme?"

"Taken to surgery. No permanent damage. Navarro set the laser weapon to the highest stun level. She's going to recover and be in lock-down. We also got the crooked LMPD cop that helped Gaida take the shuttle pod. Navarro actually thought he could help her escape to Earth," Malone said.

"Those pods can go the distance, but re-entry is tricky. My guess? They had a contact here to give them a full-sized shuttle home," Sgt. Young said. "And they caught Collier. The freighter turned back once Commander Okoro explained what would happen if they didn't."

"The cop is being questioned to find civilians bribed to work with them. Anyway, that's about it. Emme killed Ahmad and the other colonist. She was poised to rise to power in the humanoid colony and get mega rich besides." Malone let out a whistle. "Ambitious."

"And brilliant. With their resources, Emme would have been positioned to negotiate with big companies and governments, build her own nation in secret." Zen pondered the potential of such a scheme if she'd succeeded.

"Super-villains are real, like in the comic books," Sgt. Young said.

"Like I said, we got more to worry about. That reporter is dogging my footsteps trying to get the exclusive you all but promised him," Malone said.

"I meant giving him first dibs when we closed the case on Ahmad's murder. Hell, I had no clue we'd uncover such a mess." Zen hit a button. The bed whirred as it rose until she was sitting up.

"Yeah, well... We gave a standard press statement. Told him Emme will be charged and left out the rest," Malone said. He grimaced as if not looking forward to the thorny task.

"He's no dummy. Jacques can sniff out half-truths and missing details like a hunting dog," Sgt. Young retorted.

"We're going to do behind-the-scenes work before he puts the pieces together. Get out ahead of any reports he releases to control the narrative," Malone replied.

"You're talking like my father, Ramirez," Zen said.

"I'll accept the compliment."

"I didn't mean it as one," Zen wisecracked. Then her face turned sober. "Where's Peter?"

"We debriefed him for four hours. Pretty sure he bought the lies Gaida told him. He wasn't in on the secret mining operation, the colony, or Gaida's real intentions," Malone said.

"Delta and the others?"

"Delta was critical, but the In Situ medical team stabilized her. She's made a fast recovery. She's a cyborg, after all. Orion is salty as ever," Sgt. Young put in with a grunt and roll of her eyes.

Zen sat straight and winced at the sharp pains all over her body. She waved away Malone's attempts to fuss over her. Once she caught her breath, she let out a slow exhale. "We can't let the US or anybody else destroy hundreds of lives. I know they're not human, at least not in the sense we know. Debates in Congress and at the UN will drag on for years. In the meantime, someone would give an order and wipe them all out. We can't stand by and watch a massacre."

"Don't get worked up, Zen. You heard Dr. McCoy." Malone's touch was gentle as he tried to get Zen to lie back.

She resisted. "No, Malone. We're talking about lives. Tell him, Wyvette. Those folks have dreams, live in families—"

"I've seen it, babe. Virtual tour. Restricted to myself, Commander Okoro, and the In Situ directors only for now."

"Then you understand that the world has to re-write, redefine the concept of personhood. This opens up entire new fields of study in neuropsychology, social structures, and more." Zen's pulsed raced at the possibility of furthering her own sociological and behavioral research.

"Delta and her community have a powerful advantage. Helium 3 is just one part of it. They've discovered rare minerals not found on Earth that have huge potential. Only they know the location and have the tech to mine them. Space-Cor, multiple conglomerates. and countries are salivating over the prospect of cutting deals with the humanoids," Malone said.

"So, they're not going to be harmed?" Zen looked at him.

"No way. And my officers, along with Space Command, will make damn sure of it," Sgt. Young replied before Malone.

"Okoro made that clear," Malone added.

"I'll bet the White House, Russia, and more are losing sleep over the implications of all this," Zen said.

"Clive is juggling back-to-back briefings with them, the Pentagon, NASA officials, the UN Global Space reps, and more. He'll be talking to you soon, if he doesn't pass out from exhaustion first," Malone quipped. "I'd head back to help but I'm not leaving without you. You'll be in a seat next to me on that shuttle. Astra knows you're fine."

Zen teared up at the mention of her daughter. "I can't wait to see her face, hear her beautiful voice."

"You will." Malone caressed her right cheek with a large finger.

"Clairmont's story hit Earth a few hours ago. You're famous again." Malone laughed at her grimace.

"I can just imagine how happy Clive and my old boss at DOJ are about *that*." Zen let out a resigned sigh. More lectures about her ability to turn a simple investigation into a global crisis.

"Just Dr. Zen being Dr. Zen," Malone said.

The door slid open and Peter walked in with Ewan Lewis behind him. Peter hesitated, keeping a distance from them all. He looked sallow and drained. Lewis came around him to stand to one side.

"Hello, Dr. Batiste. I'm so glad you're okay. So very glad," Peter said.

"No freaking thanks to *you*." Sgt. Young took a breath as if preparing a verbal assault. She stopped when Zen raised a hand.

"I wanted to help Emme. She said Imirah would arrange to have her killed, like she'd killed Hassan Ahmad. I never thought she was capable of..." Peter's words came out in a rush of desperation to explain himself. He walked close to her bed. "I'm sorry. I swear, I thought Imirah was the killer. I was helping someone I cared about, trying to protect her from danger. I've been a fool once again."

"You were in Maryland sixteen years ago. A guest lecturer at Georgetown and St. Mary's. The brilliant young genius wowing the scientific and academic world," Zen broke in.

Lewis came forward, hands out. "Dr. Batiste—"

"I'm not talking to you," Zen said to him and looked at Peter again.

"'Yes, I met Emme there and fell in love. Or fell into an obsession that I mistook for love." Peter looked at Zen with an expression that seemed to beg for sympathy.

"I know what you are." Zen pushed away from the pillow at her back to sit straight.

Malone blinked with confusion. "Zen, wha—"

"Ma'am, take it easy." Sgt. Young stood.

"Okay, everybody stay cool," Lewis called out.

"Dr. Batiste, Zen. I've made terrible mistakes," Peter croaked.

Zen cut off his next words when she sprang for him. Before anyone could move, she'd put Peter in a choke hold. One arm circled his neck, her other hand applied pressure to his neck. She felt strength surge into her as rage pushed her to the brink. "You killed them. Two other girls disappeared. You and that bitch murdered Alexis Batiste. She had a name, you bastard."

Shouts came through to Zen as muffled background noise swathed in bubble wrap. Nothing mattered except retribution for losing her baby sister. Images of her mother collapsing at the news Lexi would never come home. Memories of loud sobbing at the funeral. A polished casket being wheeled off to the cremation chamber. Then she snapped back to the trauma unit. Multiple strong hands yanked at her. Peter struggled until he got her grip loosened.

"I didn't... kill her."

"You're a lying psychopath!" Zen struggled to regain her hold. The desire to snap his neck overwhelmed rational thought.

"She's not dead. Listen to me. She's not dead!" Peter croaked, barely able to speak.

Shock threw Zen off balance. She staggered, and her grip on Peter's neck slackened. Sgt. Young managed to pull Zen in one direction while Lewis yanked Peter free. Both men tumbled to the floor from the force of the struggle. Malone alternated between shouting at Zen and waving back nurses who had rushed into the room. A Space Command security officer pounded next, but skidded to a halt at Malone's command.

"You... you..." Zen panted from exertion and the emotional waves that buffeted her. She couldn't put together the words to express her revulsion, her fury at Navarro's disgusting attempt to evade justice.

Peter slumped against the wall like a toy with dead batteries. Lewis released him after a few minutes and took a few steps away. "I knew you'd eventually start to suspect I has something to do with your sister's death. I used the investigator training OSI put me through to track what happened to her. I had to know as much for myself as for you. The treatment chopped up my memory. Then we came here and Emme started dropping hints about my past, the things I did back then. Horrible things I can't recall. I just... But I didn't kill Alexis. Ask your father."

Lewis rubbed his square jaw while staring at Peter. Sgt. Young had let go of Zen and stood in stunned silence. Zen clung to her for physical support as what Peter was saying sunk in. Alexis. Dead. No—alive somewhere. And her father knew.

"Get him the hell out of here. Now!" Malone roared. He gestured to the security officer, who grabbed Peter by both arms. Another officer arrived in the meantime. "Put Dr. Navarro in lockup. I'm going to talk to you, Lewis. And you better damn well give me answers. You."

"Sir," the newly arrived officer barked in reply.

"Don't let Agent Lewis use his phone or any kind of communication device before I talk to him."

"Yes, sir."

"Isolate him in an interview room. Everyone else out," Malone huffed as he smoothed down his shirt.

"I'm going to check my patients first." The nurse supervisor motioned the other nursers forward without waiting.

Two hours later, things had settled down. Zen lay on her side in the hospital bed, curled into a ball. Sgt. Young took turns standing next to her and pacing around the room. Malone murmured into his phone in a corner. Then he ended the call.

"Sarge, give us a minute or three," Malone said in a quiet tone. His olive complexion had paled, his dark hair still tousled from the fray.

"Nobody gets in." Sgt. Young gave Zen a worried glance. Then she marched out to stand guard.

"Baby..."

Malone's voice faded into a silence. He eased beside her onto the bed facing her and gathered her into his arms. Zen buried her face against his chest. She sobbed; her moans of pain dampened against the fabric of his shirt. Ten minutes later, her cries trailed off into sniffles. Her limbs felt weak from an outpouring of grief held in too long. Malone kissed her forehead when Zen finally looked at him.

"I'm going to talk to my father now," she said. She wiped away tears with the backs of both hands.

"Maybe a cooling-off period is a better plan. Tomorrow morning?" Malone brushed fingers along her thick braided natural hair.

"No, now. Before he has a chance to hear from Lewis and get his story lined up." Zen sat and swung her legs over the bedside. "You can't keep Lewis locked in a cell much longer. The man has rights."

"We're on the moon and I have full authority. I can do what the hell I want," Malone said with a frown.

Zen rubbed a hand on his furrowed brow to smooth away the fierce expression. "My fight, Ramirez. Let me handle them."

Malone nodded and stood. Together, they went to Commander Okoro's office. Sgt. Young followed them. After a short conference with the commander, he left Zen and Malone alone in his office. Sgt. Young went out with the commander, but assured them she'd be right outside. They used Commander Okoro's satellite link to video call Zen's father. James Batiste's brown face looked ashen when it appeared on the screen. Zen recognized rows of his favorite books in the background. He was in his office, but not the one at home. For an hour, Malone sat beside her, silent as James made his confession. Anguish twisted his usually strong visage. Alexis, his Lexi, had been more troubled than Zen had ever guessed. Zen had been too wrapped up in her own life. College. Graduate school. Marriage and pregnancy. All before Zen had turned twenty-five. To say Lexi had "fallen in with a bad crowd" didn't do the full story justice. Lexi led the bad crowd into much worse than drunken parties, sex, and rebellion. Her father's solution? Save her from prison or worse. A new identity, a new life on a space station. Only the White House and officials with the highest security clearance knew it existed. James begged for forgiveness, for understanding, and to help protect Zen's mother from more heartbreak.

"You're a parent, so you must know how I felt. I couldn't let my daughter, my child..." James squeezed his eyes shut and covered his face with a large hand.

"I don't want to hear your excuses. Using your connections to cover up crimes. All those years of pretending to be the upstanding Dr. James Batiste, defender of world peace and justice." Zen's flat tone contrasted with the contempt sitting in her stomach like a jagged rock.

James dropped his hand to stare at her. "We're talking about Lexi, Zen."

"You had strong reasons to think she killed at least one person. She used people for her own purposes. Manipulated others because she could. I didn't know her at all." Zen spoke more to herself than in response to her father. Every memory of past conversations, their childhood, and family life seemed distorted through a new lens.

"Zen, listen to me. Come home so we can talk in person. I know you'll understand."

"I'm done with you for now. Good-bye, Daddy." Zen ended the call, cutting off her father's pleas.

Malone sat in stunned silence, staring at the blank screen. Seconds later the image of a space station blinked on, floating in the black vastness in space. He took Zen by the hand and squeezed it. "I know what you're going to do. It's done. She has a new life. Think of the consequences. What good will it—"

"Don't, Malone. Just don't." Zen looked at him. "I'm going to the Celestial Space Station. And I'm going to find my sister."

[1] The Lodestone Puzzle – Book 1 of the Dr. Zen Mystery Series

Don't miss out!

Visit the website below and you can sign up to receive emails whenever Lynn Emery publishes a new book. There's no charge and no obligation.

https://books2read.com/r/B-A-YISG-TRXPB

BOOKS 2 READ

Connecting independent readers to independent writers.

Also by Lynn Emery

Dr. Zen Mystery
The Lodestone Puzzle
The In Situ Murders

Joliet Sisters Psychic Detectives
Smooth Operator
Hunting Spirits
Dead Wrong
Dead Ahead
Die Trying
Spirited Sisters

LaShaun Rousselle Mystery
A Darker Shade of Midnight
Voodoo Lily
Between Dusk and Dawn
Only By Moonlight
Into the Mist

Third Sight Into Darkness
Devil's Swamp
LaShaun Rousselle Mysteries Books 1-3

Triple Trouble Mystery
Best Enemies
Devilish Details
Pretty Dangerous

Standalone
After All
Louisiana Love City Girls Boxset
A Time to Love
One Love
Sweet Mystery
Night Magic
Good Woman Blues
Gotta Get Next To You
Soulful Strut
Tell Me Something Good
Tender Touch
Louisiana Love Box Set

Watch for more at www.lynnemery.com

About the Author

Mix knowledge of voodoo, Louisiana politics and forensic social work, and you get a snapshot of author Lynn Emery. Lynn has written over twenty novels so far, one of which inspired the BET made-for-television movie AFTER ALL based on her romantic suspense novel of the same name. Holly Robinson Peete and DB Woodside starred as the lead characters.

Her romantic suspense titles have won and been nominated for several awards, including Best Multicultural Mainstream Novel by Romantic Times Magazine.

Get exclusive offers each month in Lynn's newsletter and a free short story when you sign up! Go to:

https://www.subscribepage.com/s1y8j8

Visit www.lynnemery.com to see a full list of Lynn Emery novels.

Read more at www.lynnemery.com.